THE PHOTOGRAPH

Penelope Lively

THE
PHOTOGRAPH

Viking

VIKING
Published by the Penguin Group
Penguin Group (USA) Inc., 375 Hudson Street,
New York, New York 10014, U.S.A.
Penguin Books Ltd, 80 Strand, London WC2R 0RL, England
Penguin Books Australia Ltd, 250 Camberwell Road, Camberwell,
Victoria 3124, Australia
Penguin Books Canada Ltd, 10 Alcorn Avenue,
Toronto, Ontario, Canada M4V 3B2
Penguin Books India (P) Ltd, 11 Community Centre, Panchsheel Park,
New Delhi–110 017, India
Penguin Books (N.Z.) Ltd, Cnr Rosedale and Airborne Roads, Albany,
Auckland, New Zealand
Penguin Books (South Africa) (Pty) Ltd, 24 Sturdee Avenue,
Rosebank, Johannesburg 2196, South Africa

Penguin Books Ltd, Registered Offices:
80 Strand, London WC2R 0RL, England

First American edition
Published in 2003 by Viking Penguin,
a member of Penguin Group (USA) Inc.

1   3   5   7   9   10   8   6   4   2

PUBLISHER'S NOTE
This is a work of fiction. Names, characters, places, and incidents either are the product of
the author's imagination or are used fictitiously, and any resemblance to actual persons, living
or dead, business establishments, events, or locales is entirely coincidental.

LIBRARY OF CONGRESS CATALOGING-IN-PUBLICATION DATA
Lively, Penelope
    The photograph / Penelope Lively.
      p.   cm.
    ISBN 0-670-03205-0
    ISBN 0-670-03362-6
    1. Widowers—Fiction. 2. Adultery—Fiction. 3. Sisters—Fiction. 4. England—Fiction.
I. Title.
PR6062.I89 P48 2003
823'.914—dc21   2002032420

This book is printed on acid-free paper. ∞

Printed in the United States of America
Set in Berling   Designed by Francesca Belanger

THE PHOTOGRAPH

Glyn

K ath.

Kath steps from the landing cupboard, where she should not be.

The landing cupboard is stacked high with what Glyn calls low-use material: conference papers and student references and offprints, including he hopes an offprint that he needs right now for the article on which he is working. The strata in here go back to his postgraduate days, in no convenient sequential order but all jumbled up and juxtaposed. A crisp column of *Past and Present* is wedged against a heap of tattered files spewing forth their contents. Forgotten students drift to his feet as he rummages, and lie reproachful on the floor: "Susan Cochrane's contributions to my seminar have been perfunctory. . . ." Labeled boxes of photographs—*Aerial, Bishops Munby 1976, Leeds 1985*—are squeezed against a further row of files. To remove one will bring the lot crashing down, like an ill-judged move in that game involving a tower of balanced blocks. But he has glimpsed behind them a further cache which may well include offprints.

On the shelf above he spots the gold-lettered spine of his own doctoral thesis, its green cloth blotched brown with age; on top of it sits a 1980s run of the *Yorkshire Archaeological Journal*. Come to think of it, the contents of the landing cupboard are a nice reflection of his own trade—it is a landscape in which everything co-exists, requiring expert deconstruction. But he does not dwell on that, intent instead upon this, increasingly irritating, search.

He tugs at a file to improve his view of what lies beyond and, sure enough, there is a landslide. Exasperated, he gets down on hands and knees to shovel up this mess, and suddenly there is Kath.

A brown foolscap-size wallet file, with her loopy scrawl across the flap: *Keep!*

She smiles at him; he sees her skimpy dark fringe, her eyes, that smile.

What is she doing here, in the middle of all this stuff that has nothing to do with her? He picks up the file, stares. He cannot think how it got here. Everything of hers was cleared out. Back then. When she. When.

Hang on, though. Here underneath it are a couple of folders, also with her handwriting: *Recipes.* Since when did Kath go in for serious cooking, for heaven's sake? He opens the folder, flicks through the contents. Indeed, yes—cuttings from newspapers and magazines in the late 1980s, but petering out fairly rapidly, which signifies. He investigates the second folder, which contains receipted bills, many of them red-flagged second demands, which signifies also, and an incomplete series of bank statements, indicating a mounting overdraft.

It would seem that this assortment of her things got pushed in with his papers by mistake during the big clearing-out operation. The hurried, distracted clearing-out operation. Elaine had volunteered to sort out and dispose of Kath's possessions. She missed this lot. And here they have lain ever since, festering.

Well, no, not exactly festering, but turning a little brown at the edges, doggedly degrading away as is everything else in here, doing what inanimate objects do as time passes, preparing to give pause for thought to those whose business is the interpretation of vanished landscapes.

The wallet file is brown anyway, so degradation is not much apparent. He dumps the folders on the floor and goes to sit on the top step of the stairs, holding the file.

He opens it.

Not much inside. Various documents, and a sealed brown envelope containing something stiff. Glyn sets this aside and goes through the rest.

A jeweler's valuation for a two-strand pearl necklace and a pair of drop pearl earrings. Originally her mother's, he seems to remember. Kath wore the earrings a lot.

Her medical card. And her birth certificate. Aha! So this is where that was, the absence of which caused considerable nuisance back then, necessitating a visit to Somerset House. No marriage certificate, one notes. That too had gone missing, making difficulties. And is still lost, it would seem. Not that that is, now, a problem.

Her O-level certificate. Seven subjects, A grades in all but one. Glyn scans this with some surprise. Well, well. Who'd have thought it?

The injunction on the file's flap was presumably to herself. This was the repository for items she knew that she must hang on to, but—knowing herself—that she knew she was only too likely to lose. He experiences a stir of fondness, which disconcerts him. And he has been entirely diverted from the hunt for that offprint, which is a matter of some urgency. Fondness is overtaken by annoyance; Kath is getting in the way of his work, which was not allowed, as she well understood.

There is also a National Savings Certificate for £5, bearing a date in the mid-1950s. When she was about eight, for heaven's sake. And some checkbook stubs and a Post Office savings book showing a balance of £14.58, and a clutch of letters, at which he glances. The letters are from Kath's mother, the mother who died when Kath was sixteen. Glyn sees no reason to be interested in these and pushes them back into the file unread.

He is left with a semiopaque folder which turns out to hold a sequence of studio portraits of Kath. She is looking at him in glossy black and white, now made manifest entirely. Young Kath. A backlit Kath with bare shoulders, head turned this way or that, eyes to the camera or demurely lowered, provocative smile, contemplative sideways gaze. These would date from the aspiring-actress days, long before he knew her. Very young Kath.

Glyn studies these photos for quite a while.

Kath.

He returns everything to the file. There is now just this brown envelope. He notices for the first time that something is written on it. In her hand. Lightly penciled.

"DON'T OPEN—DESTROY."

And for whom is this second instruction intended?

He opens the envelope. Within are a photograph and a folded sheet of paper. He looks first at the photograph. A group of five people; grass beneath their feet, a backdrop of trees. Two members of the group, a man and a woman, have their backs to the photographer. Of the other three, Elaine can be identified at once, visible between the two whose faces cannot be seen. Near to her stand another man and woman, whom Glyn does not recognize.

One of the back-turned pair is Kath—he would know that outline anywhere, that stance. The someone else, the man, is at first a bit of a teaser. Familiar, surely—the rather long dark hair, the height, a good head taller than Kath. A slightly hunched way of standing.

Glyn brings the photo closer to his face for more minute inspection. And then he sees. He sees the hands. He sees that Kath and this someone, this man, have their hands closely entwined, locked together, pushed behind them so that, as they stand side by side in this moment of private intimacy, this interlocking of hands would be invisible to the rest of the group.

Except to the photographer, who may or may not have been aware of what had been immortalized—the freeze-frame revelation.

And now Glyn recognizes the someone, the man. It is Nick.

He turns to the folded piece of paper that accompanied the photograph. He feels as though gripped by the onset of some incapacitating disease, but this paper requires attention.

Handwriting. A brief message. "I can't resist sending you this. Negative destroyed, I'm told. Blessings, my love."

No signature. None needed. Neither for Kath then, nor, now, for Glyn. Though confirmation is needed. Somewhere he will have an instance of Nick's handwriting. A signature. A letter from way back when he was a consultant, or some such nonsense, on that landscape-history series Nick published and of which he endlessly and ignorantly enthused, as Nick always did.

The disease now has him by the throat. The throat, the gut, the balls. What he feels is . . . well, what he experiences is the most appalling stomach-churning, head-spinning cauldron of emotion. Rage is the top note—beneath that a seethe of jealousy and humiliation, the whole primed with some kind of furious drive and energy. Where? When? Who? Who took this photograph? Who presumably passed it on to Nick and destroyed the negative?

The telephone rings, down in his study. Such is Glyn's powered state, his consuming purpose, that he is at once on his feet and halfway down the stairs to pick it up and snap: "I am not available. Sorry."

I cannot be doing with you right now, because I have just

learned that the woman who was once my wife had an affair with her sister's husband apparently—at some time yet to be identified. I am evidently a dupe, a cuckold. My understanding of the past has been savagely undermined. You will appreciate that for the foreseeable future this requires all my attention.

The phone stops. Of course. The answerphone is on.

Glyn returns to the top of the stairs. He sits holding the photo and the sheet of paper, looking from one to the other. Kath is everywhere now, the landing is full of her, and the staircase, and the big brimming treacherous cupboard; there are dozens of her, from different times and at different places, all talking at once, it seems. She curls up against him in bed, chattering about some film she has just seen. She puts her head round the door of his study, sunnily smiling, offering coffee. She skids ahead of him down a Cumbrian hillside, a small brilliant figure in a red jacket.

Questions are pouring through his head. When and where and who? But also—who else? Who else knew about this? Did Elaine know? Did Elaine connive? Was this matter common knowledge? Was he the innocent, the fool? Did people mutter to one another, throw him patronizing glances?

And for whom did she pencil that scribble on the envelope: "DON'T OPEN—DESTROY"?

For herself?

For me?

Did she plan this, step-by-step? Did she plan this moment? That she would fall from the landing cupboard, set me ablaze?

Well, no. Because Kath was not like that. Kath never planned. Kath never looked beyond tomorrow. Kath seized the days as they came and discarded them when done.

No, she came across that file one day, into which she had shoved various items. She flicked through them—looking for something, maybe—and saw that envelope. Took out the photo and the sheet of paper, thought "Oops!," scribbled on the envelope, shoved everything back.

But why not just kill the photo, there and then?

Because she might want to look at it again. Because it meant something to her. Something? A great deal? Everything?

This file was a safe deposit in which she stowed away things that she needed to keep for reasons of expediency or convenience or . . . sentiment.

Why not segregate the categories? One file for documents, another for matters of the heart.

Because Kath never operated like that—in a careful, considered, rational way. She simply pushed these things into the same file because she wanted or needed to hang on to them. And on the occasion when she wrote these words on that envelope, perhaps the phone rang while she was riffling through the contents. She put everything back, then had a sudden thought. She pulled out the envelope, quickly scribbled on it, returned it to the file, put the file in the drawer or the cupboard or wherever she kept it at the time, and forgot about it. She picked up the phone, cried out, "Oh, *hello* . . . How lovely to hear you, I'm so glad you've rung. I was going to . . . Listen, what are you doing today? I've got this sudden yen to go to—" And off she spun into another spontaneous activity, some more uncalculated hours.

But in writing these words—in thinking of writing them—she had some subliminal notion of a person who might at some point be going through her things, might come upon the envelope, might open it.

Me.

So she tells me not to open it.

And does she expect me to comply? Or does she assume— with a little curve of her mouth, a tiny shrug, a roll of the eyes— that I will open it?

Be it upon his head, she thinks. I *told* him not to.

All in a matter of seconds. As the phone rings. As she picks up a pencil.

Glyn has been sitting on the stairs now for so long that his backside is beginning to ache. He gets up, returns to the cupboard. He picks up from the floor the landslide of files and puts them in a pile on the windowsill. Kath's file he lays to one side, along with that envelope and its contents. He sets about a search of the area behind the files, which is silted up with miscellaneous papers alongside which, finally, there do appear to be some offprints.

That initial incandescent shock and rage have given way now to a sense of consuming purpose. He knows what he is going to do—but first things first. He is still raking over what he has seen and all that that implies, but at the same time he will grimly keep to its appointed course this day, which has turned out to be a day apart. He will find that bloody offprint.

He burrows through the detritus of thirty-five years. Paper, paper, paper. Entire forests that have died for him. Oak, ash, and thorn have perished to sustain his career—well, no, Scandinavian pine, more likely. In this heightened state he finds himself able to think in complex ways. Thoughts hurtle in parallel; thoughts shunt one another aside. He homes in on the photograph: when? who? He spots a box of slides, remembers a lecture he has to give, pulls them out. *Where* was the photo taken? Where are they standing, the pair of them? No offprint, so far. He returns the stack of files to their place and moves up to the next shelf. Newspaper cuttings, bulging boxes; another forest has been felled. He imagines the axes—no, chain saws, it would have to be. There were trees in the background of that photograph, he remembers. What kind of tree? A clue; check later.

He takes down a box, opens it. Notes—reams of handwritten

library notes from the days before photocopying facilities. Work. His own laborious hours of work. Heaven knows how many hundreds of thousands of hours of work the contents of this cupboard represent: his work, the work of others. And his work is in its turn the reflection of the work of countless nameless dead. "A landscape historian deconstructs the physical evidence of work done by generations of nameless people. The daily application of a faceless horde, century after century—laboring away hour after hour, year after year, hot, cold, wet, hungry, with aching limbs. Digging and shoveling and hauling. Fetching and carrying. Hacking and chopping. Loading, stacking, lifting. Herding animals, tending animals, butchering animals. Felling trees, quarrying stone. Turning wood and rock into houses and barns and churches and cathedrals. Heaving stone and glass up into the sky. And all this manipulation of the physical world carried out by scurrying, driven people, set only upon survival, upon working in order to eat in order to live from one day to the next, in order to feel the sun and the rain and the wind, get a bellyful of food, catch a few hours' sleep, wake to see another day."

When did I write that? he wonders. Not bad, eh? He seems to remember saying it to camera, when they did the first television series. That heady time. Those were the days. Being whisked around with that attendant entourage—the pretty, feisty girls with clipboards, and the director and the camera people and the sound people—and himself always at the hub of it all. Holding forth on hillsides and halfway up cathedrals and realizing that he loved every minute of it. Being recognized by strangers once the programs had gone out: that sideways glance in the street or on a railway platform. Snide remarks from colleagues, for which he didn't give a damn. Jealous, weren't they? Oh, it was a helter-skelter, full-pelt time, that was.

But work, all of it. Well, there's work and work. And I've been wet and cold too, thinks Glyn, and I've done a spot of digging, though I pass on shoveling and hauling, and hungry hasn't much come into it. But there's not a day of my life in which I haven't worked.

And here Kath comes in, dead on cue.

It is her voice that is clearest. What is said. Why is it that words hang in the mind forever? A sentence that is spoken over and over again. In his head, Kath is words quite as much as she is flesh and blood.

"You're not going to come with me?" The tone shoots up—a high emphatic note: ". . . *with* me?" And now he sees as well as hears. She is sitting at the other end of the table in the kitchen in Ealing, a letter in her hand. It must be summertime; her skin is very brown against her white shirt. That gold chain is round her neck. Her hair is damp from the shower, flattened against her neck.

"You're not coming with me to Devon for a lovely weekend with the Barrons?" Now she gives him that teasing look—never pleading, oh, never that, just a take-it-or-leave-it quirky glance. "Plenty of landscape in Devon."

And he explains—no doubt for the second or third time—that there is this conference.

"Never mind," she says. "Too bad. Toast?"

Kath did not work. Kath was not fettered by obligation, by responsibility, by having to be in a certain place at a particular time, by having to do things she might not especially wish to do. In the mind's eye, Kath is forever breezing down the street, smiling, traveling light, while all around her is perforce and necessity: the postman dealing out mail, door-to-door, the van driver heaving cartons into the corner shop, the patrolling traffic warden, the gang busy with hydraulic drills and JCB, the estate agents displayed at their desks, the driver of the taxi panting at the lights. All except Kath, who is bound for some destination of her choice, to do something she prefers to do.

And even when Kath did work she did not appear to be doing so. When she had a job—in those interludes when she was employed, gainfully or otherwise—it was because she had elected to do so. It had seemed suddenly interesting or entertaining to help out in an art gallery or a craft center, to get involved in a music festival, to do picture research for a publisher. And when the interest and entertainment faded, somehow Kath was no longer there. She had simply melted away, from one day to the next—perhaps with a vague apologetic smile, perhaps not.

Glyn knew these episodes, because he was sometimes on the receiving end of the inquiring phone calls, which could range from perplexity to indignation.

How did she do it? Well, thinks Glyn, she managed nicely for ten years because she was married to me. I paid the bills. I fed her and housed her and clothed her, pretty well. But before that? After all, Kath was a fully fledged adult by the time she came into my hands. She was thirty-six, she had been on the loose for twenty years, given that the home more or less broke up when the mother died. The girls each had a bit from her, of course, but not enough to live on. Well, not quite, but enough to scrape by, perhaps, in a hand-to-mouth sort of way. With the occasional top-up from somewhere or someone. I suppose that is the answer. And Elaine, being Elaine, set to and learned a trade and worked for the next forty years—very lucratively, these days, one understands—while Kath, being Kath, did not.

Glyn is still ferreting away in the cupboard, but if the offprint comes his way he is in danger of missing it entirely, so dense are his thoughts. He is finding that these thoughts are nothing new, but that everything is somehow skewed by what has just happened. This illness that he now has—this fever—has given everything a twist. Kath is both what she ever was, and she is also someone else. He is looking differently at her—he is looking differently for her.

She toiled not, neither did she spin. She did her own thing. In that sense she was in tune with the spirit of the day. But in other ways she was not. She didn't care a jot for achievement or status—neither for herself nor in others. She laughed at pretension. The hedonistic climate of the times suited her well, but the confrontations of the day were of no interest. I don't remember Kath ever getting exercised about the international situation or how she should vote. Feminism passed her by. Women's rights meant nothing to her because she had them anyway. Nothing had ever been denied to her because she was a woman. Being a woman enabled her to sail through life, setting her own course, following mood and fancy.

But not every woman can do that, thinks Glyn. Oh dear me, no. And why could Kath do it?

Because.

And at this point consideration gives way to imagery. He no longer thinks about Kath but sees her, experiences her. He sees her breasts. Small, neat breasts—little cones tipped with those surprising chocolate-brown nipples. He could not take his eyes off them, once, and they surge again, full frontal, at this moment. That bush—a rich, silky pelt exactly matching her hair. Those legs. Her slim feet. And her face. Oh yes—her face.

Kath could do it because she was a startlingly attractive woman. Not a conventional beauty, but with looks that were maverick and mesmerizing. The small face with those delicate features—the set of her nose, green eyes that seemed to catch the light, mouth tilted when she smiled. If she was present, you noted that everyone's glance strayed towards her. Men, women. Even children. Kath had an affinity with children. They drifted her way, and she to them. Perhaps if . . .

God, no. Kath as a mother? She with the attention span of a butterfly. Just as well it was never on the cards. And, anyway, I never wanted children.

He has reached the top shelf of the cupboard now. More files; more boxes of this and that. *Oxfordshire Drove Roads—1984*. He opens the box: maps, photographs, and Kath once more. Not as such, not standing somewhere sometime holding someone's hand, twisting the past, but lightly laid across that time, staking a claim.

"Why are we here?" she says. "It's getting terribly muddy."

She has climbed onto a five-barred gate and sits there, squinting into the sun. She is wearing jeans and a T-shirt with no bra. Glyn can see the shape of her nipples through the thin material; this sight distracts him from the matter in hand, which is close inspection of the Ordnance Survey map. If there were a nearby haystack he would take her into it and be done with it. But when did you last see a haystack? He does not yet know this woman very well, but soon will, if things go according to plan.

They have been following a track between fields, the grassy surface of which has now given way to rutted mud and puddles. Glyn is interested in the width of the track. He considers this, resolutely ignoring Kath's nipples. One thing at a time. "We're here," he says, "because I think this track may be an early drove road. I need to check it out. I did mention this when we set off."

"So you did. I keep forgetting you're *working*." She laughs. That laugh. Like no other. "It feels like a country walk. But, actually, would you mind if I stay put here while you check out the rest of it? I'm going to sunbathe behind the hedge."

And she is over the gate, into the field, and is sprawled with her back on the grass, T-shirt off, bare-breasted to the sky.

He shoves the box back onto the shelf, and as he does so he spots a cache of papers behind. Offprints—aha! And, yes, here at last is the quarry: "Basic Patterns of Settlement Distribution in Northern England," *Advancement of Science*, 1961.

Had he started at the top, that file would never have come to light. Or not on this particular day. The day would have proceeded as it should; he would now be at his desk downstairs, getting on with the work in hand.

Glyn sweeps up all that he needs, closes the cupboard, and goes down to his study. There he sets the offprint to one side. He will get back to work in due course, dammit.

He takes out the photograph.

Look again. I may have missed something first time round. Kath is wearing a full skirt, and some sort of black top that shows a lot of her neck and back. I think I remember that top. She has dangly earrings. Those too I remember.

Nick wears dark trousers and a short-sleeved check shirt. Neither item strikes a chord, but I remember well that characteristic somewhat too long hair and the way it flopped across his forehead. Here, it obscures his face, which is turned to one side, looking not at Kath but towards someone else. Towards Elaine, it seems.

Elaine faces the camera. She is speaking, perhaps—her mouth is slightly open. Maybe she is speaking to *them*. She wears trousers and a casual sort of sweater thing, a bag slung over one shoulder, a denim hat.

The other two I do not recognize. A tall thin man. A shortish woman with dark curly hair. Also dressed in light, casual clothes, which tells me only that this is summer, and that the occasion is distinctly informal.

Quite a little party. And then there is the photographer, of course. Him; her.

Where am I? Well, patently I am not there. I was absent, elsewhere, about other business.

And where are they all? The background is anonymous. A belt of trees. Grass on which they stand. Sky—blue, the odd white cloud.

An outing. A little excursion. "Listen, let's go to . . . Drop everything, why don't you! It's a heavenly day. Elaine's coming, and Nick of course. . . ."

When? Judging by Elaine's youngish face we are looking back into the 1980s. Thereabouts.

But one would like to know precisely when. No—one would not *like* to know, but one feels driven to know. I am driven to extract from this vital piece of evidence all that it can tell about how things were back then, since it appears that they were not as they seemed to be at the time, nor as I have believed them to have been ever since.

When was this photograph taken?

And who was the photographer? The person who collected a wallet of developed film, idly inspected the contents, looked more closely at this print, did some quick thinking, cut the negative from the strip, passed on the print to *him*.

Tacit collusion. By whom?

The person who can tell me, of course, is Elaine. Who may or may not have been in collusion herself—and that I need to know—but who will certainly be aware of the identity of all members of the party on that interesting little outing.

And now it is Elaine who fills the room. He sees and hears her, in various incarnations. He has known Elaine for a long time, in different ways. Crucially, she is Kath's sister, and it is as such that he now examines her.

Well, they weren't all that close, of course. Elaine the elder by far, and the two of them poles apart—in looks, inclinations, personality, everything. But there was something going on between them—that odd mix of tension and commitment between siblings. Elaine sniping away about Kath being Kath, which she never apparently came to terms with—but then coming over all protective. Kath suddenly nipping off to see Elaine for no good reason, ringing her up late at night.

None of my business, anyway, thinks Glyn. It was up to them. But now suddenly it is his business. Where does Elaine stand over this matter? Does she know? Did she know?

He scrutinizes Elaine—Elaine of that time, successful garden designer, burgeoning businesswoman, Nick's wife. Longtime associate of his own—he and Elaine go way back, after all. But Elaine is tiresomely inscrutable. She speaks and looks and does as she always has: no clues. Perhaps she was ever thus—quite a cool customer, Elaine.

She was in this room, once. Back then. When. After. "Will you go on living here?" she asks.

And when he replies she makes no comment. She offers to see to Kath's things. Which she did, though not, evidently, achieving a clean sweep.

As if he needed a house move, on top of it all. Yes, of course there would be . . . resonances. But there will be resonances anyway. One would have to learn to live with them.

He dismisses Elaine. She has nothing to offer, or at least not in this form. He pulls his notes towards him, switches on the computer: it is midafternoon and enough of the day has been dissipated.

That photograph smolders in its envelope, and in his head.

Dispassionate appraisal is Glyn's working method. Appraisal of evidence, consideration of the available facts. A system which has produced several books, many articles, a torrent of lectures and papers and reviews. Opinion comes into it as well, of course, and Glyn is known for forceful opinion and vigorous defense of his position. But detachment and the balanced view are paramount.

A dispassionate view of Glyn himself, at this moment, would show a man of around sixty staring at a computer screen, a shock of dark hair, flicked with gray. A square, rugged face that has evidently seen a good deal of fresh air—the reddened, weathered look of a farmer. Large brown eyes, chunky brows. Mouth pulled down at the corners, indicating perhaps embattled concentration. He thumps the keyboard, making a lot of errors: a two-fingered typist. Once in a while he reaches for a paper from the pile beside him, scowls sideways at it, bangs away again.

The room is a workshop, that is clear enough. It is lined with bookcases, crammed from top to bottom: books vertical, books horizontal. Tables and chairs piled with papers. Filing cabinets. There is little that is decorative or nonfunctional: a pair of Staffordshire dogs on the mantelpiece, a luster jug on the windowsill, a worn Persian rug on the floor. A framed Ordnance Survey map of a patch of Yorkshire from the mid-nineteenth century. Some aerial photographs of green sections of landscape. A color photograph of Glyn himself, a couple of decades younger, handsome on a windblown hillside, with scrawled signatures beneath his feet: "Greetings from us all: *Changes in the Land* team, 1980."

Pull back further—take a more distanced view—and the room is subsumed within a house that stands in a tree-lined street of detached homes with small gardens: a 1930s development, the prewar extension of the southern English city that can now be seen—pull back further yet, up into the ultimate dispassionate eye, the sky itself. And there is the city, there is the accretion of stone, brick, wood, glass, and metal. There is the cathedral, riding high amid the central jumble. There are the ravines of roads, the encircling discipline of chimneyed terraces, a belt of parkland, the white cliffs of office blocks, and on the outskirts the neat geometry of the university at which Glyn is employed.

No people here; the insect-crawl of cars. Glyn's house is lost now, digested into the urban mass, a tiny box in a row of similar boxes. And the mass itself, the inscrutable complex muddle, bleeds away at its edges, getting sparser and sparser until it is lapped entirely by space. Or rather, by spaces—squares and triangles and rectangles and oblongs and distorted versions of such shapes, edged sometimes with dark ridges. Dark spongy masses, long pale lines slicing away into the distance. Here and there a miniature version of the city density, a little concentration of energy at the confluence of lines. And then eventually space gives way—there is spillage, seepage, a burgeoning unrest that condenses once more into city format: the enigmatic fusion of now and then, everything happening at once.

If you know what you are looking at, that is. If you are Glyn Peters, who has got up now from his computer and is pulling out the wide shallow drawers of a cabinet. He finds what he wants—a map and a large aerial photograph. He spreads the two on top, side by side, pores over the aerial spread, seeing not space and shape but an assemblage of time. He sees centuries juxtaposed, superimposed, carving each other up, pushing one another out of the way. He sees the labor of medieval peasants etched beneath the rigorous lines of eighteenth-century enclosure; he sees a motorway slammed across a Roman road; he sees the green mound of a Norman castle thrusting up from the clutter of a city center.

He sees himself, staking out private territorial claims. Been there, done that. There is Bishops Munby, where he spent the summer of 1976, supervising the excavation of a lost medieval village. He can see that field still, with its eloquent lumps and bumps and declivities, its record of the little buildings that had been here, the village street, the string of fishponds. Days of sun, days of rain, the wandering inquisitive cattle, the makeshift canteen in a tent. The evenings in the local pub, the jolly student-labor force. He sees the girl from Durham, Hannah someone, young lecturer, with whom there had been a mutually satisfactory arrangement over that time: frayed denim shorts and long brown legs, glinting a conspiratorial smile as she trowels away at a wall.

He is down there ten years later, amidst that industrial conurbation, matching street patterns against the early survey maps. Solitary work, the place eddying around him, people casting a glance at the man with his clipboard and knapsack who prowls to and fro. A time of furious application, with his big book in the pipeline, his head buzzing with projects. And Kath's voice comes in here, rising off the glossy surface at which he is staring, which is overlaid now by that rank-smelling hotel in which he used to stay, Kath's voice on the phone: "I'm off to France for a couple of weeks with some people, since you don't seem to be around this summer." A pause. "Do you love me?" she says. He is writing up his notes in his hotel room: and there is Kath, a hundred and fifty miles away. She is reverberating still. But he hears only her; he himself is extinguished. What did he say to her? Goodness knows.

He looks up from the spread photograph and stares out of the window, struck by this. Odd. All that swilling speech in the head comes from others, never from oneself. It is they who say things: you do not reply. There is no exchange; vital evidence is missing. And I've never been what you might call lost for words, thinks Glyn.

Interesting. The operation of memory would seem to be largely receptive: what is seen, what is heard. We are the center of the action, but somehow blot ourselves out of the picture. Glyn rakes around some more and finds that he cannot much hear his own voice. Just occasionally, in delivery of some lecture, or holding forth to a camera, but that will be because the lines have been committed to paper and so are familiar. But in all those scenes with others, he is silent—he who seldom was.

It occurs to him that there is perhaps a telling analogy to be made here with the silence of the dead. The myriad dead with whose lives he is concerned, whose affairs he tries to reconstruct from what they have left behind—brick and stone and the disturbance of the landscape and a blizzard of paper in a thousand archives. That great mute mass, who perpetrated everything but cannot tell you how it was for them, whose voices can only be heard at second hand, filtered, diluted, distorted. Yes, a pungent paragraph in some article. Make a note of it. The idea is not watertight—what about diaries, letters?—but it is worth playing with.

He continues to stare into the unkempt rectangle of his garden, in which a pigeon patrols the shaggy lawn and a squirrel pours down the trunk of the cherry tree in one fluid movement. He seldom steps into the garden, nowadays, and the house itself is simply bed and workstation. When in need of company he lines someone up for a bite in a pub—colleagues, one of his research students. For more extended solace there is Myra, who works in the University Registry. A discreet relationship; Myra has long accepted that a permanent commitment is not on the cards and that what is between them must remain a private concern. Myra cooks a mean Sunday roast, her bed is deep and soft; he keeps shaving kit and a toothbrush in her bathroom cabinet.

Glyn is now watching the squirrel, mindlessly. The squirrel loops about on the grass; from time to time it freezes, quite motionless, tail curved. Then it shoots into a bush and is gone.

Glyn surfaces, angry with himself: he is not a man who gazes out of the window at squirrels while working. This is the inertia of emotional strain, he decides. And it will not do.

He drives himself back to the computer. The aerial photograph remains spread out on the top of the cabinet; it has served its purpose, and other purposes which he had not intended. He jabs away once more at the keyboard; text piles up on the screen. And eventually honor is satisfied; the substance of this article is there. Final grooming can be left until tomorrow. Right now, he needs to get back to what has happened. He needs to get things into perspective, order his own responses, consider a strategy.

It is evening now—a long, light evening of early summer. Glyn goes into the kitchen, opens the back door. He has been cooped up inside all day; maybe fresh air will do something to alleviate his state of mind. He takes the old basket chair out onto the small paved terrace. He fixes a plate of bread and cheese, with a dollop of pickle, an apple. He opens a bottle of red wine.

He settles down out there, in the benign light of this fine evening. All around, the suburb is noisily appreciative: lawn mowers, children playing. Glyn is impervious to this; he is not here at all, not here and now, but grimly focused on an elsewhere.

He is at the scene of that photograph. He does not need the thing itself, he knows what he saw, just as the words of the accompanying note are printed in his mind.

Right, let's be objective about this. What is there to see? Two people holding hands, in a way that would appear furtive. To hold hands suggests, well, familiarity at the least, but not necessarily a carnal relationship. The language of the note is intimate—"my love." It is also conspiratorial. The implications of the way in which the photograph was passed on by whoever took it further compound the suggestion that something was going on that had to be kept under wraps. In other words, they were fucking.

Since when? For how long? And does this raise further questions? Was this part of a pattern? Did Kath skip merrily from one lover to another? And did everyone know this except for me?

Evidence, he thinks, I need evidence. Well, I can look for evidence. But first things first. What do I know that is certain?

He scrutinizes his marriage.

He considers the bald narrative, which would run something like this. On Saturday, August 25, 1984, Katharine Targett and Glyn Peters were married at Welborne Register Office. They took up residence at 14 Marlesdon Way, Ealing. In 1986 they moved to 29 St. Mary's Road, Melchester, by reason of Glyn Peters' appointment to a professorial post at the University of Melchester. They continued to live at this address for the duration of their married life.

There should perhaps be a preamble to this: Glyn Peters met Katharine Targett at the house of her sister, Elaine, whom he had known for a short while. A brief courtship ensued.

The facts. And Glyn is of course a facts man, par excellence. But he looks at these facts with fair contempt. They tell him little. They tell him only what he knows, and it is what he does not know that matters now.

It is the subtexts that signify, the alternative stories that lurk beyond the narrative. The fragmented versions of those years; his and hers. His own version has different facets. There is his life with Kath and his life without her. The times when they were together—eyeball-to-eyeball across the breakfast table, limb-to-limb in bed, out and about as a conventional couple—and the times when they were apart, when he was just himself, as he ever had been. Walking, talking, working, living a life of which she knew little, now that he comes to think about it. The sealed life of professional commitment.

And what about Kath's subtext? For, of course, she too led this dual existence. And he knows nothing, now, of either, it seems. And her evidence is irretrievable, wiped, lost.

While his own is now fatally distorted. There is what he

knows, and there is the lethal spin imposed by the photograph and that scribbled note.

When was this going on—her and him?

Glyn lays those years out for inspection.

He places them in order. There were the immediate postwedding years in London, before he got his Chair. The house in Ealing. The daily term-time tube trek to the college; teaching; snatched hours in the library. The vacation escapes—field trips, conferences, extended library time. And what was Kath doing? He remembers a spell helping out in a gallery, a period when she got involved with some festival and would vanish for days on end, a brief flare of enthusiasm as a tyro jewelry-designer in someone's studio. But what about the rest of that time? Tracts of it. He samples his own returns from the college, of an evening, or from some excursion elsewhere. Is Kath waiting with a drink in her hand and something fragrant in the oven? Well, no—but that was never Kath's style. If she was there, then often others were there also—that network of her chums, who now merge into one another in recollection. And if she was not, there was no knowing where she might be. A note on the kitchen table, perhaps: "Back later. Kisses. K."

The move to Melchester, to this house. To a life of intensified activity, for him. And now Kath is more elusive yet. She discovers a talent for interior decoration; she stencils, she stipples, she rag-rolls. The walls of this house are a legacy from Kath. Glyn sees her up a stepladder, in jeans and a baggy shirt, her hair caught back in a cotton kerchief: "Hey," she calls, "get this! How's this for a designer home!"

The house is full of her. Coming in through the front door—"Hi! You're here—great!"; in the bath, scented, foam-flecked, humming to herself—and he is deflected by desire; burrowed beside him in sleep—waking with a little grunt of protest as he reaches for her. He has lived with these ghosts for years—they were tamed, under control—but now things have shifted; he summons her up in anger and frustration. There she is, as ever; but unreachable in a different way.

He sees her at some gathering in the university, being the professorial wife, which is not Kath's scene at all. He sees the attentive glances of his colleagues, and tracks her progress through the room with complacent pleasure; she is herself, as always, but here she is also his—an asset, an accolade. Other men's wives are dimmed in Kath's wake.

And she has no idea. Afterwards, she says, "Sorry—I disgraced you. They were all in party frocks and I wore my denim skirt. It's probably grounds for divorce."

He examines those years. And everywhere there are perforations. There are holes through which Kath slips away. That year he was in the States for a month. Where was Kath? He has no idea. Was she alone here, perfecting her domestic skills? Unlikely. And if not, who was she with?

For suspicion smokes, now. Who else may there have been?

When first he knew Kath there were a couple of other blokes sniffing around, who had to be seen off. He cannot remember experiencing jealousy, merely a brisk and businesslike intention. Once he had seen her, he had known that he had to have her, and not just for weeks or months but for good. Marriage, this time. The absolute certainty of this surprised him—the onslaught of need. So those others had to be cut out, and the best way of doing that was by establishing possession as swiftly and as indisputably as possible. He assumed success.

That brief time is now compacted into an impressionistic blur of things said, things done. He is on the phone to her, hour by hour, talking, talking, but he cannot hear a word of his own, now—just her. She laughs—that laugh with an odd little catch to it: "Glyn, *honestly* . . ." she says. "Oh . . . it's you," she says. That

breathless, urgent note. "I *am* listening," she says. "I'm listening fit
to bust." And they are in his car, he is whisking her here, there, and
everywhere, because he doesn't want to let her out of his sight; he
has her in the corner of his eye, her profile, the dark fronds of her
hair against her skin. He takes her hither and thither—his siege of
Kath is woven into the pattern of his working life. Kath climbs
Iron Age hill forts, she tours industrial sites, she attends lectures.
"We're going *where?*" she says—incredulous, laughing. She is not
always pliable. Sometimes she has slid away; the phone does not
answer, she's terribly sorry but she can't make it. But evasion
serves only to fortify Glyn's persistence. "I'm doing things I've
never done in my *life*," says Kath. "I don't know what's come over
me." But she does know, she must know; Glyn has come over her.
He is an unstoppable force; he has taken himself by surprise, as
well as her. Who would have thought that he could be in this
driven state about a woman?

Elaine stands by the mantelpiece. They are alone. Kath is out
of the room; Nick is—heaven knows where.

"So it's you and my sister, is it?" she says.

He spreads his hands—propitiating, placating. He has nothing
to say, for once.

And the matter is never raised again. Kath announces that
they are getting married. Elaine is at once brisk with plans—the
reception in our house, leave the nitty-gritty to me, do you want a
buffet or sit-down affair? She goes into cheerful overdrive, marshals lists, caterers, cars. "It's too much," Kath protests. "We could
have a get-together at that pub by the river, just a few of us."
"You're only getting married once," says Elaine. "At least I trust
and hope that you are."

When they come out of the register office, Elaine is on the
pavement with a camera. "Stop!" she calls. "Right there. Like that.
Big smiles, please. Kath—give your skirt a tweak, it's crooked."

Glyn has by now consumed the bread and cheese, pickle, the apple, and two glasses of red wine, without noticing. The light has started to drain from the garden; all around, the neighborly sounds are subsiding—lawn mowers docked, children summoned within. Glyn has never had much truck with his neighbors; a student of communal life and activity, he is himself oblivious to community. So what next-door does or does not do is of no interest, and anyway he is off now onto the next level of churning thought.

He has reviewed the years with Kath, and has found small comfort. Now, he turns to Elaine.

He is going to show the photograph to Elaine. And the note.

She does not have to know. She does not need to know. She is better off not knowing. But I know, and I cannot bear to know alone. I need some community of outrage, or grief, or retrospective jealousy, or whatever it is that I am feeling. So I am going to show her.

Most of all, I need to know if she knew. Back then. If she has known since.

It is a while since he saw Elaine. Quite a while—a couple of years, perhaps more. So there is every reason to call her up, suggest lunch, a drink. . . . Such is the imperative of his condition that he is minded to get in the car next day and drive right over to her place—only sixty miles, after all. But that would not do. Nick might well be there.

He will have to be patient. A phone call. An arrangement.

Elaine

K ath.

Kath always swims into view just here, as Elaine waits for the traffic lights to change, with the Town Hall in Welborne High Street plumb opposite. Kath comes down the steps, again and again and again, with her hand on Glyn's arm. Kath—a married woman, for heaven's sake. Elaine sees her today quite clearly, just as she saw her back then, through the lens of the camera, having nipped out ahead to take the opportune photo: the competent elder sister who has masterminded the day. Kath is laughing. Someone has thrown confetti and there are bits in her hair; she comes down the steps laughing, forever and always.

Actually, just so long as I'm around, thinks Elaine. The lights change, the car moves off, Kath disappears. Kath is biddable now, docile, as she never was in those days. She comes and goes, and sometimes she comes when she is not wanted, but she is under control.

Elaine is in any case preoccupied. She is driving on autopilot now, nose towards home, and in her head she is back at the site she has recently left, where there is a garden to be designed. Elaine thinks laburnum alleys. She wipes out the laburnum and substitutes wisteria on wrought-iron hoops, underplanted with alliums. She thinks water features and woodland walks and walled vegetable areas. The wife wants a *potager*. Well, she shall have a *potager*. The husband, from the sound and the look of him, would rather be at the golf club, but he is very rich and has just spent a lot of money on a mansion in Surrey which must perforce be appropriately decked out.

The wife wants decking too. She has been watching television gardening programs and knows what's what in garden fashion, or thinks she does.

The wife will not get her decking if Elaine has anything to do with the matter. She will have to put it across to the wife that what is all very well for a semi in Birmingham will not do for a 1910 Surrey stockbroker holdout with Lutyens-style features and two acres of grounds. The grounds are a mess, but they have interesting bones. Elaine spotted the archaeological remains of what must once have been a Gertrude Jekyll–inspired sunken garden, complete with rill and fountain. She will have that restored.

Definitely no decking.

"You're *so* judgmental," says Kath. "Don't be so disapproving. Be *nice* to me." She has come rooting back, superimposing herself on the Surrey garden. She is just a face and a voice, like the Cheshire cat. She does this. She has said precisely that, many times before, head slightly tilted, fiddling with an earring.

Elaine sends her away.

No decking, and the water feature will be the restored Jekyll-style rill. None of your excavated pits lined with heavy-duty polystyrene. The wife will not have heard of Gertrude Jekyll but Elaine will blind her with science, and since this couple are paying rather a lot of money for Elaine's name and know-how, and because she is not some fly-by-night television presenter but a highly esteemed doyenne garden-designer with major projects to her credit, along with various glossy publications, they will probably feel outflanked and start to doubt their own desires. In a few years' time, they will be displaying the sunken garden, the wood-land walk, and the wisteria pergola, and dropping Elaine's name to the husband's business associates, who won't have heard of it but know a class job when they see one.

Elaine does not usually much care for her clients. She prefers them when they are the faceless apparatchiks of large corporations. The gardens of Appleton Hall, acquired by one of the big banks as a staff-training and conference center, were one of her most satisfactory commissions. No opinionated but unknowledgeable pair breathing down your neck and squabbling with each other about what they really wanted—just a businesslike brief, a budget, and get on with it. She is proud of the gardens of Appleton Hall—the parterre with the box hedging, the blue-and-silver border, the jewellike glimpses of surrounding landscape framed at the end of grass walks.

Elaine does not design gardens for suburban semis. The owners of suburban semis would not be able to afford her fees; there is a host, a multitude, of outfits around now which attend to the likes of them. Over her working life Elaine has seen garden design go from a rarefied activity catering only for the wealthy few, to a cottage industry available to anyone with a bit to spend on property embellishment. Gardening is a mania now, it seems. Time was, the nation's gardeners were either obsessive specialists growing prize sweet peas in back gardens, or patrician experts presiding over bosky acreages. Nowadays, every house-proud couple knows their ceanothus from their viburnum.

Elaine is amused by this phenomenon. Her trade is now fashionable, instead of being either fuddy-duddy or elitist, depending on the perception. This is good for business, though she is well aware of bustling competition. But at sixty she is starting to wind down; she is being more choosy about commissions, she is capable of saying no when the job looks too problematic or too boring.

Once, she took everything she could get; that was when she was starting out, fresh from the years of learning plantsmanship, fresh from the time working for derisory wages in famous gardens to learn how it was done. She would design anything, back then: landscaping for a hotel forecourt, plantings for a new housing estate. She had to, as the most junior apprentice and general dogsbody for a slick little firm operating in one of the leafier parts of outer London.

Those years have been expediently glossed over in the CV that she supplies to prospective clients. Since then there have been bigger fish to fry, and her brochure lays them out for inspection. The brochure has had to be frequently updated. The first one of all was a fresh and innocent affair by comparison with the designer product of today. It was compiled with Nick's help, tricked out with little decorative floral motifs done by a girl illustrator he knew, and printed by the people he used when he first set up the publishing house. Back in those heady early years of marriage, and of work: her work, his work.

Elaine is now on the last stretch of the drive home. She passes the junction with the road that leads to their old place, the house in which family life was carried on cheek by jowl with a small publishing business and an embryonic garden-design venture. The busy, cluttered place in which every room housed filing cabinets, someone sitting at a desk, stacks of books. The kitchen where Polly was enthroned in her high chair or crawled about on the floor while people made out invoices and answered the phone.

The old house sends out signals, an unquenchable Morse code that is always to be heard around here. She is not thinking of the house, but nevertheless fragments of that time tumble haphazardly in her head, mixed with consideration of planting schemes for the Surrey mansion. A bog garden? Species roses for that long bank? *Hydrangea paniculata* against the walls? And, alongside, the thought that she must do a major supermarket shop tomorrow. Now, as the fragments tumble, Nick swings into focus, perhaps because she is approaching that pub that they used to go to of a Sunday lunchtime, way back. There he is still, sitting at one of those tables with fixed benches, on a summer morning, wearing a dark-green short-sleeved shirt, hair flopping, holding a pint mug which he waves around, in full flow about this new project.

"Roads," he says. "Lost roads. Prehistoric, Roman, cattle roads. An entire series. Canals and railways have been done to death. The Lost Roads of Britain—how about that!"

Oliver is present. The other half of the firm—friend, crony, partner. He is silent, in this clip from that time. He sits there, also with beer mug in hand, in quizzical silence. Not surprising—Nick in full enthusiastic spate was not to be stemmed. Sensible, pragmatic Oliver, who looks at the bottom line and deals with the nuts and bolts of the business, leaving editorial flair to Nick. Good old Oliver. Dear Oliver, Elaine sometimes felt, when Nick was being especially wayward or perverse, when he was in obsessive pursuit of some probably unviable plan. For Oliver was there then to provide reassurance and solace and to suggest that it will all blow over, like as not, and if it doesn't, well, we'll get it sorted out. Sometimes the shifty thought used to come that she might be better off married to Oliver, and, occasionally, when being counseled by Oliver, she was distinctly stirred. But Oliver would never betray his friend, not by thought, word, or deed. And in the last resort, Elaine loved Nick, didn't she?

"You're not listening, sweetie," he is saying, still waving the beer mug, looking directly at her. "You're thinking about some blessed garden. I want you to think about roads."

She is past that pub now and the Nick of then is effaced by the Nick of today, who may or may not be at home, and if he is, she thinks irritably, you can take it as read that it will not have occurred to him that he might check the fridge and make a trip to the supermarket. Not a bit of it. He will have spent the day swanning around—reading the papers, playing with the Internet, conceivably writing a few words of a review or one of his hack travel pieces—that is, if he has any work to hand at the moment, which he probably has not. While Elaine has driven a hundred miles and spent four hours acting with constraint and civility in the face of a couple of morons.

She goes through the village. She turns off onto the side road. The old house had neighbors. The new house—well, the new house of the last ten years—is elegantly isolated, folded into a particularly appealing valley, complete with stream and woodland. They had eyed it for years, she and Nick: a little Georgian building with several acres of grounds that Elaine itched to get her hands on. And then it came up for sale. She had commissions pouring in, she was buzzing with schemes; the time was ripe to take a risk.

In ten years, a garden matures. Those covetable grounds are now Elaine's most prized creation. It is young, as yet; the pleached-lime walk is a mere stripling, the ginkgos have to grow, there is infilling to be done and mistakes to be rectified. And she would make no majestic claims for it; this is not Hadspen or Tintinhull or Barrington Court. But it is a statement of her taste and talent, it bears her signature, it is her showcase.

Past six, now swinging into the circular driveway in front of the house, she sees that everyone has gone home. Only Nick's Golf is parked there. During the day, there is quite a lineup of cars. Sonia, Elaine's personal assistant, drives from her home ten miles away. Three times a week there is Liz, who deals with the paperwork Sonia hasn't time for. The red pickup belongs to Jim, who does the heavy garden work. And then there are the relays of horticultural students serving their apprenticeship in the work-shop of a master, just as Elaine herself once did. The current apprentice is Pam, who is a little northern butterball, sturdy as an ox, and exuberantly sociable, which makes her good front-of-house material on Saturdays, when the garden is open to the public. Then, all hands are needed to patrol the grounds and to man the sales area, where plants are on offer, along with a judicious selection of garden implements, seeds, gift-shop paraphernalia, and books—not least a complete display of Elaine's own publications. On those days, the paddock next to the driveway becomes the visitors' car park. Sometimes Elaine herself is on hand in the garden to be graciously responsive to queries and compliments. Initially, she found this stimulating and good for the ego. Nowadays, she gets rather tired of being asked if this or that is an annual or a perennial, and how to prune a rose. She tends to retreat to the house and leave customer relations to the students, who enjoy it.

When she first started opening the garden, three years ago, the idea was that Nick would come into his own. Nick, after all, is nothing if not sociable and enthusiastic. The enthusiasm could surely be channeled into visitor reception and salesmanship, or at the very least, car-park duties. And indeed, to begin with Nick was all compliance. He hung about the terraces, treating middle-aged women to dollops of boyish charm; he swept little parties off to the stream garden to display the primulas; he manned the till in the shop and added everything up wrong, but nobody minded because he was so patently a beguiling amateur. Jim took over the car park after Nick directed a BMW into the boggy bit at the bottom, where it stuck fast. And in due course Nick's commitment to Saturdays withered and died. Elaine remonstrated, tight-lipped.

"Sweetie, they keep asking me what this is called or whether that will grow on acid soil, and I haven't got the foggiest idea. The girls do it much better. And we all know I can't do money, don't we?"

Oh yes, she knows that. You cannot successfully keep a small publishing house afloat without a degree of business acumen. You must be able to gauge what will sell and what will not; you need to balance risk and costs and profit margins. You require a certain facility with figures, an aspect of the activity that Nick found distinctly tiresome. He tended to avert his eyes, for the most part. When Hammond & Watson eventually crashed, despite Oliver's best efforts, the warehouse was full of unsold stock, authors and suppliers were owed, and what had started out as an enterprising small imprint with a name for topographical and travel writing had become a liability.

It took a year to sort out the mess. Nick was chastened but buoyant. Never mind. It was good while it lasted. And he had plenty of useful contacts now, lots he could do in travel journalism, stuff for the Sundays, maybe guidebooks, that sort of thing: "Listen, Oliver, what if we—"

"No," said Oliver. "Count me out, this time round. No hard feelings. We had a run for our money."

To Elaine, Oliver said, "Sorry. I should have been able to keep things under control. I feel I've let you down."

Since when, she had thought, has anyone kept Nick under control? I too should have seen the red light. From now on, there will be changes. She had felt older, harder, and, in some odd way, exhilarated.

She collects her papers and clipboard from the back of the car. She goes into the house.

Windows open to the summer evening. Music filtering from somewhere. Nick is in the conservatory with a drink in his hand and something emollient on the stereo. After his taxing day.

Elaine goes into the office. Sonia has left a pile of letters for her to sign. There is another tray of letters and faxes that she must read. She gathers these up. She puts her notes from today into the appropriate file.

In the kitchen, Pam and Jim have both left scrawled messages on the blackboard. Pam has finished tidying up the long border, but needs instructions about the box hedging and those fuchsia cuttings. Jim says the tractor mower has packed up again; he's called in the mechanic and let's hope he comes in time to get the grass done by Saturday.

Elaine walks through into the conservatory, where the plumbago is a sight to behold. Beyond, the garden is glorious in the evening sunshine. Elaine is able to pay only token respect; her head is jangling from her day and her focus is on Nick, positioned precisely as she had anticipated. He has not heard her enter, but catches sight of her as she sits down.

"Hi! You're back. I didn't realize."

"Naturally not. Do you think you could turn the music down a notch?" She starts to go through the mail.

Nick does so. He gets up to refill his glass, then has a sudden thought. "Drink?"

She nods.

"We're out of that nice Australian white you got. Let's get some more."

"Thank you for reminding me," says Elaine.

The touch of frost in the air is apparent to Nick. He gives her a wary glance. "Poll rang. Says she'll call back."

"Mmn."

Nick is now cheerfully concerned. "Don't do all that wretched paperwork now, sweetie. Relax. Enjoy this gorgeous evening. Tell you what, why don't I knock us up an omelette and a salad later on and then you needn't bother cooking?"

"Yes, why don't you . . ." says Elaine. She returns to her letters.

Nick's concern hovers in silence for a while. He gives her a furtive glance. "Pesky clients?" he asks, with professional solicitude.

"Many clients are pesky, as you put it. If I let that bother me I'd soon go out of business."

Nick changes tack. There is an element of self-preservation here.

"I've had someone called a fact-checker on my back today. Nitpicking away about could I verify this, and give a reference for that. Remember that piece I did for the *New York Times* travel magazine?"

"And could you?"

"Well, here and there I could," says Nick. "But, I mean—what a sweat! On and on she went—'Now can we look at paragraph two on galley three—' "

"An appalling imposition." Elaine's tone is level, inscrutable. She picks up another letter from the pile.

Nick's strategy is not working out quite as intended: the establishment of his own demanding agenda.

"And of course I was wanting to get to the library. I need stuff on Isambard Kingdom Brunel. I'm really excited about this book project."

Elaine perceives that Nick will probably not be invited to contribute to the *New York Times* travel magazine again. His relationships with commissioning editors are frequently short-lived: he finds deadlines offensive and briefings tiresome. The book project will remain a gleam in his eye, which is no doubt just as well, since it is unlikely to thrill publishers, there being certainly a swathe of works already on Isambard Kingdom Brunel far superior to any contribution Nick might make.

Occasionally, over the years, she has asked herself if she

should feel sorry for Nick. But Nick does not invite sympathy, because clearly he does not feel that there is any problem. When one area of activity sputters to extinction, he is blithely accepting: "Actually, it was a bit of a bore anyway, and I've got a rather good idea. . . ." Enthusiasm becomes itself an occupation. "What one should be getting into nowadays is desktop publishing. . . . I've got this marvelous scheme for up-market canal-boat holidays for rich Americans. . . . The really interesting thing would be to set up a travelers' consultation service. . . ." Once in a while, such schemes get beyond the stage of exuberant speculation, and Nick goes in tentative search of the necessary funding. But potential backers are irritatingly uncompliant. They start asking for something called a Business Plan, which has Nick running for cover. The project in question ceases to be a preoccupation, it melts into obscurity, he retreats into writing the occasional letter soliciting a book review. He becomes immersed in transitory interests. His comings and goings are unpredictable; there is always some pressing need, some undefined engagement. But he appears to be a man at ease with himself and with the world. This is hardly a case for sympathy.

Elaine has been married to Nick for nearly thirty-two years. When she looks at Polly, their daughter's firm assertive presence seems to be the expression of that expanse of time. She cannot now conceive of a world in which there was not Polly, and she cannot well remember a life without Nick. But these days it is Polly who is the most inevitable development. Polly is ineluctable; Polly of today—capable, positive, employed. Polly is a Web designer—"a here-and-now sort of job," as she herself describes it—and seems to Elaine to have been ever thus: brisk, busy, slim, trim, an adult who has somehow entirely absorbed all her former selves. Elaine has to search for the baby, the child, the adolescent. Nick, on the other hand, Nick, who has not much changed, who is simply a weathered version of his younger self—Nick sometimes appears to Elaine to be oddly fortuitous.

From time to time she wonders how she came by Nick. Why is she with Nick rather than with someone quite other? Well—because we pair off with the person we come across when the time is right. The young are like dogs on heat. In your twenties, when the hormones are roaring, it could be pretty well anyone. That someone else who is also currently available, not otherwise committed, ready to pair-bond. Oh, love comes into it—but love is an opportunist. Love can be expedient.

There was Nick, when Elaine was twenty-six. There he was, always the animated center of any group, always good-humored, always game for any proposition, gleaming with good health and well-being. In other species, choice of a mate concentrates upon physical attributes—the indicators of good genes. Nick signaled good genes, if you went by surface appearances. And Polly does have his height, his good facial bones, his teeth that do not decay. But Polly, thanks be, does not have his lack of application, his idleness, his capacity for diversion. Polly is focused, in the language of her day and of her trade.

A question of timely collision. The two of you being in the same place at the same moment. The intersection of trajectories. The conjunction of Nick and Elaine took place during the 1960s, a good time in which to be young, according to legend. It now seems to Elaine that Nick was more resolutely young than ever she was. Even at the time, she felt herself to be on the margins of progressive action, reading about it in magazines, observing posses of contemporaries who had clearly got it right. And, when first she met Nick, he was a member of just such a posse: the center of attention at some party where she was a more tentative bystander. But he had noticed her, he had sought her out—this appealing, entertaining, personable man, two years younger than she was but never mind. "Maybe he likes mother figures," a friend had joked, causing offense. Elaine had been cautious; for months their association had been spasmodic, undefined. And then something habitual had crept into it, and an unstated assumption that this was probably permanent. Over a pub lunch one day he said, "You know, honestly, we should get married, we really should." Thus had she come by Nick.

Nick has not matured well. Sometimes Elaine feels that he has not matured at all. Behavior that is engaging in someone of twenty-five becomes less so at forty, let alone at fifty-eight. Where once she was beguiled, she has for many years been exasperated, though exasperated in the tempered, low-key way of long-standing acceptance. It could be worse, she has thought: he could be a drunk, or a crook, or a philanderer. He is merely feckless, and short on judgment.

He is on the sidelines of her life, in a crucial sense. She shares a bed with him at night, she eats a certain number of meals in his company, but he is excluded from the onward rush of things. He is not part of the faxes and phone calls, the consultations with Sonia, with Jim, with the gardening apprentices, the juggling of time and energy. He knows little of her cross-country journeys to client meetings or the production process of a book. "You're going where?" he says. "Warwick? You should look at the canal near there. Longest flight of locks in the country—amazing!" He steers clear of the books after an unwise surge of interest a few years ago: "You know, we could do these ourselves. *I* could. Desktop publishing. Cut out the middleman. Simple . . . OK, OK . . . it was just an idea. . . . Forget it."

Oh no, she had thought. No way. I've been there once. Not again. And this is my operation—books and all.

The sun is going down. The evening light has intensified over the garden. Elaine spares a moment for an appreciative look. Next year, some late tulips down by the yew hedge would be a good idea, to light up that dark corner. She returns to the letters. Nearly done now, sorted into two piles—one for Sonia to deal with and another with those to which she must draft a personal reply. An invitation to speak at a literary festival; yes to that—books will be sold and it is useful publicity. Would she attend the end-of-year prize-giving at a horticultural college as principal guest? Probably—for similar reasons. Could she please visit the garden of a couple in Shropshire (". . . a bit out of your way, we realize, but we'd love to put you up for the night . . .") who have written four pages about their tedious planting theories and probably have no conception of her consultation fee, or indeed that such a thing is appropriate: over to Sonia. Faxes from clients; faxes from contractors; a blizzard of promotional material that must be glanced through at the very least, in case there is something she should know about.

Nick has refilled their glasses. He is about to sit down again.

"How about that omelette?"

"Omelette?" Nick sounds surprised. "Ah. Yes. Omelette and salad. Right, then. Shall do."

"Good," says Elaine. She picks up some stuff about a new brand of fertilizer, skims through it, throws it in the wastepaper basket. Nick is still standing there. "What's wrong?"

"Nothing. For a peculiar moment you looked like Kath. OK—supper coming up." He goes.

This is profoundly irritating, for reasons that she cannot or perhaps does not wish to define. She does not look like Kath, and never did, which is why Nick has called the moment peculiar. They both know that she and Kath were about as unlike as sisters can be. Nevertheless, she knows what he means. She has seen it herself, in the mirror. Something about the mouth. A particular expression. Some genetic quirk—an arrangement of lip. When, otherwise, it always seemed as though she and Kath shared no genes whatsoever.

How odd, that Kath should survive thus—in the twist of someone else's lip. What would she have to say about that? She'd make some throwaway remark—one of those oddball witticisms.

She'd laugh—that wry little laugh. Hanging on like this in the shape of my lip, thinks Elaine. And in my mind. And in Glyn's and I daresay in Nick's and I suppose in Polly's and in those of a great many others. Many different Kaths. Personal Kaths. She is fragmented now. The dead don't go; they just slip into other people's heads.

It occurs to her that there is an eerie connection between Kath's presence in her mind nowadays and the way things were in their childhood, when Kath was a permanent, peripheral feature of the domestic landscape. Back then, when she was relegated simply by that matter of age, the wedge of years that sat between them, prescribing and directing. A twelve-year-old does not play with a six-year-old, or that particular twelve-year-old did not. A person of sixteen is not much interested in someone of ten. Elaine remembers the closed door of her own room, the edgy contrived accommodation of family holidays. That time consisted of the long years when Kath was merely a tiresome feature, an occasional source of jealousy, a local climatic effect to be ignored or irritably tolerated. She got more than her fair share of parental attention: "Do remember she's only five . . . seven . . . nine. . . ." Her existence meant that there was always this unstable element within the household, generating concern, requiring other people's energies and help.

And then that time came to an end. Quite suddenly, it now seems. Kath grew up. One day she was no longer that annoying appendage but a person. She had fledged, grown wings—or rather, she had metamorphosed. This girl had appeared. From the child chrysalis there had emerged this spritelike creature—elfin, gamine, all the well-honed terms applied. There she was, slim and quick, with long legs and small perfect body and that pointed face with the thin, neat nose and those lake-green eyes and the high curving brows and the brown-black crop of hair—the ensemble that had everyone looking, and then looking again, homing in on her when she came into a room. You saw people glance, and then keep glancing back, with surprised interest, attention, pleasure. And she had no idea. No more idea than has a bunch of flowers, a picture on the wall, a jewel—anything that seizes the eye, that gives a momentary uplift.

"You're *so* unalike," they began to say. "No one would realize you're sisters." This by then would, perhaps, have been better thought than spoken.

Nick is now in the kitchen. Elaine can hear his inexpert clattering with pans and plates. She is still here in the conservatory sifting the final tranche of paperwork, which does not require much attention, so that she is also elsewhere, in another time and place, dispatched there by Nick's provocative remark. He did not of course intend to provoke. Nick never does. That is one of the things about Nick—something that is in itself an aggravation.

She hears her mother's voice. This is unusual; her mother is not much with her these days, nor has been for many a year.

"Our ugly duckling is turning into a swan," says their mother. "Look at her!"

And Elaine, home from college for the vacation, takes a look and sees that this is so.

"People have said she ought to think of going to stage school," their mother continues.

Elaine is consumed with annoyance. Typical! she thinks. Typical Mum. Typical people. "Why?" she snaps.

Their mother blunders on. She has come to be mildly afraid of Elaine, but has never learned how to step cautiously.

"Well, because she's so pretty, I suppose."

"And can Kath act?"

Their mother refers to a supporting role in a school nativity play, some while back. She speculates that after all you go to stage school to be taught how to act, don't you?

Kath did go to stage school, in the fullness of time, perhaps because of their mother, perhaps because of these anonymous people with their unconsidered opinions, and much good it did her. But by then their mother was dead.

The trouble with Mum, thinks Elaine, was that she took everything at face value. Literally, in that instance. Her views were simplistic, if one is being entirely honest. Not her fault. A restricted education; a life centered upon family and home. And Dad, not exactly stimulating, was he? I don't remember any kind of discussion ever taking place, except about what color to paint the kitchen, or where to go for the summer holiday. They were comfortable and unambitious. Mum looked after Kath and me, put food on the table, and saw that everything was in prime *Good Housekeeping* condition; Dad went to his office, brought home a salary, piled up a pension. They were entirely satisfied.

No, I'm not being patronizing—I'm being objective. I'm seeing them as they were, which doesn't mean I wasn't fond of them. And yes, I know that they lived as the vast majority of the population lives, and what's wrong with that? All I'm doing is taking the detached view. Mum was fine, but she had her limitations.

And she died. At forty-three. They hadn't reckoned on that. Well, who would?

I remember Kath phoning me: "Mum's got something horrible wrong with her." That was the first I knew. It was months only, after that—four, six? I went home as often as I possibly could, but it was a hectic time, my first job—even at weekends I had work to catch up with. And Kath was there.

Yes, I *know* she was only sixteen. But she'd always been closer to Mum than I was. She'd been agitating about leaving school anyway, even before Mum got ill. Well, she could have gone to sixth-form college or something later, couldn't she? But she wouldn't, would she?

I saw to the funeral, didn't I? It's all a bit hazy now, but there are moments that float to the surface. Dad sitting there blank-faced, helpless—this was right outside his remit. Me saying, "It's all right, I'll sort it out, don't worry." Phoning priests and undertakers. Twenty-two-year-olds don't have much experience with such people, but I managed. I remember feeling quietly pleased with myself—thinking, If I can deal with this I'll be able to deal with other things.

Kath seemed to be in a kind of trance, over all that time. She hardly spoke. And her looks went. It was as though she'd been blown out, like a candle. She became this ordinary teenager—peaky, with a little monkey face. She was like that for a year or so, and then gradually it all came back, and people were glancing again, and there began to be boys by the shoal, of course. She ran wild rather, I suppose. Dad was like an automaton, just doing what had to be done, day by day. And then he took up with Jenny Peterson down the road, or rather she took up with him, and they got married.

Kath says, "I can't go on living there. Jenny doesn't like me." She has been saying this over and over, down the years. She says it very precisely—she sounds distant, calm. But that is all she says. Listen as she may, Elaine can now hear no more.

What did I say?

Look, there was no way I could have had her move in with me. I was in that bedsit in Chiswick, saving up every penny for a mortgage deposit. She was going on nineteen by then. We were poles apart—not just the age thing anymore, but tastes, inclinations, everything. We'd have driven each other mad. And it wasn't as though she didn't have friends. Kath always had friends—droves of them.

I kept in touch, didn't I? Not that it was easy, the way she flitted around. You could never be sure where she was or what she was up to from one week to the next. That was the drama school time. Which didn't last long. One minute she was all wide-eyed about it, and the next thing you knew it was all off: "That? Oh, wasn't working out. Some people I know have asked me to come and live in their squat in Brighton."

It was the 1960s. Kath suited the sixties—the sixties suited her. Letting it all hang out, doing your own thing. It was the right climate for her—she was young at the appropriate time. Whereas I wasn't. To be industrious and achieving was to be out of step. And gardening had no cachet at all, back then. It meant old men with allotments, or middle-aged ladies in Gloucestershire. Kath waltzed about the place—to be honest, I don't even know what she was doing, half the time—while I knew just what I wanted to do and what I wanted to be.

Of course I was concerned about her. Of course. But she was a consenting adult by then, wasn't she? It wasn't for me to tell her what to do and what not to do. Even if there was no one else, Dad having opted out altogether. And if you did say something, she had this way of sidestepping.

"You're *so* judgmental," says Kath. "I come all this way to see you and you tell me I need a haircut. Be *nice* to me. Listen, I'm learning to drive—how about that!"

The money Mum left me went towards the deposit on the flat. I told Kath she should do the same with hers, but she didn't. Naturally not. She lived hither, and thither, wherever she happened to fetch up. A room in someone else's house, flatshares, a friend's sofa . . . Goodness knows what happened to the money. I suppose she just nibbled away at it, over time. Not that she was extravagant. At least, only in odd ways.

Kath is on the doorstep. At least, on the doorstep there is this great sheaf of flowers, a cornucopia of lilies, and through it peers Kath, smiling, sparkling: "Surprise! When I woke up this morning I knew the one thing I wanted was to come and see you!" And all Elaine can think of is that there must be £20 worth of florist's goods there, which will die within days.

Of course I didn't *say* it. Not outright. I suppose I may have hinted—I mean, she was always skint, jobless more often than not. Possibly I murmured something.

When Kath is full and strong in the head, there is frequently this sense of a mute subversive presence, of someone playing devil's advocate. Elaine knows perfectly well how things were, what happened, who did what, but there is often now this interference that distorts and confuses. As though one were not in control of the facts.

Nick is shouting from the kitchen. The omelette will be on the table in a couple of minutes.

Elaine gets up, puts the paperwork back in the office, visits the downstairs loo. There she takes a quick look in the mirror for signs of Kath, and can see none at all. Her mouth is her own once more. Moreover she is not displeased by what she sees: a face that has improved with age, settled into something more arresting than ever it was in youth. What was never pretty has now become handsome. Shapely nose and jaw, wide-set eyes, discernible cheekbones. Thick brown hair; not much gray as yet. Wearing nicely, thinks Elaine—that's what comes of a rewarding occupation, not to mention a lifetime of fresh air and moderate physical labor. Reinvigorated, she goes to join Nick in the kitchen.

The omelette is leathery and the salad indifferent. Nick has never bothered with the acquisition of domestic skills. Nevertheless, he presents this meal as though he were a gracious and benevolent host: "There! And I've opened a bottle of red. Now relax!"

They eat. Nick talks about Isambard Kingdom Brunel, and about the engineering complexity of the *Great Britain*, which reminds him to remind her that his car has to go into the garage tomorrow to have a new exhaust—any chance of borrowing hers? He leaps from thence to reflection on an idea he has for a series of handbooks on geological walks: "Region by region . . . Follow the Blue Lias from Yorkshire to Dorset, go Cambrian in Wales . . . You'd need a team of researchers, of course."

Elaine hears all this but her attention is upon her own concerns. She roves between contemplation of today's commission, notes for further action, and various flotsam that sneaks unsought into the crevices. Regal lilies with a backdrop of drystone walling become entwined with the rehearsal of a stroppy phone call to a recalcitrant compost-supplier; a vision of *Sorbus vilmorinii* is swept aside by an unquenchable memory of walking with Polly along the Cobb at Lyme Regis, prompted by a glance at the flowered dish on the dresser, bought back then. Polly is eternally eight and a half, wearing pink shorts and T-shirt. "Can I have a choc bar?" she says. Elaine is pondering whether or not to splurge on this piece of Victoriana by which she is tempted. "*Can I?*" Where is Nick? Why is he not involved in the dish and the choc bar? But Nick is not there, and the moment is finite; at some point she must have returned to the antique shop and bought the dish, but that she cannot remember, and she no longer knows if Polly got her choc bar. Probably, being Polly.

And now this incarnation of Polly is replaced by another— prompted by nothing in particular, it would seem, just part of a chain of imagery. This Polly has shrunk by a few years. She is four, or thereabouts. She is dancing. She is dancing with Kath, in the living room at the old house. There is music—a tape, the radio? Elaine can hear the music: "Here we go round the mulberry bush, the mulberry bush, the mulberry bush. . . ." Melodic, compelling. Polly and Kath face each other, holding hands—small Polly, grown-up Kath—and they whirl about the room. "Here we go round the mulberry bush. . . ." Their faces are rapt, smiling, intent. Polly gazes up at Kath, and they whirl on and on. Forever, apparently.

Definitely a wisteria walk for the Surrey mansion, but would alliums be right for the underplanting? Tomorrow she must get to work on the new book proposal, must have a session with Pam, must talk to the accountants. She looks across at Nick, who is still in full flow, and these considerations are eclipsed by the sight of his left ear, which prompts the resurrection of their wedding night, or rather the morning after their wedding night, when she awoke to find herself staring in surprise into a pink whorl on the pillow alongside her. She had never studied an ear with such intimacy and intensity before; so this is marriage, she had thought.

Now, she finds herself wondering if she could pick out Nick's ear from any other. Would she recognize it, unattached? If, say, it were sent to her in an envelope, as kidnappers are said to do.

"Of course there are guides galore to good walks," Nick is saying. "But a thematic line would be something new. One could go on to botanical, historical, you name it—" He breaks off. "Why are you looking at me like that?"

Elaine abandons the thoughts provoked by the ear, challenging as they are. "Will you undertake these walks yourself?"

"One hasn't really got the time. A team of volunteers is what I'm thinking of. I'm wondering if the garden girls—"

"No."

"There could be an expense allowance, of course."

"The garden girls, as you call them, are horticultural trainees, not freelance ramblers." Elaine gets up. "Do you want coffee?"

"OK, if you're making it. I may do a bit of preliminary scouting around tomorrow. Locally. Just to get ideas. So all right if I take your car?"

"No. I have to go to the supermarket. Unless you'd care to do that."

Nick pursues this line no further, as was to be anticipated. He changes tack. "Not to worry. I'll do it when mine has been fixed. Actually, we're going to have to think about replacing mine—there's too much going wrong."

"And what will we replace it with?"

"I thought one of those new Renaults might be fun," says Nick eagerly. "Like in the ads, you know? Red. I've always wanted a red car."

"I wasn't talking about the replacement car. I was asking what money we would be using."

This is bad manners. There is a tacit agreement that the fact that it is Elaine who pays the bills is not openly contemplated. At least, it is a tacit agreement so far as Nick is concerned.

He pulls a face. He shrugs. He gives her what she thinks of as his beaten-puppy look. It is a look that used to disarm her twenty years ago, but has somehow lost its potency in recent times.

Elaine makes coffee. There is silence now in the kitchen, which also serves as a workplace, with reminders on all sides of what goes on there: the blackboard on the wall with its chalked messages from the labor force, the publishers' posters of Elaine's books, the windowsill dense with a propagating frame, pots of this and that, the copper jug crammed with *Iris sibirica*. For Elaine, the silence is barely apparent, her preoccupations still loud. The blackboard reminds her that it is probably the tractor mower that

requires replacing rather than Nick's wretched car; the irises provoke concern about an overdue bulb order. But these thoughts
float above more insistent background noise, which is not to do
with things that have happened and things that have not happened and the way things are. She is feeling irritated, burdened,
and a touch belligerent. She puts a mug of coffee in front of Nick,
with unspoken comments. You are complacent, she tells him. You
have always been complacent about me, above all. A mistake. I
have not always been as I have perhaps seemed. There have been
times when I have been a long way away from you. One time in
particular, I suppose. Take note.

The phone rings. "I'll get it," says Elaine crisply.

Polly. "Hi, where have you *been*, I tried you earlier. . . ." Polly is
at once in full flow. Elaine pictures her, feet up on the sofa in that
small Highbury flat ("the mortgage payments are wicked, but it's
so nice, and it's two minutes from the tube station"). Polly has had
a punishing day, she is wiped out, no one would *believe* the trouble there's been with these new clients, she's just off to chill out
with some friends over a meal. She'll call again before the weekend, maybe she'll shoot down for lunch on Sunday, depending on
how things are—anyway, this is just to check in, this week has
been crazy, take care, see you.

Polly's voice invades the kitchen like a message from another
planet, which in a sense it is. Elaine knows plenty about her
daughter's life: the feverish mix of work and play, the determined
application to everything she does. Polly is a thirty-year-old Web
designer. By the time she is a thirty-four-year-old Web designer
she intends to be running her own business and will be thinking
of a baby. As yet, the putative baby has no putative father, but all
in good time. Elaine finds herself admiring Polly's strategic approach to life. Months and years are mapped out, a matter of tar-
get achievements: new carpeting for the flat when I get my salary

increase, a job move next spring, split up with Dan by Christmas if things don't seem to be going anywhere. It is an approach mirrored by the question apparently asked by potential employers: "What do you expect to be doing in five years' time?" Or perhaps the question has conditioned the outlook of a generation. Elaine herself, at thirty, would not have cared to hazard a guess about what she might be doing in five years' time. Or rather, she would have felt that to do so would be tempting providence. Certainly, she could not have given the confident and ambitious reply that is evidently de rigueur. She admires this combination of pragmatism and positive intent; this is a climate that would have suited her too. As it is, her own success has been achieved by hard work and a degree of opportunism rather than any calculated ascent.

"Poll hard at it?" says Nick. He chuckles. "I was filled in earlier on. A job for some big outfit, apparently. It's all go, isn't it?"

For Nick, Polly remains a source of benign amusement, just as when she was six or sixteen. Polly, over the years, came to treat her father with impatient tolerance, like some wayward older brother. She bustled around him: "Dad, your desk is a shambles, I'm going to do something about it." She would contemplate him, her mouth knotted with disapproval: "You *cannot* wear that tie with that shirt." There was affection here; when Polly did not care for people she did not bother to sort them out. And Nick, congenitally disposed to delegate anything that did not appeal to him, made no objection. Nowadays Polly deals with his income tax for him, such as it is. She prescribed Chinese herbal medicine for his hay fever and has chivied him into membership of a health club. That undertow of irritation has been replaced by a sort of protectiveness, as though he were some flawed but valued institution. Elaine finds this attitude both annoying and perverse.

The thing about coming home, says Polly, when she dashes down for a night, or a meal, is that everything's always got to be exactly the same. Don't you see? I mean, you can have some new curtains occasionally, if you like, within reason, but basically it's got to stay put. I've got to be able to touch base. Totally self-centered, I know, but you don't *mind*, do you? The occasional innovation I will allow—actually, a makeover of the bathroom would be no bad thing—but basics have to stay the same, right? No blue rinses, Mum, OK? And if Dad ever goes in for gray flannels and a tweed jacket I'll slaughter him.

Whenever Elaine hears this mantra, she is both touched and slightly mutinous. All right, all right, she thinks, I take your point. But you've got nothing to worry about, have you? Oh dear me, no. Any radical steps taken around here are to do with planting schemes or office equipment, with which presumably you would be in sympathy.

Nick has finished his coffee. He is now leafing through the newspaper in search of the television programs. Elaine picks up her address book and pulls the phone towards her. She must call a client who is only available in the evenings. Nick glances across the table.

"That reminds me. Glyn rang. Said he'd try you again tomorrow."

"Glyn?" she says. "Oh . . . Glyn."

Elaine and Glyn

Why this restaurant? Why not come to the house? Why, anyway?

Elaine drives into the car park behind the Swan, finds a space. She tidies her hair, checks her face. It is a long while since she saw Glyn; longer still since she ate a meal alone with him.

The Swan is apparently a halfway point, as near as makes no odds. Thirty miles for each of them to drive: Glyn, brisk and practical—"So, thanks for your kind offer, but if you don't mind . . . It'll be good to see you." And the phone is put down without further explanation.

So here she is. And as she walks into the Swan's dining room—dark paneling, red-checked tablecloths, limited clientele on this weekday lunchtime—she sees that here too is Glyn. He rises to greet her: the polite kiss. "You're looking well, Elaine."

Glyn is surprised. Elaine must be sixtyish, for heaven's sake, but she does not look it. Any more than one does oneself, come to that.

She sits down, making a crisply critical comment about the hotel's garden, which is visible beyond the window. He takes note of her: becoming haircut, clothes that are casual but smart. There was always a compelling vigor about Elaine; she still has it. Fellow

eaters glance at them. If things were otherwise, he could be enjoying this occasion—a pleasant get-together with a woman he has
known for many years. But this is no indulgent arrangement.
There is an agenda; it is smoldering in his pocket, distracting him
as the waiter proffers menus, as Elaine asks some question.

So what is this lunch about? Elaine knows at once that Glyn is
in a heightened state. Mind, you need close experience of Glyn to
be aware of that—not a man who was ever less than charged. But
there is something up today. She can sense it: an absence of concentration, a restlessness. It is apparently an effort for him to give
a rundown of his latest project, a reticence which is unusual. So
what is afoot? Maybe he is about to remarry and considers it
proper to tell a former sister-in-law in a formal manner? Perhaps
he has been elevated to the peerage—well, he is a prominent academic, occasionally outspoken on public issues. Possibly—here
Elaine's interest is sparked—possibly he has some professional
scheme requiring garden-history expertise, as he did . . . back
then. If that were so, one might well find oneself available. All the
rage, these days—lost gardens. Prime-time television and all that.
No bad thing to become involved.

The waiter returns. Choices are made, the meal is ordered.
"Nick sends greetings," says Elaine.

Glyn becomes busy with his napkin. He butters a roll. "And
how's business, Elaine? Lots of work?"

"All I want."

"Good, good. You're a fortunate woman. You embellish the
landscape and get paid for it. As opposed to those of us who frit-
ter away a lifetime asking questions about it."

"You too get paid," says Elaine.

"True." He reaches across the table, pats her hand. "I'm glad
things are going well. You deserve it. You're a worker, always were."

Glyn is a physical-contact man. An arm-round-the-shoulders man, a hand-on-your-elbow man. The pat reminds her of that: his mode of emphasis.

"I'm certainly not complaining. Only when it comes to the more perverse clients."

"Ah, that's a hazard of the trade. Capability Brown had plenty to say about his. Repton too. Dealing with patronizing eighteenth-century aristocrats. Bear in mind that it is they who will vanish without trace. Your creations will outlast the merchant bankers or whoever they are that plague you."

He continues along these lines as the first course arrives. He talks of some stately-home magnate who had a lake dug and then didn't care for the effect and had the lot filled in again. He moves on to cite instances of vast expenditure on historic garden cre-ation. Elaine had forgotten his compendious resources, that capac-ity to conjure up facts, figures, anecdotes. Compelling enough, in its way, but there is the hint, just now, of a routine.

Glyn is treading water. He would like to get on with the mat-ter in hand, his mind is on that and on nothing else, but good manners would seem to insist that the niceties are observed. A pe-riod of general chat. A decent interval of white noise.

"Fascinating," says Elaine. "What a mine of information you are, Glyn—I'd forgotten. I'm flattered at being lumped in with Repton and Brown. Can't say I've dug any lakes lately, but perhaps my day will come."

Glyn plows on. This is conversation, of a kind: comments are made, opinions exchanged, occasionally there is glancing refer-ence to some past shared experience. Plates are taken away; more food arrives. Now, thinks Glyn. In two minutes, when she's fin-ished eating.

Elaine is talking of Polly. Glyn stares at her, trying to focus.

The daughter. That's right, the daughter. "—Web designer," Elaine is saying. Glyn inclines his head, all interest.

"Do you know what a Web designer is?"

Glyn spreads his hands, defeated.

Elaine puts her knife and fork together, dabs her mouth with her napkin. "Actually," she says, "I don't think you heard a word of that, did you?" She gives him a long, speculative look. "Come on, unload. I've got a feeling we're not here just to chat, are we?"

"Ah . . ." Glyn pushes his plate to one side. Right, here goes. Suddenly, he feels once more in control, back on course. Some questions will be answered. He reaches into his pocket. "Actually, you're right, Elaine."

Elaine sees and hears that this is something of another order. This is not marriage, or ennoblement, or garden history. She feels a creep of disquiet.

Glyn is holding something out to her. She takes the photograph. She takes that scribbled note. She looks first at the photograph. She looks at it for quite a while. Then she reads the note.

She says nothing. She holds them, one in each hand, looking, not speaking. Then she looks across the table at Glyn.

"In a file in the landing cupboard," he says. "Must have been there since she—since then. They were in this." He pushes across the table towards her that envelope. "DON'T OPEN—DESTROY," Elaine reads.

"So . . ." says Glyn. "So here's a turn-up for the books." He watches her.

Elaine looks back at the photograph. Something strange is happening—to her, to the figures that she sees. She sees people who are familiar, but now all of a sudden quite unfamiliar. It is as though both Kath and Nick have undergone some hideous metamorphosis. A stone has been cast into the reliable, immutable pond of the past, and as the ripples subside, everything appears different. The reflections are quite other; everything has swung and shattered, it is all beyond recovery. What was, is now something else.

"Or perhaps you knew?" says Glyn.

"No, I didn't know. Assuming that there was indeed something to know."

"Well, what does it look like?"

Elaine has seen enough. The hands. The handwriting, the language. She picks up the photograph and the scribbled note and puts them in the envelope.

"I suppose it looks like—what it looks like. And, no, I didn't know."

"Then I'm sorry. This is as much a shock to you as it was to me. I'd begun to think I was the only one in the dark."

Elaine makes no comment. The ripples are widening; the reflections become clearer. But, at the same time, they are not clear at all; they are ugly, distorted, deceptive.

"When was it? Where were you all?"

"It must have been in the late 1980s—'87 or '88. We'd gone to the Roman Villa at Chedworth. I forget quite why. Mary Packard was there, and the man she was with then. Do you remember her?" Elaine speaks dully. She would prefer not to speak at all.

Glyn shakes his head. He is not interested in Mary Packard. "Who else was there? Who took the photograph? And passed it on to Nick?"

Elaine is silent. At last she says, "Oliver."

Oliver. Even as she speaks, Oliver falls apart and is reassembled—in a nanosecond, in a single destructive instant. He too becomes someone else. The Oliver who has been in her head these last ten or fifteen years disintegrates and is replaced by a new and different Oliver, one whom she does not know. Did not know.

"I see. Him. Nice, reliable old Oliver. In collusion, apparently."

The waiter is hovering, menus in hand, proposing dessert. Elaine feels now as though she had fallen from a great height and were picking herself up, gingerly testing limbs. "Nothing else," she says. "Just coffee."

Never mind Oliver, thinks Glyn. I'll get to him in due course. The point is that there are now two of us in this. He looks guardedly at Elaine; she has been rocked all right, he saw that in her face, but there is no sign of collapse. Well, Elaine is not the type to run weeping from the room.

"I'm sorry," he says. "It's a slap in the face, isn't it? I've had a few days to digest. Not that I find that makes a great deal of difference."

"Difference to what?" This is not so much a question as a prompt. Talk, thinks Elaine. Just talk and let me consider. Let me do some steady breathing and take stock. I seem to be intact, more intact than I would have expected.

"—point is the suggestion that nothing was what it seemed to be," Glyn is saying. "That what one has been carrying around in the head is apparently fallacious. That one was, that we were, unaware of a significant fact, namely, that your sister—my wife—at one time had an evidently intimate relationship with your husband, to put it baldly. Suddenly everything has to be looked at in a different light."

"Some might prefer not to look," says Elaine.

"Unfortunately, I don't find that possible. Do you?"

A pause. "Probably not."

"I can't tolerate a misconception. Everything is thrown into doubt. At least that is what I'm finding. Everything." He stops abruptly. He is finding also that he does not wish to pursue this line. Personal breast-beating was never on the agenda. There was an entirely practical motive for this meeting, and that has now been satisfied. He knows what he needs to know. Or rather, he has begun to know what he needs to know. He is sidetracked now by a new line of thought.

"Professional conditioning, to some extent, I suppose. We don't like the status quo to be upset. Some new and vital piece of information comes along and the whole historical edifice is undermined. Take carbon-fourteen dating. They've got everything nicely worked out—what is contemporary with what, a chronology set in tablets of stone—and then along comes dendrochronology and the whole thing is shot to pieces. Stonehenge is earlier than the Pyramids, the Neolithic isn't when they thought it was. Throw it all out. Think again." He gives Elaine an interrogatory glance. "You know about carbon-fourteen dating?"

"As much as I need to know at this moment."

"Recent history is less vulnerable. More a question of constant raking over of the ashes. Reinterpreting. Arguing. The sudden reversal is less likely. It's the early stuff that is the shifting sand. Let alone when you get back to paleontology. A minefield. That said, nothing's sacrosanct. There's always the possibility of startling new evidence that moves the goalposts. The drought summer of 1975 made possible aerial photographs that showed up a whole range of early settlements on the southern gravel terraces that were completely unsuspected. Prehistoric-population estimates had to be entirely revised. You follow me?"

"I take your point. Your personal goalposts have been moved, right now."

Glyn stares across the table at her. "Is that not how it seems from your perspective?"

Coffee has arrived. And with it, for both of them, a further presence. Kath is around. Or rather, several Kaths have arrived. For Glyn, she is for no apparent reason sitting on the roof of a narrow boat, somewhere in a Northamptonshire reach of the Grand Union Canal. Her arms are wrapped round her legs, she wears rope-soled canvas shoes, her tattered straw hat has a bright-blue scarf tied around the crown. And what was he doing? Steering the boat, presumably, which Kath never learned to do, and if the other couple he hazily remembers to have been there on that weekend outing are present, they are not evident in this slide. Kath sits alone, and she is gazing at a couple of children running along the towpath. Quite small children—oddly, he still sees them also. Kath gazes, and presumably he, Glyn, was yanking away at that wheel and anticipating the next lock, while Kath's mind is patently on something quite other.

Elaine is experiencing several Kaths, which tumble in her head. Kath is not under control, she will not be dismissed. She is a continuous effect, as she was in childhood, a glimmering presence, flickering away there on the perimeter. She cannot be disregarded; "Here I am," she says. "Here I was. Look at me."

And Elaine looks. She sees a new Kath, who is colored by what Elaine now knows. She is angry with this Kath: angry, resentful, frustrated. But she is also baffled and a touch incredulous. Why? Why Nick? Kath hardly noticed Nick. Or so one thought. Nick was simply a person who was around, as far as Kath was concerned. Familiar, and inevitable—my husband. But apparently all the time . . . or some of the time.

Elaine summons up that day, the day of this photograph. In a snatch of time—as she stirs her coffee, sets down the spoon, lifts the cup to her lips, drinks, returns it to the saucer—she recovers those hours. But there is not much to recover—tracts of it have gone down the sluice, it seems. She sees neatly restored ruins, a mosaic pavement, a glassed and labeled fragment of Roman cement on which is the paw print of a Roman dog. She sees a grassy bank, the surrounding woodland. She sees Kath walking towards them in a car park, Mary Packard and her companion behind: evidently they all met up at this place. The arrangement, and its reason, are gone. But can be surmised: Kath's phone call—"Listen, Mary and I have this plan. . . . Yes, yes, tomorrow as ever is . . . *Of course* you can drop everything, both of you, bring Oliver too. . . ." And now a picnic comes floating up: Nick is rummaging in the coolbag, he looks up at her, he says, "Is there any fruit, sweetie?" Mary Packard and Kath lean over the railing that surrounds the mosaic, laughing at something. Mary Packard's man is so irretrievably consigned to the sluice that Elaine cannot supply him with features or a name; he is just a lurking presence. But Mary Packard is loud and clear: Kath's longtime friend, the crony, the soul mate, the abiding element amidst the ebb and flow of Kath's associates. Short curly hair, emphatic manner, a potter by occupation.

Glyn is trying to sort out the years, but to no great effect. He could do with pen and paper, but that would hardly be appropriate just now. What was he doing in '87 or '88? Which was the year he was up in the north for much of the summer—did this take place then? More accurate dating will be necessary. And there is a sense in which Elaine has failed him. She did not know, which removes the biting thought that he was the sole innocent, that all around were wise to what was up, and tacitly pitying, or jeering. She did not know, but others may have done. Oliver, patently. He will see to Oliver all in good time. For now, first things first.

"You think '87 or '88?"

Elaine puts down her coffee cup. She is silent, staring at the table. She is considering the query, it would seem.

But no. "Does it matter?" she says.

"It does to me."

She shrugs. "Sometime then."

"Can't you be more precise?"

"No."

"Oh, for God's sake, Elaine—"

"And don't snap at me."

He is contrite. "I'm sorry. Sorry, sorry. Look, I'm not snapping at you, I'm snapping at . . . at what apparently happened."

"Retrospective snapping will get you nowhere," says Elaine. And furthermore, she thinks, let's be clear about this—we don't have a common cause, you and I. All right, we've both been wrong-footed, we're both outraged, but that is the beginning and the end of it. Whatever comes next is a personal matter, for each of us.

"Why Nick, one asks?" Glyn's contrition has evaporated; this is speculation with a note of insistence.

"Why indeed?"

"And if Nick, who else?"

"Is this wise?" says Elaine.

"Is what wise?"

"Questions."

"Possibly not. But what else can I do?"

She meets his eye. "Nothing?"

"I am not a do-nothing man. I am conditioned to ask questions. Will you do nothing?"

She inclines her head. No answer.

"I'm sorry you had to know this," says Glyn.

"I didn't have to know it, strictly speaking."

This takes effect. There is compunction, but also defiance. "Right. OK. You've got a point there. But you might well have done the same."

"And you had to know if I knew."

Does this mean he is exonerated? No way of telling. He is evasive, now. "Whatever . . . Here we are. There it is."

"There it was," says Elaine.

"A fine distinction, to my mind. If a distinction at all."

She considers, apparently concedes the point. "Perhaps. But asking questions won't change that. Could even make it more so."

"So be it," says Glyn.

Determination, or perversity? There is a pause, both of them possibly weighing this up.

Elaine steps in. "I suppose there is one question that springs to mind."

Glyn waits, wary; something in her tone has him on his guard.

"Did Kath ever know?"

"Know . . . what?" Glyn is prevaricating. Both of them are well aware of this.

Elaine gives a tiny shrug, a steely glance.

"Well, there wasn't so much to know, was there?" He shoots up his eyebrows, that Glyn expression of deprecation, surprise—whatever is appropriate.

"Maybe not," says Elaine. "But did she?"

"No. She had no idea."

Elaine reflects, and decides that this is probably true. There is silence between them. Something has been let loose; she has broken a taboo.

"Long time ago . . ." says Glyn. He avoids her eye. Is this necessary, for heaven's sake? An aberration, after all, surely that has long been understood?

Yes, indeed—time out of mind ago. But not entirely out of mind, and that is what is at issue. We were both there, after all, thinks Elaine; nothing can change that. We are the same people. Up to a point. She watches Glyn; it is astonishing to her that, once, she burned for this man.

Glyn is experiencing something of the same sensation. Before them both there hangs that time of the Bellbrook garden project. Both shed eighteen years, and see one another again for the first time.

Elaine sees a muddy wasteland, girdled with Portakabins, littered with bulldozers, piles of bricks and planks. She sees the aerial photograph of the same site before this invasion, which has been handed to her, with its provocative patterning of lines and depressions. She sees the television team that is here to record the shadowy presence of the gardens of a vanished Jacobean mansion discovered on the building site of a new housing estate. And especially she notes the talkative personable presenter of this program in the making. A landscape historian, she has been told—the first time she had heard of such a trade.

Glyn sees the inviting potential of this unusual site. He assesses the contractors' crane, from which it is proposed that he should make the opening commentary, with the camera panning away to a bird's-eye view of the garden's outlines disappearing beneath the geometry of suburban streets and crescents. And he turns from consideration of subsequent shots to inspection of this expert on garden history and design who has been called in to elucidate the visible evidence. "This is definitely a parterre," she is saying. "And it looks to me as though the vista runs along that axis. . . ." He steps across, hand outstretched: "Glyn Peters. Great to have you with us. Now. Tell me—"

She tells. She gets out pencil and paper and sketches a possible design for this extinguished landscape. "Assuming that this pattern is complemented by an identical layout on the other side of the central path, which it must have been, you've got the whole thing extending—oh, a couple of hundred yards or more, most of it built over already. I do feel that some sort of central basin and fountain is implied. . . ." Glyn eyes her. He rather likes what he sees. Something in her eyes, and the curve of her mouth. He feels a distinct flare of interest. He is all exuberance and enthusiasm. He lays a hand on her arm: "Wonderful! Thank goodness they brought you in. Listen—let's take off to the pub while they set up the cameras and then we can really talk."

He talks. He is an exhilarating and refreshing companion.

They are noticed in the Crown and Cushion of some unmemorable high street. He recounts entertaining anecdotes of filming experience, he is compelling about field systems and drove roads, or so it seemed at the time. Elaine remembers thinking with approval that this is enthusiasm bolstered with the authority of knowledge. This is a man who knows what he is doing. She likes that Welsh intonation too.

And thus by the time they return to the site there is a definite rapport, an alignment firmer than that required by this transitory professional association. Glyn wonders if he might pick her brains at some point about early park plantings; Elaine finds that she would have no objection at all to this. Addresses are exchanged. "Are you married?" Glyn inquires. "Of course," comes her brisk reply. "Aren't we all?" He laughs: "In my case, no, as it happens."

The filming takes place. Glyn holds forth from the contractors' crane; at ground level he strides around this scene of devastation, conjuring up the elegant formality of another century. He describes clipped topiary, fountains, graveled paths. In between takes, he rejoins Elaine: "You're a magician! I'm reinventing the text as I go, thanks to you." Elaine observes with amusement and fascination. This beats client meetings any day, she thinks.

In due course, a week or so later, she sees Glyn again. He is anxious to show her the grounds of a derelict mansion in Northamptonshire that he has come across. She drives many miles to this assignation, which for some reason she describes to Nick, dismissively, as a consultation with turf suppliers. Glyn and Elaine trespass the grounds of the mansion by way of a crumbling wall and a thicket of brambles, with much laughter and exclamation. When Glyn puts both hands on her waist to jump her down from the wall she realizes that, should the question arise, she is likely to commit an infidelity for the first time in her married life.

All the signals were there. No doubt about that. It was not a question of if, but when—when this undeclared interest would tip over into an admission. She had thought that Glyn did not seem a man to hold back. And she had known that, when the time came, she would not either. She is astonished by this now. She feels as though it were some other woman who was caught up in that flurry of sexual interest. Which is made more mysterious by the fact that in all the subsequent years of their association, she never saw Glyn in that way again. It was as though his allure withered the moment he was with Kath.

There had been other meetings. Two? Three? Not many more than that. All are hitched to the lingering background of some significant place. Maiden Castle: they climb the grassy ramparts, he takes her hand to help her up the steep slope, meets her eyes, the tension sings between them. They are on an ancient stone bridge over a little river, leaning on the parapet while Glyn talks. She no longer hears a word of this, but sees his face still as he turns to her, stops talking, puts his hands on her shoulders, kisses her on the mouth. She feels the flick of his tongue.

But he had come to the house, also. Had he not . . . Well, had he not, we would not be here today on this freighted occasion, thinks Elaine.

Glyn visits Elaine at home. He wants to see a book Elaine has mentioned that has early photographs of the grounds of Blenheim Palace. When the suggestion is made Elaine notes that he could quite well consult this book at some library. On the day that Glyn comes to the house Nick is out, by coincidence, and Polly is of course at school. Glyn and Elaine spend hours together—eating lunch, talking, looking over those convenient photographs. The tension is there again—enhanced, wrung tight. The air crackles with what might be, what may be.

And somehow Glyn does not leave but stays on into the evening. Polly returns, and so does Nick, who easily digests an unanticipated visitor, as always. Elaine is just putting together a meal for everyone when the door bursts open and here is Kath, on one of those unheralded surprise visits.

The evening is prolonged and convivial. Nick is in high spirits. Glyn scintillates. He turns frequently to Kath. And when at last he leaves, Kath leaves with him. He has offered her a lift to the station.

Elaine stands at the window, watching the retreating lights of Glyn's car. She thinks, So that's that. He had only to set eyes on her. Wouldn't you know?

Glyn's voice jolts her back to the restaurant table and the matter in hand. "*That* has nothing to do with this," he is saying emphatically.

She looks at him.

"If you are suggesting that Kath took up with your husband because briefly, long ago, you and I . . . eyed one another . . . then I'm telling you that she had no idea. No idea at all. Not from me." His return look is a challenge.

"Nor from me," says Elaine. "All right, she didn't know. I'm merely noting a symmetry."

For Christ's sake! thinks Glyn. What did she have to drag this up for? Irrelevant. And symmetry be blowed. I hardly laid a finger on her, as I recall. All that was wrapped up when I married Kath. Never referred to again. Why revive it now? Surely there's no question . . . He shoots her a glance, but it seems to him that Elaine's expression is one of controlled dislike rather than latent interest.

In fact, Elaine's somewhat wooden look is the product of distraction rather than dislike. She is assessing her own condition. Within the last hour her perception of the past has been questioned, her understanding of three people has been shown to be faulty; yet she is surprised to find that, far from feeling diminished, she is filled with a sense of grim purpose. Glyn is rapidly becoming superfluous.

"My dear Elaine," he is now saying, "that really is water under the bridge"—a propitiating smile—"we both know that. Not that I haven't always had a great affection for you. But it has no bearing on . . . this other thing." He changes tack. "This would seem to be . . . Well, the evidence suggests a great deal. But there is only one person now who can tell us exactly what."

"Are you planning to have a word with Nick, then?" Elaine is icy.

"Perish the thought. That is your prerogative, if you so wish."

Quite, thinks Elaine. But you're not going to leave it alone, are you?

"Nick is your concern," he continues, dismissively.

"He is indeed. And what is yours?"

Glyn stares at her. He has the intense and concentrated look that she remembers from those times when he would be expounding some new theory, holding forth on a current investigation. He does not reply.

Nick is oddly insignificant, Glyn is finding. He is puzzled himself by this. An initial urge to seek him out and punch him on the nose has given way to a kind of indifference. His business is with Kath, not Nick.

The restaurant has emptied. At the edge of the room, staff loiter.

Elaine folds her napkin, puts it on the table. Glyn cocks an eyebrow in the direction of a watchful waiter. The bill arrives.

"Well," she says, "thank you for the lunch."

He grimaces. "I wish the circumstances could have been different."

"It seems that they were decided a long time ago."

Except, of course, that they were not. The photograph might

have lain unrevealed in Glyn's landing cupboard; Glyn might have found it but chosen to remain silent. Alternative scenarios flicker in their minds—significant but, now, irrelevant. I know, thinks Elaine, and that's that. Now for what is to come.

"Just one last thing," says Glyn. "Can you let me have Oliver's present address?"

Oliver

Glyn?

Oliver has not set eyes on Glyn in years. He seldom thinks of him, except in a subliminal way in which past acquaintances can sweep briefly into the mind, and as rapidly evaporate.

But now here is Glyn, fair and square in the office, sprung by Sandra's terse remark: "Someone called Glyn Peters rang—left a number. Please call back."

"Right," says Oliver. He sees Glyn now: that square face, the thick brown crop of hair. He hears the voice, with its tinge of Welsh. Assertive, confident, but always rather compelling. The man addressing you as though you were a seminar, but you listened.

Something in Oliver's voice has evidently alerted Sandra. "Who is Glyn Peters?"

"Glyn?" says Oliver casually. "Oh, Glyn was Elaine's brother-in-law. You know . . . Elaine, wife of Nick, my erstwhile partner. Can't imagine what he wants."

And, indeed, he cannot.

Sandra has picked up on a point here—the professional eye for detail. "Was?"

"Kath . . . died," Oliver explains. He gets busy at his screen. "We need to have a talk about the new layout for *Phoenix*."

"OK," says Sandra crisply. "Right away, if you like." He has got her back on course; she is now applying herself to the design problems of the alumni magazine of an Oxford college.

Precision is the name of our game, thinks Oliver. He thinks this with pride. Accuracy. Every comma and full stop in the right place, each paragraph correctly indented. Footnotes, indexes, contents pages. Not a letter out of place. The discovery of a typo in one of his publications can give him a sleepless night. He is more satisfied than ever in his life. Desktop publishing was made for him. No tricky editorial input, no headaches about marketing and distribution. Just take the commission from the client and set about creating the immaculate product. He loves the screen on which he can conjure this precision: the compliant technology, the wonder of being able to twitch lines and letters this way and that. He is always reluctant to delegate; he surreptitiously checks and rechecks the work of even their most reliable operators. Even, it must be said, that of Sandra herself, who is a bird of his own feather. When they are alone together in the office they sit before their screens in companionable absorption, and Oliver knows that Sandra is experiencing a pleasure complementary to his own— creating text, marshaling text, positioning headings and notes. They are both getting the same buzz. It is almost like sex, he thinks.

Which is perhaps how their alliance came about, the reason that a business relationship shifted into something more, so that here they are now together by night as well as by day, in amiable conjunction, an agreeable conjugality. Oliver thinks of Sandra as friend rather than lover. Best friend. Friend with whom he makes friendly love, in the king-size bed in the first house that he has ever owned. No more seedy flats. No more fridges in which lurk nothing but a wedge of moldy cheese and a pint of sour milk. Clean shirts to hand. Spare lightbulbs and loo paper.

Oliver is still astonished to find himself one half of a couple, at this relatively late point. After the long bachelor years, the occasional forays in halfhearted pursuit of someone, the withdrawals into not especially discontented solitude. Sex on tap is indeed a luxury, though, truth to tell, both of them are somewhat less inclined these days. The cheerful roistering of their early time together is pretty well a thing of the past. But, in any case, lust was never really the driving force where his gathering interest in Sandra was concerned. More affection, appreciation—and along with these the realization that, yes, it would be rather good to go to bed with her.

And thus it was that one day he put a finger on Sandra's knee—a nylon-clad knee from which her skirt had ridden up as she sat bolt upright in her desk chair. "I've been wondering . . ." he said.

And Sandra did not slap his face, or his hand, or rush from the room. She made a correction on her screen, turned to look at him. A long, steady look. "As it happens," she said, "so have I."

Sandra is nothing like the girls he used to run after, time was. She does not have long blond hair or legs to her armpits. She has full breasts and quite muscular calves. Her face is rather flat, all on one plane, it seems; large gray eyes, the mouth a trifle thin. Her neat cap of brown hair is streaked with gray—becoming silver glints. She is quick and calm and cool. Oliver has never seen her truly fazed, that he can recall. An essential quality in a business partner and also, he now finds, one conducive to a tranquil home life. The fridge is always stocked, the bills are paid, the insurance policies are in order.

Actually, Sandra is nothing like the people he used to know.

She is nothing like Nick. As business associates, Sandra and Nick might as well be from different planets. She is nothing like Elaine.

She is nothing like Kath. Above all, she is nothing like Kath.

As if, thinks Oliver.

Oliver used to know all sorts of people. Quite a few of these were women in whom he was currently interested, but usually not sufficiently interested to make a great issue of it. He took them out from time to time, and then, usually, they went off with someone more pressing. The rest were people with whom he had a drink or a meal every now and then. Some of these were fallout from the days with Nick. Nick and Elaine. The business generated a vibrant social life; there were always people turning up at the house, those whom Nick thought potential contributors to some series and had invited along with a gust of enthusiasm—picture researchers, photographers, freelance designers. Temporary assistants came and went, hired by Nick and then gently fired by Oliver when it was realized that resources couldn't run to this. Oliver had his own office in the converted barn that adjoined the house, and a scruffy flat in the nearby market town. In his office he dealt with what Nick called the boring part of publishing: the negotiations with printers, with distributors, with accountants. Over in the house, the fun went on. Nick seldom came to the barn, though Oliver was frequently in the house, summoned to meet this brilliant photographer, this amazing writer. He spent many hours at that kitchen table, while ideas were bandied about over glasses of red plonk. Often Elaine was there. Polly was a baby in a high chair, then a toddler, eventually a schoolgirl.

Sometimes Kath came.

Oliver did not contribute much to those fervent creative sessions around the table. He would come up with quickly calculated figures when appropriate; occasionally, when the level of unreality was getting high, he would be quietly insistent about costings and

projections. But not too insistent; he had learned that it was better
to have a chat with Nick at some later point, by which time he
might have gone off the whole idea anyway. Besides, Oliver enjoyed those occasions. He enjoyed the heady to-and-fro of ideas,
Nick's flights of fancy, the provocative range of people. He liked
the fetching girls with portfolios of artwork—and tried his luck
with these, every now and then. He was properly impressed by
the erudite experts on this and that, who might or might not be
just the author they were looking for. He was well aware of his
own role and image: the sweet voice of reason, sensible Oliver,
who'll sort out the paperwork and get this off the ground. But it
seemed as though he had taken on a degree of protective coloring;
he too was caught up in the creative process. He was a modest but
essential adjunct to all this excited planning. He contributed by
his very presence, and thus became a part of the fluctuating society around Elaine's kitchen table. He stepped out for a while with
a girl Nick brought in to do design. He struck up a friendship with
a man who knew all there was to know about windmills. He became someone people invited along to Sunday lunch gatherings,
he was a useful extra car-driver for spontaneous excursions. That
was a breezy time; there was always some new venture in the
pipeline, other projects charging ahead, fresh people conjured up
by Nick. Thus it was perhaps that Oliver's natural pragmatism was
set aside, that he failed to be alert to the warning signs until it was
too late. Then there were the unnerving weeks when he went over
the figures again and again, looking for some lifeline, and could
find none.

"I feel I've let you down." It was to Elaine that he had said this,
not Nick. And he remembers being surprised by her calmness in
the face of what was happening. Her husband was about to go out
of business, but she seemed quietly buoyant. "We'll be all right,"
she had said. "I've got some plans. What will you do, Oliver?"

He too had had a strategy in mind. He had seen what he could do, even as Hammond & Watson was laid to rest. He had taken happily to computers. That was the way to go. Word processing, printing on demand. He had sidestepped Nick's bustling ideas for future collaboration and slid away. Sometimes he thinks of those years with a touch of nostalgia; mostly he relishes his present certainty and control. Satisfaction lies in an impeccable page, and healthy accounts.

Sandra knows little of Nick, or of Elaine. Least of all does she know anything of Kath. She is aware that Oliver's previous business venture had to do with mainstream publishing, and that his partner was the inspirational and creative member of the team and ended up if anything a mite too inspirational and creative, which was why the thing folded.

Both Sandra and Oliver are reticent about other times. Sandra is divorced, but Oliver knows little of why or when. "'Nuff said," says Sandra crisply. "Over and done with." Equally, she does not press Oliver for information. There is tacit agreement between them that both have lived other lives and that a mutual respect for privacy is appropriate in a late liaison such as theirs. Oliver finds that he is distinctly incurious about Sandra's past. This fact has occasionally given pause for thought; it seems to indicate a detachment that is perhaps not quite right. He reminds himself of Sandra's qualities and of the reasons why life with her is so compatible—her unruffled efficiency, her household management. Her compact, nubile body—nicely sexy when you wanted to see it that way but not a daily disturbing provocation. Her panache behind the wheel; he has come to dislike driving. Her *bœuf en daube*.

Given all that, an obsessive concern with Sandra's previous life seems superfluous, and indeed childish. Leave that to young lovers.

And Sandra too steers clear of inquiry. Though just occasionally an edge creeps into her voice which perhaps indicates suppressed attention. She comes across an inscription in one of Oliver's books: "Happy birthday—tons of love, Nell."

"One of your ladies, I suppose." Crisp, but a statement, not a question. The matter is not pursued.

Where Nick and Elaine are concerned, she is apparently uninterested. The business was wound up; Oliver went his own way. That will do, it seems, for Sandra.

Nowadays, Oliver does not know nearly so many people. He has lost touch with pretty well all of those acquired during the Hammond & Watson years. His clients of today do not move on to a more intimate plane; many of them he never meets—they remain a voice on the phone, a sender of faxes and e-mails. Occasionally he and Sandra entertain another couple for supper. He has moved into that closed society of coupledom, he realizes, on the fringes of which he hung round for so many years. A member of a couple always has someone with whom to go to the cinema, to take a walk. The unattached are flotsam, eddying about the solid purposeful mass of the coupled. From time to time, he does give a wistful thought to life as flotsam: it had its compensations.

"Kath?" says Sandra.

She speaks so abruptly that Oliver is jolted to attention. He has been cruising happily, fingers tapping out a routine task, thoughts quite elsewhere. He stops tapping, and returns to the office.

"The sister. What did she look like?" Sandra is wearing that intent look that he knows so well, like a dog pointing. This can be applied equally to the choice of a cut of meat or consideration of a page layout.

What did Kath look like? Oliver is stymied. How did you begin to describe Kath? "She was . . ." he begins. "Well, she . . . she had dark hair. Not very tall."

"There's a photo I saw once in that envelope you've got in your desk at home. I noticed it when you were trying to find an old photo of yourself to show me. A girl sitting beside a pond. Is that her?"

Sandra's observational talent. He knows at once the picture she means. Kath is sitting cross-legged on the grass in front of the garden pond at Nick and Elaine's house. Her eyes are screwed up in the sunlight, she has bare arms and legs, and a radiant smile, beaming straight at the camera: she is entrancing. Yes, Sandra would have noticed that photo.

"That's her," he says. "Yup."

"I see." Sandra looks reflectively at him. "She was extremely attractive, then?"

"Yes," says Oliver. "She was. Yes, you could say that."

"I'd taken it that the photo was of some girlfriend."

Oliver is almost shocked. "Oh dear me, no. No, no."

Sandra gives him a little smile. She turns back to her screen. Kath has been dealt with, so far as she is concerned.

It still seems incredible to Oliver that Kath will not suddenly walk into the room. Never again. That is what she did, back then. No one was expecting her, Elaine didn't know where she was, what she was doing, and then there she would be—smiling, laughing: "Are you all terribly busy? Can I come to lunch?"

He sees her arriving thus with a great tray of peaches in her arms. She has bought up the entire stock of some greengrocer. "Here . . ." she says. "I couldn't resist. Let's gorge." And Elaine has pursed lips. Oliver can read her thoughts: extravagant, exaggerated, they'll go bad before they can all be eaten.

Elaine was strange where Kath was concerned. You could feel that she was unsettled when Kath was around, there was that sense of concealed tension. She watched Kath a lot—but, then, everyone did that. And she chivied her. Criticized. Elder-sister stuff—but there was a compulsive edge to it. Though it all seemed to roll off Kath; she would smile, deflect. "All right, I'll reform, I promise. . . . Listen, I want to tell you about this amazing place I've found—"

Kath. What a shame it was, thinks Oliver. What a crying shame. When Kath comes into his mind, it is always like a sudden shaft of light. She is talking about a place she's been to, a person she's met, she is all zest and animation, a group springs to life when she is there. There was nobody, Oliver thinks, but nobody, less likely to be . . . dead.

He sometimes wonders why he did not fall in love with her. Plenty did, after all. But no. Kath always seemed out-of-bounds. Sacrosanct, in some curious way. Not for him. She was never less than warm, friendly, welcoming. But then she was like that with everyone. Almost everyone. If Kath didn't care for a person she simply moved away; you never saw dislike, disapproval, but she would have created a space, turned aside. What a talent, thinks Oliver. But that was how she seemed to run her life. When things no longer suited her, she moved on, moved off. Or so one understood. He remembers Elaine's terse inquiries: "You mean you're not working at that gallery anymore?" and Kath's light responses: "Things weren't going quite so well. And I've met this nice man who wants me to help with a festival he's running."

Occasionally, when Kath turned up, there was a man with her. Hardly surprising. Oliver can barely remember these men. One cast an eye over them, of course. Envious? Well, no, not that—but with a kind of proprietorial concern. Was this fellow worthy? And since the same man seldom came a second time, and more often than not she was alone, there was no reason to get exercised about the matter. It seemed remarkable that no one had snapped her up on a permanent basis, but clearly she had this talent for evasion.

Which made Glyn Peters all the more surprising. Oliver remembers well the advent of Glyn Peters. One became aware of an intensity about Elaine, a tautness. And then one day there was Kath and she had this bloke with her, very much at home apparently, knees under Elaine's kitchen table as though he had a right there, one eye on Kath all the time, holding forth. Oliver had been wary at first, hackles raised; gradually he had found himself intrigued, even slightly mesmerized. The man had a way with him, no doubt about that. Not surprising he'd been a hit on the telly, apparently. He had that knack of talking whereby he seemed to be addressing you personally, as though you were especially equipped to appreciate all this intriguing information. Oliver can hear him now, giving them all a breakdown on medieval crop-rotation systems, on how to date a hedge; he would glance in your direction, and you felt flattered, singled out, recognized as a connoisseur.

Was that what Kath had felt? Elaine put her head round his office door one morning—brisk and to the point: "A date for your diary, Oliver. Kath's getting married. We'll have a bit of a party. You met Glyn a few weeks ago—remember?" And that was it. Well, well. Lucky Glyn Peters. How had he done it? Oliver remembers Kath at one of those kitchen gatherings, the table awash with food and drink, Nick talking, Glyn talking most of all, and Kath sitting slightly apart, on the window seat, her legs curled under her, Polly alongside. Polly was always wherever Kath was. Kath is plaiting Polly's hair—Polly's long schoolgirl hair. She combs the hair and looks towards Glyn, a speculative look, as though she is asking him something, asking herself something. They are shortly to be married. Oliver inspects Kath for indications of consuming passion; but there is just this querying gaze. Puzzled, almost.

You could not but be absorbed by Kath, even if you did not fall in love with her. There was what she looked like, and there was what she was. She was . . . What was she? thinks Oliver. She was an entirely nice person. Nice? What does that mean? A non-word. You couldn't imagine Kath doing anything mean, or malevolent, or despicable. She was nice to people—hang on, that word again—she was friendly, and interested, and kind. And a provocative thought arises: Was she able to be that way because of what she looked like? Because the world smiles upon the physically attractive and they can smile back? But the world is also well stocked with malign beauties, and ever has been, from Snow White's stepmother onwards. A ravishing woman can also have a vile temperament. So that theory won't wash.

When Oliver remembers Kath, that luminous quality predominates. The way your spirits lifted a notch, just because she was there: the day seemed more promising, the adrenaline ran stronger. And really, Oliver thinks, that is distinctly odd. Perverse, even. Kath had gaiety and verve, but she was not especially wise, nor clever, nor well informed. If one is being realistic, one would have to say that her contribution to society was nil. She did nothing useful, had no sustained employment, was neither creative nor industrious. She had no children, if children are to be seen as fulfillment of a social purpose. She simply was—as a flower is, or a bird. People are meant to be more than that, are they not?

Oh, come on, thinks Oliver, this is getting heavy. It's enough that she was a startlingly appealing person, in every way.

She could surprise you, take you unawares. Once, he was with her in the courtyard between the house and his office in the barn; they were sitting on the bench there, waiting, it seems, for someone or something—the framework of the moment is gone now. And she turned to him and said, "Are you happy, Oliver?"

He had clenched in alarm. He had wanted to protest that he wasn't the sort of person who answers that sort of question, or to whom that sort of question is put. He had gazed at her beseechingly: was he supposed to say, "Are you, Kath?"

She had gazed back, thoughtful, expectant, really wanting to know, it seemed, as though his reply might solve some problem. And when he went on saying nothing she smiled—that smile, that great smile that always made you smile back, willy-nilly: "I bet you are. You've got more sense than to be unhappy."

When he realized that there was something going on between her and Nick, he had been disturbed. More than that—incredulous, alarmed, offended. How could this be?

The first intimation had been a look, quite simply. Nick watching Kath in the way that others watched her, those coming across her for the first time, people who hadn't known her for years, as Nick had. Elaine had not been present; Oliver had been uneasily glad of that.

After that, small disconcerting signals. Nick covertly attentive when Elaine was on the phone to Kath, pretending to read the newspaper. Kath visiting less, rather than more. Elaine saying one day, "Ages since Kath showed up—where's she got to now?"; Nick's furtive look, his apparent casual lack of interest.

And then one day Oliver had gone to the Blue Boar in Welborne to meet a man for a drink—a piece of fellow flotsam from that footloose uncoupled time—and there at a table across the room were Nick and Kath. Quite evidently intent upon one another. Oliver had been all of a dither. What to do? March up to them, jolly and unconcerned: "Hi there—what a coincidence! Tom's with me—you know, Tom Willows—we'll join you." And then he had hesitated, headed in one direction and then another, and they had looked up and the expression on their faces was not one of cheery innocent welcome but of dismay. Oliver had flapped a hand, mouthed some dismissive greeting, bolted for an alcove as far from them as possible. "Isn't that your partner?" said Tom Willows, puzzled. "No," said Oliver. "I mean, yes. Business meeting—no need to get involved. Pint?"

Later that day Nick came across to the barn. "Just to have a word about print runs for the new series, and to ask what you think about this jacket artwork—fantastic, isn't it?" The usual Nick, all lit up with plans and ideas. "I think we should really go for broke on this one, don't you—?" And, at the end of it, turning to go, he had shot Oliver a look—a wary, propitiating look: "Oh . . . and, Olly, incidentally, you didn't see me this morning, OK?"

I don't want this, Oliver had thought. I don't want any part of this. This is nothing to do with me.

But it was, now.

No one else must know: that was paramount. He knew, who had no wish to, but there must be no others. Above all, not Elaine. Above all, not Glyn Peters—a man who struck Oliver as being quite likely to come charging in with a horsewhip.

The matter was never raised again between him and Nick. Except that once, tacitly. The business with the photograph. That had been his warning shot. Nothing said. Just that silent indication: Watch it, stop it. And, eventually, he assumed, that was just what had come about. It ended, as these things do.

Oh well . . . long out of the way, all that, thinks Oliver. Laid to rest, thanks be. No harm done, in the end.

"I'm off out," says Sandra. "I've got to go to the bank. Mind the shop for half an hour, will you?"

And she is gone. Oliver makes himself a cup of coffee. He yawns. He is drifting rather this morning—he will need to go over those pages carefully. He stares out of the window for a moment, remembers that call. He picks up the phone.

"Oh—Glyn? Oliver Watson here, returning your call."

Elaine and Nick

Nick goes to a health club these days. This is on account of his paunch, which has been causing him disquiet. He is also disturbed about his bald patch, and while he is aware that visits to the health club will not do much for that, he feels that all the same there may be some general knock-on effect. Nick cannot understand how he has come to be fifty-eight. This is ridiculous, frankly. Time has been stalking him, but the thing to do was to give it the cold shoulder, pay no attention. And now suddenly it has reached out and clobbered him. He does not care for what he sees in the mirror; he is pained and affronted.

At the health club, Nick jogs and cycles and pumps. He plows up and down the gold-dappled blue waters of the pool. He is bored to desperation while doing this, and the jogging and pumping make him ache, but he is satisfied with his own strength of mind. He weighs himself frequently, finds that he can definitely chalk up the loss of two and a half pounds, and buys a new pair of jeans to celebrate the fact. Elaine has made it plain that she thinks men of his age should not be wearing jeans, which is unkind, he feels; why should he give up the habit of a lifetime?

The boredom of the health club is somewhat tempered by

idle observation of those around him. Most are much younger—in their twenties or thirties. Many of the girls are tattooed—a butterfly on the shoulder, a spray of leaves on the thigh, a star on the ankle. To pass the time, Nick makes a mental inventory of these tattoos, which means he needs to look quite closely at the girls, though he is careful to do so discreetly, knowing how easy it is for men to be misconstrued these days. He has listed clover leaves, and ivy and daisies, and a single rose. He got a fleeting glimpse once of a dragon round the midriff, which needs a confirmatory sighting. The girls themselves are of course pleasing, though that is about as far as it goes. He can honestly say that while there is the odd *frisson* of sexual interest, he is not tempted. Occasionally, he exchanges a few words with one of them in the cafeteria—Could I take that paper if you've done with it? Were you wanting this chair?—and the girl will be polite enough, though not what you might call encouraging. In transitory glum moments, Nick wonders if he is emasculated by the paunch and the bald patch.

But Nick is not constitutionally glum, never has been.

All his life, he has woken up each day with a renewed surge of interest. When he looks back—which in fact he does not much do—he has this gratifying sense of busyness, of teeming schemes and projects, of some unquenchable source of stimulation. Admittedly, plenty of schemes and projects never came to fruition, and indeed he has forgotten now what most of them were, but it is the general effect that counts. He has never been bored—or, if he has, he has quickly sidestepped. Which is why he is proud of his tenacity at the health club.

And he has plenty still to do. He has two or three ideas on the go that just need some more research. A gazetteer of eighteenth-century follies; the definitive series on hill walking; a photographic survey of World War II pillboxes. Truth to tell, it is a blessing that with Elaine doing so well for years now the pressure is off, he can take his time, play around with any new inspiration, and look really carefully at what might be involved. And there's no need to do too much hack stuff, where the money, to be honest, is neither here nor there. Quite a good idea to keep one's hand in with the odd piece of journalism, but no point in becoming a slave to it.

"There is something we have got to talk about," says Elaine.

Her tone of voice sets an alarm bell ringing, but only a muted one. This matter of upgrading his car? Probably. Nothing that can't be sorted, if he goes about it in the right way.

It may be that the demise of Hammond & Watson was all for the best, in the long term. Of course it was tremendous fun, at the time—that nonstop activity, new books brewing, those heady moments when the first bound copies arrived, the pursuit of likely authors, all the comings and goings. But there had been also the endless niggling, tiresome background irritations of accountants and suppliers, and all those bloody figures which apparently forbade one to do this or that. Admittedly, Oliver took much off one's back, but they were always there, like some po-faced inappropriate guest at a party, clouding things.

No, he doesn't regret those days so very much. The time since has been something of a liberation, Nick now realizes. He has been able to give proper consideration to a project, drop it if it seems likely to become a bore in the end, instead of being obliged to plunge ahead because a publishing house must publish, after all. And then sometimes one got tired of the book or the series in midstream. No, he can take things as they come—do background work on some idea when he feels inspired, and accept fallow periods when nothing much springs to mind, but that's not so bad because there are always plenty of agreeable ways of passing the time. He is aware that Elaine gets a bit uptight about this way of doing things, but it is so shortsighted of her. As he has tried to explain—but she never quite seems to get the point—you are actually much more productive if you pace yourself. He had never realized that was the case back in the Hammond & Watson days, when he used to be scurrying around like some demented ant—day in, day out. Of course, Elaine's own style is one of relentless work. He's always telling her she should let up a bit, take a few days off. But no—if it's not client meetings and site visits, it's paperwork with Sonia or sussing out some new supplier. And when she's not doing any of that, she's out in the garden, fossicking away.

"Oh . . . right," he says. "Over supper, OK? I was just going to the health club."

"*Now*. I'm away tonight."

Mind, he'd be the first to agree that Elaine's industry is remarkable, and that her success is a great blessing. All credit to her—he would never have believed that the outfit she's got now could have arisen from those small beginnings. He got a bit of a shock the other day when he heard her discussing last year's turnover with Sonia. And incidentally, given that, it really is a bit stiff to be getting all flaky about replacing the car.

Just occasionally, Nick looks at Elaine and is disconcerted. He gets this odd feeling that she is someone else, a person he doesn't know all that well. Which is absurd; she is the woman with whom he has been getting into bed every night—well, most nights, admittedly Elaine is elsewhere rather more often nowadays—for God knows how many years. How long have they been married? He'd need to work that one out. And of course this is nonsense—Elaine is as she ever was, just older. But sometimes this stranger glances across the table at him.

She's in the top league now, it seems, in her trade. There's talk of a lecture tour in the States, and she's designing a garden for next year's Chelsea Flower Show. She's busy. Which means that she is not always as attentive to what Nick may be saying or doing as she once was. Maybe that accounts for the sense of alienation. But it's not a problem.

Nick has always given problems a wide berth. Problems should not be what life is about. When running a business, you hire someone else to deal with nuts and bolts, as good old Oliver did. Nick is always saying to Elaine that she should pass on much more to Sonia than she does, or bring in some troubleshooter. And, above all, you never allow yourself to get rattled if things aren't working out the way they should. Just move on. Cut your losses and forget about it.

This is the best policy for personal life also, Nick reckons. The snag is that other people tend to ambush you, from time to time. They create difficulties. They misunderstand, they misinterpret. It has to be said that Elaine has a tendency in that direction. Some small thing can be absurdly inflated, an obstacle found where there need be none. Such as this nonsense about the car.

"In the conservatory," says Elaine. "Sonia will be here in a minute."

He follows her. Really, this is getting a bit out of hand.

How long *have* they been married? He must remember to check that out with her, though obviously now is not the moment. Nick is well attuned to Elaine's state of mind, and it is clear that this morning is a bad patch, for some reason. The strategy will be, as ever, to be nicely propitiating, lower the temperature, and change the subject and, with any luck, whatever is riling her can be laid to rest.

Nick is definitely fond of Elaine. Absolutely no question about that. He cannot imagine being married to anyone else. Time was—and he is prepared to admit this—he used to look around a bit, once in a while. But everyone does that when they're younger, don't they? There's nothing of that kind now, hasn't been for many a year. Elaine suits him nicely. Their sex life has rather gone off the boil, but presumably that's true of anyone of their age. Though Elaine of course is a touch older than he is, not that he's ever made anything of that.

Nick can't quite remember how he and Elaine came to get married. No wonder he's not certain how long ago it was anyway. An awful lot of years, that's for sure. He's never gone in for mulling over the past. What's done is done. You can't change what's happened, so why keep hauling it out and looking at it? And he has never wished himself not married to Elaine; just occasionally it has been therapeutic to . . . look outside a bit. Back when he met her there was such a crowd of people about, melded now into an impressionistic blur. Lots of girls. Somehow it was Elaine he married rather than someone else, and he is inclined to feel that that has been nothing but a blessing. All right, she can be edgy at times, such as right now, but one can handle that. And she has always kept things running—he is absolutely prepared to hand it to her there, if it weren't for the way she has got her own business off the ground they might well be in a bit of a pickle at this point. No, Elaine deserves all credit, no question. If she gets rather fraught on occasion, well, that's understandable. She's under a fair bit of pressure, and the thing is to be understanding and accommodating.

"Actually," he says, "I've given it a bit of thought—this car question—and I reckon we don't need to go for brand-new. A year or two old would do me fine."

"We're not talking about your car."

■ ■ ■

It has to be said that Elaine can be just a mite governessy. Ever has been—and getting more so, Nick fears. One is going to have to be tolerant. It was never a good idea to make a stand when she got ratty about something quite trivial—best just to back off and, with any luck, it would blow over. In the past, he could always placate her, talk her down, be especially friendly and helpful and all that. Lately, this approach somehow doesn't seem to cut so much ice. The best thing is just to keep his head down, go his own way, which is, after all, what he has always done, and take care not to get into antagonistic situations. Elaine likes to run a tight ship, she likes to know what's going on around her, but nowadays she is pretty well taken up with the business, and frankly there's no need for her to be bothered about Nick's day-to-day arrangements. It would be a lot more sensible if there were some more fluid system over cash flow, and then he wouldn't need to involve her when something crops up like this matter of the car. He's suggested this more than once, but Elaine can be funny when it comes to money. Distinctly shirty.

"Oh . . . right." He gives her a questioning look. An open, sunny, at-your-service sort of look.

Damn. That means the car matter has simply been put on hold, stashed away in one of Elaine's mental "pending" files, and he will have to allow a judicious interval before he brings it up again. Which is a blasted nuisance. The Golf has over eighty thousand on the clock, one thing after another is going wrong, and he wouldn't really want to do a long trip in it. Which means that he has got to get it replaced before he can go up to Northumberland and have a few days pottering around Lindisfarne and Alnwick and places like that, which he feels might be inspirational.

• • •

Elaine is silent. Nick waits. Back in the house, the phone rings, stops. Sonia has picked it up. Outside, Jim rides the tractor mower to and fro, to and fro.

"So the mower's running OK now . . ." says Nick.

Which is all to the good. Bad news if it was packing in. God knows what those things cost. Not as much as a car, though, surely? But of course it's not the car we're here about, apparently. There's something else.

When Elaine comes on all heavy like this, the thing is to play it down. Nick does not like rows. In fact, he never has rows—not with anyone. If a row situation threatens, he somehow just is not there anymore. This technique has worked with Elaine, up to a point. It is difficult for anyone to get satisfactorily confrontational with someone who will not confront back. Nick is aware that he is rather skillful at marital peacekeeping, at the avoidance of overt hostility, at the adroit use of diplomatic initiatives. On occasion, he has wondered if he ought not to be exploiting this experience, this facility. When lifestyle publications became a boom industry, he thought of stepping in with a really definitive book on married life from the man's point of view. With a pushy title—*How to Stay Married*, that sort of thing. A combination of wry humor with practicality. And a literary slant as well—cite some famous abiding marriages and look at the ups and downs. D. H. Lawrence and what's-her-name. Tennyson was married for donkey's years, wasn't he? Dickens—no, that went off the rails. One would have to get it all up, but that could be quite amusing. In fact, the thing was definitely a promising idea, but somehow it was a project he had never felt able to run past Elaine. Normally he gave her a progress report on any scheme he was working on—not that there was ever very much of a comeback, not much constructive input from her, put it that way. Sometimes you could even feel that she wasn't giving the sort of attention that she should be. Anyway, he'd somehow had this sense that she wouldn't really get the point of the marriage-book idea, so it was never mentioned and eventually he'd abandoned it. It was something one could always pick up again, if there was nothing much else in mind.

But Nick knows that he is sensitive to the coded language of married life. He can negotiate. And so he is not going to allow whatever is at issue just now to get out of hand. Easy does it.

"Kath," says Elaine.

It is curious how her name instantly summons her. She is right there, for an instant, looking at him. And he feels . . . Well, there is a pleasant sense of well-being, a little lift of the spirits. Kath could always do that. A whole troop of Kaths flit about him, stemming from different times and places. She is dancing with Polly— a child Polly. She has just married Glyn, and stands hand in hand with him, beaming. She sits cross-legged in the garden here, making a daisy chain. She . . . And then again she . . .

"Kath?" he says.

They seldom talk about Kath. At least not deliberately, as it were. She crops up, often enough. Naturally. Some casual mention. "Wasn't Kath there when . . . ?" "Didn't Kath used to go to such-and-such . . . ?" Polly talks about her quite a lot. She and Polly were always thick as thieves.

So why, all of a sudden . . . ?

"You and Kath," says Elaine.

■ ■ ■

There is this heave of the gut. The room seems to swing a little. The troop of Kaths is quite gone. It is just him and Elaine, sitting there in the conservatory, with the tractor mower going up and down outside, a bee buzzing in the blue plumbago. Everything is quite real and precise, unfortunately. It is Tuesday morning, about half past ten. He should be on his way to the health club. Instead, he is here, with a sick feeling in his stomach.

What is going on? Not . . . Surely she can't have . . . How could . . . ?

"I've seen a photograph," says Elaine. "And a note from you that was with it."

Oh God. It comes rushing into his head as she speaks. That photograph. Of course. He can see it. He remembers laughing when first he saw it. And he couldn't resist sending it to Kath. She didn't keep it? The silly girl didn't go and hang on to it?

"I see you know what I'm talking about," she says.

Jesus Christ. But . . . Hang on, how did . . . ? Oliver. It was Oliver who handed over the photo. And one—well, one sort of squared Oliver. And he said he'd binned the negative. So has bloody Oliver . . . ? Otherwise it has to be that it has somehow turned up. Where?

"Glyn found it," says Elaine.

Now the whole place whirls. The floor rocks. That bee makes a shrill, insistent din, like a dentist's drill. This shouldn't be happening. But it is.

Get a grip. Take control. This is bad, but it is nothing that cannot be contained, like everything else. Naturally Elaine is upset; she has had a shock. It will take a while for her to digest this; he is going to need all his resources.

"Ah . . . Glyn," he says.

Now it is Glyn's turn to come surging in. Nick can see him plain, and he is looking like thunder. Nick cannot hear what he is saying, which is probably just as well. Glyn—a nasty complication there. But first things first.

"Look, love," he says. "What we have to do is get this thing into perspective. OK—I'm not going to defend myself or tell lies. I wish it didn't have to be like this, but now that it is . . . well, I'm just going to be entirely honest. Yes, Kath and I once, just for a while, we—"

"I don't want to know," says Elaine. "I don't want to know when, or where, or for how long. It's enough that it was."

"Listen," he says. "It was a flash in the pan. A silly, idiotic, passing thing. It was all over, long ago. Long before she—"

"No doubt."

"It makes absolutely no difference to *us*," he says. "Neither then nor now. It was a stupid mistake. Kath herself would say that. Believe me. I know she would."

"Very likely."

This isn't going right. He has struck the wrong note, somehow. And Elaine is unnerving him. She just sits there, quite calm, staring him down. Right now he feels more strongly than ever that there is a stranger there, not her.

The bee is silent. Jim and the tractor mower have gone. The ground is steady, the room no longer rocks, but it feels alien. Everything is just the same, but not the same at all.

"What can I do?" he says. Very quiet voice. Careful, sorrowful.

"I want you to go," says Elaine.

He gazes in total disbelief. "Go where?"

"That is entirely up to you. Away from here. Away from this house."

He is about to say, "But this is my house," when he remembers that it is not. It is Elaine's house. Elaine put down the deposit, Elaine pays the mortgage.

"So long as you are here," says Elaine, "I shall be reminded of this every time I look at you. I shall have all the feelings that I am having at the moment. And I don't propose to remain in this condition for the foreseeable future. I have better things to do."

"But I live here," says Nick.

"At the moment."

Scuttling thoughts. No, not thoughts—panicky explosions in the head. But she can't! Yes, she can. What will I . . . ? Where can I . . . ? This is so unfair. Years ago. I haven't committed a *crime*. I mean, lots of people . . .

Stay cool, that's the thing. Sweet reason. Elaine is a reasonable woman. She must see that this is . . . exaggerated. Of course it's shaken her up, of course she's angry. She has every right.

Quiet voice, still. Gentle, persuasive. "Listen, I absolutely understand how you must be feeling. And I'm with you. I'm wiped out by this myself. But we can manage. We can't let it spoil everything. In time, we'll be able to live with it."

"You apparently have been doing so for years, quite comfortably," says Elaine. "Personally, I don't feel so confident about that."

Back in the house the phone rings again. It stops. Nick sees Elaine shoot a glance at her watch.

"Honestly, sweetie," he says. "This is all a bit over the top. What we need to do is wind down, sleep on it, and have a little talk in a few days' time."

Elaine gets up. "In a few days' time you won't be here," she says. "I'm off shortly. I'll be back late tomorrow afternoon, and I expect to find you gone. Money is being paid into your account, and will be each month. Enough to rent a place and meet modest living expenses. Take your car. And your books. We can sort out what else belongs to you at some later point."

And she goes. Outside, Jim is back with the tractor mower. The bee is joined by a friend. The day marches on.

Glyn and Oliver

Bloody hell! What a mess. After all this time. Just because of a wretched photograph.

Oliver feels trapped. Here he is in his own familiar pub along the road from the office, and nothing is as it should be. Instead of a pint and a quiet half hour with the newspaper, he is eyeball-to-eyeball with Glyn Peters. The pint is there, but he is not enjoying it. Glyn is a heavy presence, grilling him. He leans insistently across the low shiny round table, moving beer mats with one finger. He fixes Oliver with those glittery dark-brown eyes.

"What I need to know—" he says.

You'd be a damn sight better off not knowing, thinks Oliver. Just leave it alone. Nothing to be done about it now. All over with. And, no, I don't know how long it went on for and I don't want to know and nor should you. It's nothing to do with me, never was. Anyone would think I was some sort of accessory to the crime.

"Why did you photograph them?" demands Glyn.

For heaven's sake! "Look, I didn't see until after I got the prints. I just snapped the whole group, standing there chatting to each other. I hadn't noticed that Kath and Nick were—" He shrugs.

And when you did, thinks Glyn, you got into a right old panic, didn't you? Your business chum and his sister-in-law. And you all matey with everyone—always in and out of the house . . .

Years since he set eyes on Oliver Watson. The man much the same as ever—that slightly apologetic manner, self-deprecation tinged with complacency. Running some sort of small printing outfit these days, it seems. Little office with computers. Lady who appears to be rather more than an assistant, taking a distinct interest in one's arrival. Oliver rather keen to get them both off the premises sharpish: "Glyn Peters—Sandra Chalcott. Sandra's my partner. We'll push off to the local, shall we, and have a chat there?"

"How did you find me?" Oliver inquires. "Given that we've rather lost touch?"

"Elaine."

"You've told Elaine!"

"I needed to establish certain facts. There was no alternative." Glyn is impatient rather than defensive.

"Nick?" says Oliver, after a moment.

"That's up to Elaine. I am frankly not much interested in Nick."

Oliver takes a swig of beer, which does nothing for him. He wishes he were back in the office. He wishes Glyn were anywhere but here. He is irritated, and also faintly apprehensive. There is something evangelical about Glyn's approach to this, the sinister evangelism of the obsessed.

Glyn hammers on. "You must have seen a good deal of Kath, over the years?"

"Well . . . yes. She was often around." What is this leading up to? Good grief . . . is he going to accuse me of having it off with her too?

Glyn leans back in his chair. He places his fingers tip-to-tip, rests his chin on them, becomes reflective and confidential. "Let me tell you, this revelation has stopped me in my tracks. You must understand that. I am confronted with . . . an unreliability about my own past. My past with Kath. I am not interested in recriminations. My concern is purely forensic. Do you follow me?"

"Not really," says Oliver.

"I want to know if Kath was in the habit of infidelity. I want to know about her."

Oliver is shocked. But you were married to her, for Christ's sake, he wants to say. It's a bit late in the day to start talking like this.

Glyn finishes his beer, rises, gestures at Oliver. "Drink up."

"Actually, I won't have another," says Oliver. "I've got an afternoon's work to do." But Glyn has ignored him, and is already heading for the bar.

When he returns he is in full flow before he has sat down. "I have to look at this as I would at any other major piece of research. Every clue must be followed up. . . . I have to take a detached view, lay everything out for inspection, pay attention to even the most marginal pieces of information. . . ." Isolated phrases reach over, rising above the background buzz of the pub; Oliver wears an attentive expression, and allows himself to drift. What's with the man? Was he always like this? Well, yes—somewhat. And the voice—great delivery. Generations of Welsh preachers behind that. "Method, patience. You start out with an open mind, prepared for whatever may turn up. Which doesn't mean that you don't follow a hunch, do you see? Now, seeking you out may take me nowhere, but it was worth doing. Kath is now my area of study—"

"But she's not an area," Oliver interrupts, goaded. "She's a woman. Was."

Glyn jolts to a halt. He stares. Annoyed, it would seem. But the mood switches. "Point taken," he says. "That's the whole trouble, isn't it?"

Oliver looks down into his unwelcome second pint. No answer to that one.

"So tell me, then. Was she known for this kind of thing?"

"Not to my knowledge."

"Before she married me she had . . . admirers. Par for the course."

"Quite," Oliver agrees.

"I'm concerned with a subsequent pattern of behavior."

Oliver is finding it hard to believe that this conversation is taking place. He surveys the room. He eyes other pairs of men, presumably having a comfortable postmortem on some business assignment, or talking politics or sport or last night's television. While he is landed with the manic concerns of a bloke he thought he no longer knew.

"You must have had a general impression about her, as a person."

No comment required, it would seem.

"Did you know her friends?"

Enough, thinks Oliver. "Look," he says. "Kath is . . . dead. Not here. Can't put up any sort of defense or explanation. Is this fair?"

Glyn spreads his hands. "But that is the whole point about the dead. Precisely. They are unaffected. Untouchable. Beyond reach. The rest of us are still flailing around trying to make sense of things. Addicts like myself choose to do so as a way of life."

"Well," says Oliver. "That's your view. Not mine, I have to say."

Glyn takes stock. This is not going anywhere. Impossible to get one's point across. Stonewalling—that's what the man is at. Why? What's his agenda? Is there something he knows? If so, he's been pretty quick on his feet. Had no idea what I wanted to see him about until half an hour ago. Whatever . . . no point in spinning this out.

He smiles—genial, equable. "And I respect your position. But I'm sure you appreciate that I've been somewhat thrown by this."

Actually, Oliver does. At least, at this moment he does. It must indeed have been a slap in the face. He manages a wan reciprocating grin.

Glyn downs his beer. "Well—good to have met up again after all this time. Pity it had to be about this."

Oliver mumbles some similar sentiment.

They get up and move towards the door. Outside, Glyn pauses. "The other couple—on that occasion. Woman called Mary Packard, I believe. Friend of yours?"

Oliver shakes his head, wanting to make a bolt for the office.

"Artist of some kind, is that right?"

"Potter," says Oliver desperately. "Lived in Winchcombe." Oh, treachery. But what is Mary Packard to him? Anything to have done with this. "Have to dash," he says. "Client due shortly. Good to see you."

Polly

Kath! I can't believe all this is about *Kath*.

I mean, basically she was just such an amazingly nice person. I adored her. So possibly I'm prejudiced, but that's how she was for me. I thought she was wonderful. Of course, that rather went down like a lead balloon with Mum. She and Mum . . . Oh well, old history now. Except that apparently nothing is. But it was all more on Mum's side, you know. Always Mum being uptight and critical, and Kath going her own sweet way. I suppose that was the problem—Kath just carried on regardless and other people were left to look on, and they didn't always look kindly. Though what business it was of theirs, frankly . . . I mean, Kath just lived life to the full and what's wrong with that, say I?

She was *so* attractive. That face. And the way she moved and sat and stood—you always found yourself watching her. Not that she was the slightest bit vain, never bothered about clothes or hair—well, she didn't need to, but the point is she never realized she didn't need to. Just didn't much care. Of course you can only be like that if you *are* that compelling, so I suppose in a way she did know, kind of unconsciously—it comes full circle.

But she wasn't full of self-confidence—not a bit. It was more that she was . . . well, she had some kind of glow. And dash—

always off somewhere, meeting someone, jumping in the car. She didn't hang around. Almost as though she didn't dare to, when one thinks about it. As though if she stopped, something would catch up with her. Anyway, "self-confident" isn't the term—definitely not. But she must have *known* the effect she had. Men, after all . . . It was more as though that just didn't have any effect on *her*. Or any sort of ego-boosting effect. She didn't really seem to have an ego, come to think of it. Self-centered she was not, if that's compatible with always doing pretty much what you want. Hmm . . . more complicated than one reckons.

I remember when my first boyfriend dumped me, when I was at college. What? Oh yes, definitely he was a rat. Hey—are you having a go at me? Well, good, then. Anyway, it was Kath's shoulder I wept on, of course, rather than Mum's. Kath said, "That's what they do." And sort of shrugged, with that little odd smile. And I remember I said, "I bet no one's ever dumped *you*." And she thought for a moment and she said: "Not as such, I suppose, but there's other ways of going about it." I can still hear her saying that. I didn't know what she meant, and I don't now. Women dump too? Well, of course. Too right they do. I'm not talking general theory, I'm talking Kath, do you mind? And then she took me out shopping and we bought me a crazy ridiculous dress I'd never have bought on my own and had an extravagant lunch in an Italian place. That was Kath all over—turn your back on life's glitches, go out, go away, ring up a friend.

Sort of thing that made Mum go all tight-lipped. Not Mum's style, you see. There was something tortoise-and-hare about Mum and Kath. Oh, but it's the tortoise that wins, isn't it? Hmm . . . food for thought there. Not that it was a race, or even the usual sort of sisterly-rivalry stuff. Frankly, they never even seemed like sisters. But there was some kind of eerie connection. Umbilical cord—no, that's not right, but you know what I mean. I suppose it's always like that, with siblings. I wouldn't know, not having any.

When I was little, Kath was where the fun was at, whenever she came to our house, always unexpected, out of the blue. Bringing lovely silly presents that I've never forgotten—paper flowers that opened in water, and a kite like a dragon, and a ginger kitten that just about had Mum hitting the roof. She made up games that we played, and she read me stories, and she did my hair in funky styles, and she discovered face-painting for kids before everyone else was doing it. When she walked in the door it was suddenly like it was Christmas, or a birthday.

It's funny she never had children of her own. She and Glyn. Mind, I can't imagine Glyn with children. Doubt if he wanted any. It wasn't something she ever talked about. I wonder . . . Well, whatever reason she didn't, she didn't.

You can imagine not wanting children? Oh, you can, can you? I see.

Thinking about Kath, I suppose one thing that sticks out is that she never worked. Not properly, that is. I mean, for most people—for practically everyone—work is what you are, in a sense. What you have to do, day in, day out, decides everything else. How much money you've got and therefore how you can live. And it either builds you up or grinds you down, doesn't it? Personally, I consider myself pretty lucky, work-wise. I like it. I get paid not too badly for doing something I don't at all mind doing. And I get an odd sort of kick out of knowing that what I'm doing is absolutely a here-and-now sort of thing. A today kind of job. I mean, if you'd said to someone twenty years ago, She's a Web designer, they'd have gone: Eh? They'd have been thinking crochet work. It's like operating the spinning jenny at the beginning of the Industrial Revolution—or stoking the first steam engine or whatever.

Nobody's done this before, I say to myself. Nobody's spent their days sitting in front of a box with a glowing window, flicking images around. What I'm doing is precisely where the human race is at, today.

OK, laugh. I knew it was pretentious when I said it. Oh—funny—right.

No, you're not. Excuse me, but no way is estate agent cutting-edge stuff. Estate agents have been around since the Ark. There'd have been an estate agent on Mount Ararat, telling Noah this was a prime development site. Sorry, Dan.

Don't worry, you'll always make lots more money than I do. But I wouldn't want to be doing anything else. It beats stoking engines any day—if this is the new technical revolution, then we slave workers have certainly got it easier this time round. In fact, the slave workers are somewhere else now, aren't they? They're out there mending the roads and carting rubbish and heaving bricks, like they always were. Of course, it helps to have had an education a cut above the average. Three years at college and all that. I was never going to end up on the checkout at Tesco, whatever.

Kath. I've got right away from Kath. Her not working. Or not working in any serious sense. Just stuff she'd do for a few weeks or months and then pack it in—temping with a publisher, front-of-house girl in an art gallery. God knows how she managed, income-wise. But she never went in for mortgages or rent either. She just seemed to perch—here, there, and everywhere. Mum was always fussing because she didn't know her address.

No, actually some guy was *not* paying the bills. You're quite wrong there. Not that there weren't plenty who'd have been glad to. There was always someone hanging around. But Kath wasn't one for commitment, or at least not for a long time. Frankly, I think she had a problem.

Excuse me, Dan, but you are so wrong. Of course a person has a problem if they apparently can't commit themselves to a relationship by the time they're thirty-five.

And there was no question of career motivation in Kath's case. Way back, when she was very young, she was going to be an actress. Why, oh why, is it that for any girl with definitely above-average looks it becomes inevitable that she's going to be an actress? Nowadays it would be modeling, wouldn't it? Kath would be talent-spotted in Oxford Street. Back then, people must have kept saying, "Honestly, with your looks, you just have to go for acting. . . ." Until it became what she had to do.

I mean, that's so stupid. The idea that what a person looks like decides what they ought to do. You might as well say that red-haired people should drive London buses. And it happens to women more than men. Above all it happens to ultradecorative women. A good-looking guy can ride it out. He can end up as prime minister, or governor of the Bank of England, or whatever you like. I'm not saying that they do, but you get the point. If a girl is very, very pretty, then that's going to put a particular spin on everything that happens to her. She's privileged, but there's a sense in which it's a curse as well. She's directed by her looks. In Kath's case the actress stint meant that there was no college, no learning how to do anything, just muddling along until that becomes a way of life.

All right, I daresay a nice-looking girl *does* get on well in the property business. Which doesn't prove much, if I may say so.

And then she met Glyn. Do you know, I've no idea why she up and married him. I mean, he was an academic—not really her scene at all. Mum knew him first, apparently—I've never known quite how. Not that he was your straightforward scholarly type, Glyn. He was on the telly a lot, back then—climbing around Roman forts and stuff, holding forth. Actually, when I was a teenager he made quite an impression. All that talk—and a whiff of Richard Burton about him. Richard Burton meets Heathcliff. And apparently he made a dead set at Kath, soon as he saw her. But she'd had that happen before, often enough, for heaven's sake. Anyway, this time she gave in. Commitment, finally.

And it stuck. Until she—until that awful time. I've told you. They got married and stayed married. It seemed to work. Mind, it was a very coming-and-going sort of marriage—Glyn off doing what he did, and her hanging out with friends like she always had and getting involved with this and that. Kath wasn't going to sit at home doing the devoted-housewife bit. She never talked about him much. Just little throwaway remarks—"Glyn's off conferencing somewhere, so I'm on the loose. Hey, let's go up to town. . . ." And she'd sweep me off on some spree. You always had such *fun* with Kath. And do you know, even in the middle of all this, I can't feel any differently about her. I mean, because of her there's this almighty fuss—well, because of her and Dad, let's get things into perspective. And for me she's still the same person. Kath. I can't somehow relate this to her.

All right, we'll talk tomorrow. Actually, it's not *that* late, but never mind. I'm really, really worried about my parents, that's all. And now I'm wondering how far you're there for me on this, Dan.

Elaine takes the phone through into the conservatory, where Sonia cannot hear. Sonia's polite constraint is becoming a mild ir-ritation—her determined pretense that everything is as usual. The instrument bleats on as Elaine walks, as she sits down, as she looks out towards the pergola and sees that the wisteria is starting to show color. Polly's agitation seeps into her ear, creating jagged un-rest on that side of her head.

"—and it's all so long ago!" wails Polly, grinding to a halt.

"Up to a point," says Elaine. In fact, it is not so long ago. It was fifteen years ago, or thereabouts, which in the context of her life is a mere trifle. Odd things happen to time, as you get older. Time compacts. Where once it was elastic, and ten years seemed an eternity, it has become shrunken, wizened—nothing is all that long ago. But for Polly fifteen years is an age.

Polly is off again. "—and I know it's a shock and it's hard to come to terms with, but does it have to matter *so* much? I mean, you and Dad are still the same people."

"I'm finding that we are not," says Elaine.

"Mum, I can't believe this is happening."

Elaine notes that the grass is patchy under the crab apple— some reseeding needed there. Pondering the sight line down through the pergola, she wonders about the crucial focal point beyond: that acer is not earning its keep.

"I don't *understand*," cries Polly. "Well, of course I do understand, I understand entirely how you feel, Mum, *of course* I do, but . . . does it have to be like this? Couldn't you—"

"No," says Elaine. "I can't. I've explained. Just as I've explained to your father."

"But one cannot imagine how he . . . I mean, how's he to *manage*?"

Elaine abandons consideration of the acer and that sight line. It is not that she is seeking distraction, or is impervious to Polly's distress. Rather, she is interested to find that normal preoccupations continue alongside the current clamor. This is surely a healthy sign. And, today, Kath is nowhere in evidence. She does not come swimming up; she is silent. Contrite? Defensive?

"I've made an arrangement with the bank," says Elaine.

"Oh, I know, I know. Dad said. I don't mean money. I mean, how's he to sort himself out? Do you know where he is?"

Silence.

"Here," says Polly. "He's here, in the flat. Until he can fix himself up with somewhere else. Or at least that's the idea. On my sofa. The new one from Habitat."

"Ah. I see." Elaine's composure is now ruffled. "I see," she says again. "Your sofa."

"He's gone out to buy some socks. At nine o'clock in the evening. He forgot to bring any. He seems to think he can buy socks at an all-night petrol station."

Elaine is groping now. She has no comment. The socks are a blow below the belt.

"I'll have to go," says Polly. "He's back."

For Polly, it seems as though a virus is at work. Order and expectation have been violated. Nothing is as it should be. Alien data have flashed up on the screen—uninvited, unwelcome—and they cannot be dismissed. People are not behaving as they should; moreover, it appears that they never did. Polly has always believed in forward planning, which requires a reliable infrastructure. Now there are fault lines all over the place. Her mother has apparently flipped; her father is camping on her sofa, with no spare socks, and his shaving kit is all over her bathroom. She does not know whether she should rush home this weekend and exhort her mother further, face-to-face; she will have to put on hold the planned supper party for friends, so long as her father is invading her space. She dotes on them both, of course she does, but they should not be doing this. They have broken the rules. They have ceased to be the essential backdrop, the calm, still center; they have become a further perverse element, impeding smooth progress.

People split up. Naturally people split up. All around, relationships are in a state of fission—that is to be expected. But not these people, that relationship. And not because of a distant transgression, a mishap long ago, something packed away into the past, over and done with. What has got into them? Why can't they be grown-up about it?

She scolds Kath. What were you thinking of? she says to Kath. How could you? Now look what you've done!

But Kath is impervious. In Polly's head, Kath does what she always did: she flies the dragon kite; she plucks a dress from a rail and cries, "This one!"; she laughs across a restaurant table. She is beyond the uproar of the present, except in blame. And Polly cannot be angry with her. The scolding is a ritual gesture. Why? she says to Kath, just once. And still Kath is unreachable. But Polly glimpses something in Kath's eyes that perhaps she never saw before. Someone else looks out of them, someone sad. But Kath was never sad—not Kath.

Polly fumes and fusses. She rehearses further appeals to her mother. She yanks the Habitat sofa into its bed mode, which means that her sitting room is barely navigable. She knows that she will sleep badly tonight, and be fouled up for work tomorrow.

And another thing. Dan is not coming out of this well. Probably she needs to stop seeing Dan sooner rather than later.

Glyn and Kath

Glyn is concerned with time. He is also worried about the time: it is twelve-forty-five, he is sitting on the side of a Dorset hill, and at two o'clock he has a seminar in the university, which is well over an hour's drive away. He should be getting a move on, instead of which he is sitting here brooding about time.

Time is his most essential professional tool, he reflects. Without it he would be faced with a chaotic and incomprehensible medley of evidence, much like the confusing juxtapositions of the landscape itself. Time is the necessary connection between events. Time is the device that prevents everything from happening at once. Pioneering archaeology went all-out for the establishment of chronology, and no wonder.

A kestrel hangs in the wind, level with his line of vision. Beyond it, in the distance, the green complexity of field patterns is interrupted by a large, long building with tall chimneys which he knows to have once been a nineteenth-century mill, today a development of luxury apartments. Just below him the hillside ripples away in a series of ledges; these he recognizes as the eroded ramparts of an Iron Age hill fort, which is why he is here at this moment. He is working on an article for which this hill, which he has not visited for some while, can provide some useful references.

The kestrel evokes Kath. He came here with her once: another kestrel performed similarly, and Kath remarked on it. "It stays still," she had said. "The wind is rushing past it, and it stays still. How?" He sees today that other bird, and Kath's hair blown across her face, and feels her hand on his arm. "Look!" she is saying. "Look!"

Glyn is now diverted from his reflections on the functions of time; he notes that his flow of observation—unconsidered, uncontrived—is a nice instance of the tumultuous, spontaneous operation of the mind. He knows enough of the theories of long-term memory to identify his recognition of the mill and the hill fort as the practice of semantic memory—the retention of facts, language, knowledge, without reference to the context of their acquisition. He simply knows these things, along with everything else he knows that makes him a fully operational being—a being considerably more operational than most, in his view. Whereas the vision of Kath sparked by the kestrel is due to episodic memory, which is autobiographical and essential to people's knowledge of their own identity. Without it we are untethered, we are souls in purgatory. Those glimmering episodes connect us with ourselves; they confirm our passage through life. They tell us who we are.

Glyn stands up, impelled by his own circadian clock, which is muttering away about that seminar. The kestrel swings suddenly sideways and down. Glyn heads for his car, which he will recognize thanks to a further spurt of semantic memory, and which he will be able to drive because procedural memory keeps all such skills alive. Without that, we would fall over, be struck dumb, stare bemused at the driving wheel.

Precarious, he thinks, as he plunges surefooted down the steep hillside. The precarious fusion of automatic processes, all of them necessary for daily functioning, all of them operating at the same time. And indeed, even as he thinks this he is also taking note of various things about this site, carrying out the purpose of his visit. He assesses the alignment of the ramparts, and the trace of a possible entrance. He relates this place to other known Celtic sites. But these thoughts are permeated with something else—not so much a thought process as a condition of the mind, a climate: all the while, that episodic memory mode is in operation, reminding him that he and Kath paused just about here to eat sandwiches, that she found an orchid, that she called out, "Come! Something amazing!," that a shower of rain sent them running for the car.

And when was this? Neither semantic, episodic, nor procedural memory can help here. Clearly the mind rejects the concept of chronology. It is an unnatural idea, fostered by perverse chroniclers ever since the Old Testament.

And what else was going on then for Kath? Glyn gets into the car, starts the engine. Now that he knows what he knows, the Kath that he sees is infused with something dark and unwelcome. Was she betraying him at that very time? Was she thinking of Nick, as she watched the kestrel, as she caught sight of the orchid?

It is several weeks since his discovery of the photograph, the event that has come to seem a defining moment. There was before the photograph, a time of innocence and tranquillity, insofar as such a state exists. Now it is after the photograph, when everything must be seen with the cold eye of disillusion.

Well, not everything. His marriage, simply. Which is quite a lot. He is calmer. The initial consuming fire has banked down to a steady, smoldering purpose. He must reconstruct his years with Kath, scrutinize them, search for further enlightenment. He must discover if this was an isolated incident. If it was, that is bad enough; if it reveals an entire lifestyle unknown to him, then he is discredited. He is proved to be without powers of observation or perception. Worst of all, everything that he remembers of that time is shown to be faulty.

He is in the process of creating a retrospective diary of the period. Where he was, when, and for how long. And so, by extension, where Kath was and what she was doing—as far as this is possible, which largely it is not. His own files are the reference source for his activities, but piecing things together is a laborious process taking up far too much time. Kath's part is more elusive, and requires input from others.

Oliver Watson proved pretty useless. Perhaps not altogether so, because this woman Mary Packard would have to be sought out at some point, and might be more productive. But generally speaking, the meeting with Watson had been futile, like a cross-country trek to some archive in pursuit of a document that turns out to be unrewarding.

The purpose of the exercise is to identify and interrogate key figures with whom Kath was involved: friends who may be persuaded to bear witness, men who may have been lovers. Of course he is not going to come out with it, just like that. He is not going to say, "Do you happen to know if my wife was promiscuous? Did you by any chance sleep with my wife at any point?" He is going to probe. He is going to be devious, circumspect. He will go in with some pretext, put out feelers. He will know, the instant he is on to something. He will know by the inflexion of a voice, by an intonation, a hesitation, an evasive reply. He is, after all, trained to home in on significant omissions. He knows when absence of data is suggestive. He can recognize the implications of a gap in the record.

Right. Now for the list of witnesses. He will need a swathe of material: diaries, telephone directories, newspaper libraries, compliant contributors. He will need the name of the woman who ran that gallery in Camden, and information about craft centers and arts festivals—all those erstwhile haunts of Kath's. He will need patience, and his own professional skills. He is stimulated rather than daunted. This is after all his *métier:* the pursuit of information is what he does best.

But first of all he must interrogate himself. His prime resource is the leaky vessel of his own memory. At times he views it thus, quite literally—as some old pail with holes and rusted seams. Alternatively, he imagines an extensive manuscript of which there survive only a handful of charred fragments; it is like trying to piece together the Gospels from the Dead Sea Scrolls.

He makes lists. He rummages through files and old engagement diaries, and so discovers where he was and when during those ten years of marriage. This is where the leaky vessel comes in, the charred fragments. He remembers that during the summer of 1986, when he was working on early population densities and spending a great deal of time in the British Library, Kath was helping out with a music festival, or so she said. She came and went. There was a man who used to ring up a lot, one of the organizers. Glyn picks up an echo of his voice: "I wonder if Kath is around? Peter here, from the Wessex Festival . . . If you could just tell her I called."

That festival is entered on Glyn's chart, fleshing out 1986. This Peter is entered also, underlined.

The project occupies Glyn's every spare moment, along with many moments that are not strictly speaking spare at all. He examines old files when he should be reading departmental papers, or going over a lecture. His thoughts drift in that direction during meetings. Now, in the car heading towards the university and that seminar, he is in full undistracted contemplation of the matter. All right, this is obsessive behavior, and he is perfectly aware of that. But that is par for the course; Glyn does obsession, always has, a five-star capacity for obsession is what makes him a painstaking researcher, obsession has produced seminal books and articles.

He reaches the university, dumps the car, hurries to his office,

where a posse of students is camped outside his door. He switches
to charm mode, apologizes for being late, apologizes for his muddy
shoes (see, I have been out on the job), sweeps them into the
room. He must now apply himself to agrarian change in the six-
teenth century; later on, back to the matters in hand.

There is a further task which is ancillary to the fact-finding process and the pursuit of witnesses. You could call it the examina-
tion of motive, Glyn supposes. Several motives. Why did he marry
Kath? Why (to be fair) did Kath marry him? Above all, why did
Kath cheat on him with Nick? And with others, if others there
were.

Why? Why? Why? Motive is all. Motive is clarification. Motive
explains. Motive soothes, perhaps.

He is good at nailing motives. The landscape heaves with hidden motives, coded motives. It looks the way it does because people chopped trees down to build ships, because they overran the
place with sheep when wool was in high demand. It is scarred
with the effects of cupidity: shafts sunk because this man wanted
to get rich, villages swept away because another man needed to
improve his view. Motive is Glyn's speciality.

"Can you help?" says Glyn. "I'm wondering if that is Peter
Claverdon?"

He is in a dispiriting public library in a small market town. He
has arrived here after consulting back issues of newspapers, the
Internet, and by way of five phone calls to total strangers. But here
he is on a Friday evening, having driven sixty miles, about to attend a poetry reading.

His most recent informant had said that, no, there shouldn't
be any problem about getting a ticket. And, no, there is not. The
library is well furnished with computers, and rather more lightly

equipped with books. Uncomfortable chairs are arranged in a semicircle, confronted by three further chairs in a row. Eleven people are seated in the semicircle. A man has emerged from a back room and looks around, apparently checking the arrangements. Glyn has already deduced that this must be his quarry, but he consults the librarian who sold him a ticket. Yes, that is Peter Claverdon.

Glyn inspects. He now knows something about this fellow—long-term arts administrator, something of a jack-of-various-trades, peripatetic and evidently versatile, hired to mastermind arts events from musical extravaganzas to this evening's contribution to a weekend of poetic commitment. Lean build, casual dress, late fifties. And undoubtedly the guy from those remembered phone calls. Glyn experiences a stir of hostility, which will have to be kept well under control.

He chooses a seat at the back. Three more people trickle in, plumping the audience out to fifteen, which looks less amid the empty chairs. The poets arrive, shepherded by Peter Claverdon. They do their stuff. Glyn pays token attention, watching the quarry and considering tactics.

The reading concludes. Two members of the audience buy copies of the poets' works. The poets chat among themselves.

Glyn picks his moment, and advances. He introduces himself. "The name should ring a bell with you. You knew my wife."

The man looks blank, and then there is a gleam—a definite gleam of something. "Oh—*Kath*. Good heavens—Kath." Now there is compunction, concern. "What a tragedy. I was so sorry—"

Glyn's expression indicates stoicism, grief suppressed. He gestures gracious acceptance of sympathy. He allows a moment of tribute. Then he proceeds. He explains. He appeals. He has this notion to write a brief private memoir of Kath, for circulation amongst relatives and friends. There are some areas of her life about which he needs to know more. Periods when she had commitments away from home. People who knew her then. Such, I understand, as yourself. Wondered if I could take up a little of your time. A chance to color in some of the blank spaces . . .

Glyn observes the man keenly as he speaks. What is he seeing? The man is responding, definitely. But what is the response? Something flickers in his eyes. Passion recalled? Guilt? Embarrassment? Glyn is alert; he scents involvement.

When Claverdon replies, he is all compliance—he seems enthusiastic. Yes, he saw quite a bit of Kath back then. What a lovely person she was. Used to ferry performers around for us, that sort of thing. See them into their hotels, get them to the venues on time. An entire Hungarian string quartet fell in love with her.

A red herring? Glyn registers benign interest.

The audience is ebbing away. The poets are packing up. "I've got some photos, come to think of it," says Claverdon. "Why don't you come round to my place? I live five minutes from here. The poets may want to get drunk, but I'm sure they can manage on their own. I'll just point them in the direction of the White Hart, and we can be on our way."

This helpfulness is disconcerting. Glyn feels wrong-footed. What is going on? It is clear that the man did indeed know Kath. His tone, and that betraying movement of the eye, suggest that he knew her well. Just how well? Is this willing invitation some crafty smokescreen?

Peter Claverdon disposes of the poets. He leads Glyn through the market square and down a side street, talking about these photos: definitely one of Kath escorting a well-known conductor, if he can lay his hands on it. "She did some office filling-in for us a year or so later—you remember?" He shoots a quick look at Glyn, who expediently remembers. "She was a person we liked to call on—very popular girl, Kath."

They reach a terraced cottage. Claverdon unlocks the door, calling out, "Hello!"

No reply. "Ah," he says. "My partner should be back any minute. Coffee? Drink?"

A partner. Was she around then? Was she aware of Kath? Is the smokescreen for her benefit also? Glyn accepts a glass of wine, his attention now in overdrive. There is something about this guy, something he cannot quite nail. And there is a note of comfortable intimacy when he speaks of Kath.

The photographs are found, after some rummaging in drawers. And, sure enough, there is Kath. There is Kath beside the prominent conductor, who had taken rather a shine to her, says Claverdon. And here is Kath in a jolly lineup of the festival staff. Kath is next to Claverdon; Glyn finds himself scrutinizing them very closely. He cannot see their hands. Kath is beaming. She looks happy, relaxed. She is radiant. Glyn has an odd feeling of exclusion; he knew nothing of that day, of these people.

It strikes Glyn that it would be appropriate to establish himself. He is a mere cipher at the moment, where Claverdon is concerned. He swings the conversation round, and makes clear who he is and how he stands. But Claverdon knows, it seems. He nods—a neutral sort of nod, with perhaps not quite enough recognition of status. Yes, Kath said. Said you were always very busy. Said landscape history took up all your time.

She did, did she? This is provocative. Suggestive. There is the smack of intimate exchanges here. Glyn is bristling, but must keep his cool. He turns back to the matter of Kath and the summer of that festival. He mentions that he cannot remember where she used to stay. Hotel, was it? He is trained on Claverdon, watching for some giveaway.

There is the sound of the front door opening. "My partner," says Claverdon.

And into the room comes a man. A man slung about with supermarket carrier bags, a domestic and slightly out-of-breath man, who dumps the bags, aims a kindly smile at Glyn, says to Claverdon, "I thought I'd better do a Sainsbury before the weekend."

Claverdon explains Glyn. "You remember Kath Peters? Who was one of the Wessex Festival team? You and Kath were great mates. Poor Kath—"

The man is all interest. Of course he remembers Kath. Who wouldn't? He makes a face of regret, of sympathy. He starts at once on some anecdote involving Kath.

Glyn is barely listening. He feels like some kind of dupe. Partner. How was he to know the guy was gay? His time has been wasted. No point in hanging on here. He finishes his glass, waiting for the moment when he can get up and leave.

The two men are recalling some occasion when Kath apparently saved the day with an emergency sprint to Heathrow to collect a replacement performer. Glyn shifts a hand and notices his watch with exaggerated surprise. "Heavens! That late . . . I must be off."

Claverdon's partner has poured himself a drink and is settled on the sofa, talking the while. "Game for anything, wasn't she? And she was on such a high that summer. What a shame it all went wrong. She was so upset—you could see."

Glyn does not hear this; he will hear it later, much later. He is on his feet now, pleading time, distance, fatigue. "*Many* thanks," he is saying. "Good to see those pictures—" His hosts also rise; Claverdon looks rebuffed, as well he may. The partner hovers. When Glyn is outside the door, heading for his car, the image returns—the pair of them, staring at him. Well, one could hardly have set to and explained, could one?

All right, then. So why did he marry Kath? He married her because she was the most desirable woman he had ever met: he had to have her, he had to go on having her, he had to make sure that no one else had her, evermore.

So you loved her?

Of course.

Did you say so?

Probably. Surely. Anyway, that is immaterial. I never went in for those statutory exchanges.

He married Kath because it was an imperative.

"Clara Mayhew?"

"Speaking."

"Ah. You don't know me—Glyn Peters. But I believe you used to run the Hannay Gallery, and would have known my wife, Kath."

Pause. "I did. She worked for us from time to time." Further pause. "I was told she—"

"Yes. Yes, I'm afraid so. Please forgive me for bothering you, but I wondered if possibly—" Glyn floats the idea of a memoir once more. He is getting adept at the memoir; he convinces himself, the work takes shape in his mind.

"You've gone to a lot of trouble to find me," says Clara Mayhew, after a moment.

This is not quite what she is supposed to say, but no matter. Glyn agrees with her—he has indeed. He does not mention the systematic program of inquiry, and merely says that he is relieved to have struck lucky. "I believe you knew her fairly well?"

"Did I?"

This is unanswerable, which is presumably the intention. Glyn is now backing away from the idea of a meeting. Perhaps Clara Mayhew is another dead end. All the same, Kath spent many weeks and months at that gallery. He tries a shot in the dark. "I think she had a particular friend amongst the artists who used to show there, but I cannot remember the name. I just wondered if you might be able to help."

"Help?"

"Help with the name of this . . . this person. This artist."

A sigh. "I seem to recall that Kath had a lot of friends. Always in and out of the gallery."

"I just have this feeling that there may have been—"

"There was the portrait, I suppose. Did it ever get done?"

"Portrait?" Glyn leaps to attention.

"Ben Hapgood. Wanted to paint her. Mad keen. No doubt he did, I wouldn't know."

It occurs to Glyn that this Clara is bored rather than obstructive. Not a particular mate of Kath's, then. But productive—oh, distinctly productive. He becomes brisk. "Hapgood? That'll be the chap. The name certainly rings a bell. Do you by any chance have an address?"

But Clara's patience has run out. No, she does not have an address. All she knows is that the man lived in Suffolk back then. And she's afraid she really has to go, so if he will excuse her . . .

Gracefully, Glyn does so. Ben Hapgood. Right.

Why did Kath marry him?

She married him because she found him charismatic, charming, because he made it clear that he was entirely focused upon her. She married him because he offered a different kind of life, because he wasn't like the others, because he was a blast of energy.

Sex?

Of course.

You were handsome.

I was. Kath was outstandingly attractive. I was a good-looking man. There's usually some symmetry about these things, one notes.

All the same.

All the same what?

You weren't the first, not by a long chalk. So why you? Why indeed?

She married him because he insisted that she should.

This woman Clara has dropped the name Ben Hapgood into Glyn's mind. There it lies, fermenting. Glyn works away. He checks directories, he consults Web sites, he locates lists of artists, and before long he has the fellow, who does indeed still live in Suffolk. Which will mean a long cross-country drive, but what is that to a man with a mission?

But the fermentation has had further effect. Something has come bubbling up from the vaults of memory—a lost moment, a vanished moment, a moment in which Kath is sitting in the garden on that red-striped deck chair. She wears skimpy clothes and dark glasses, her head is tilted back in the sunshine. She is talking. "Ben Hapgood," she says. "He is *such* a good painter. And he's just won this important prize. I'm so pleased. . . . You're not listening, are you?" she says. And the rest is drowned out by that "You're not listening, are you?," the dark glasses turned towards him now, and a little exasperated smile. So what was he, Glyn, doing? Reading? Thinking? Also talking? Not listening, no. But now he is listening. He is listening hard.

He listens day after day, but there is no more. Kath has gone silent. He listens all the way to Suffolk, picking his way through the hierarchy of the road system, from motorways to dual carriageways and eventually onto minor roads that have him reaching again and again for the map. Ben Hapgood is not expecting him.

Ben Hapgood is expecting a person who is interested in his work, who happens to be visiting the area, wondered if he might call in . . . a person who did not give a name because, when Hapgood asked, the line unfortunately went dead. Cut off. What a pity.

So Ben Hapgood will not be concerned, apprehensive, suspicious. Glyn is already visualizing Ben Hapgood; this man who was so keen to paint Kath's portrait, so infatuated maybe, so involved. Glyn sees a man who complements Kath's dark looks, as he does himself; he sees an Ur-Glyn, more *louche*, touched with artistic glamour. He sees this man in his studio with Kath. It takes time to paint a portrait, does it not? Many sittings. Many cloistered hours together.

Did these hours of intimacy take place here? Did Kath too pick her way down these winding side roads? It would seem so. And suddenly Glyn has a vision of Kath in that little Renault, off somewhere, going places, one hand out of the window, waving goodbye: "See you soon. . . ." And he feels a spasm of pain; he is clutched by an unfamiliar sensation. These glimpses of Kath do not provoke anything much, in the normal sense of things. He lives with them; they are a part of an interior landscape, they are simply there, and that is all there is to it. This is disconcerting. "See you soon. . . ." But she will not. Never again.

He jams a foot on the brake. This is it. This is where Ben Hapgood lives. This is the white cottage with a picket fence, on the right of the lane after you have forked left.

Two cottages knocked into one, more precisely, plus a rambling range of outbuildings in which, presumably, is the imagined studio. Glyn drives up onto the grass verge (did Kath too make this same maneuver?) and gets out. He stands for a moment, gathering himself, before he moves forward and lifts the latch on the gate. Precisely as he does so, the front door opens and out steps, presumably, Ben Hapgood. Who is short, ginger-haired, smiling cheerily, and behind whom hovers a woman. Both look to be in their mid-fifties.

Greetings all round. "Glenda, my wife. And you are . . . ? I'm afraid I didn't catch—"

Of course you didn't, thinks Glyn. "Peters—Glyn Peters." He watches intently for recognition, but none comes. Fair enough—a not uncommon name, after all.

They move into a farmhouse kitchen. Tea is made. More chat. Have you come far? Hope my directions worked all right. That sort of thing. A friendly couple, unexceptional, untouched on the face of it by artistic glamour. Kath liked artists, thinks Glyn. She had a bit of a thing about artists; she was by way of being a camp follower, I suppose. He considers Ben Hapgood who is swigging tea and talking about his vegetable plot, visible out of the window. Glyn notes the wife also, and wonders how long she has been around.

Ben Hapgood supposes that Glyn would like to have a look at the studio. Glyn agrees that he would like to do so. The three of them move to one of the outbuildings. Classic studio stuff: smell of paint and linseed, canvases stacked up, others on the walls, clutter all over tables and shelves. Big easel with work in progress. Couple of old deal chairs, basket chair with grubby cushions. No chaise longue, no bed. At least, not today.

Now is the moment. He will have to come clean, blow his cover.

He does so, at length. He is charming, apologetic, a touch rueful. When he comes to the point, when he mentions the portrait, he is intent upon Ben Hapgood, with half an eye on this Glenda. He wants a reaction. He has already had a response to Kath's name—the response with which he is becoming familiar: both register pleasure, affection, regret. . . . Glyn is by now experiencing doubts. But what about the portrait? What about that, eh?

"Oh *yes* . . ." says Glenda. "She was such a marvelous subject. And Ben did her proud. One of his best—I can say that, he can't." She laughs, lays an uxorious hand on the artist's arm. The artist smiles fondly.

So. Glyn eyes them. Either they are putting up a show, these two, or *she* has not known what *he* was getting up to, or he, Glyn, is once again wrong-footed.

"She came here?" he inquires.

Yes, certainly, she came here, it seems. She stayed here a couple of times. She was such a lovely person to have around, they had a lot of fun, the children were teenagers then and Kath was so brilliant with kids, she'd suggest these crazy games, they still remember her. . . .

When?

There is consultation. Late 1980s, they think—summer of 1988? Yes, definitely, because the show at which the portrait was sold was 1989. Snapped up.

Snapped up?

Apparently. This bloke came to the opening view and just homed in on it. Or so it was said. Spoken for within the first ten minutes.

Really? *Really?*

Glyn moves quickly. He revises his position, in a split second. He sees where to go. He explains that of course all along what he had so very much hoped was to be able to acquire the portrait. He had of course been aware of it ("You're not listening, are you? . . ."), but Kath had been vague as to what happened to it— only recently had he begun to wonder if perhaps by some miracle it might still be around. . . .

Who was this man? The man who bought the picture outright, as though he had been waiting for it, as though perhaps he already knew about it, as though he knew Kath, as though he knew Kath so well that he must get his hands on her picture before anyone else did?

". . . obviously it was too much to hope that you might still have it. But someone has. Is there any chance you'd know who that purchaser was?"

And, yes, Ben Hapgood keeps a record of where his work has gone. He fishes a file from a drawer and starts hunting through it. Glenda is talking about Kath. She talks about that summer, when, it seems, Glyn was away a lot, involved with his work: "I'm sorry, I don't remember exactly what you do, Kath did say . . . so she was rather on her own, I think she was quite glad to come here, once she took the girls off camping on the coast for a couple of days. What a shame it was she never . . . not that she ever said anything, but one always sensed—"

Glyn is concentrated upon Ben Hapgood, who cannot lay hands on the stuff from that gallery—damn, did it get chucked out?—no, hang on, here we go. A Mr. Saul Clements—and here's the address and phone number. London. Sounds an expensive address. Laughter.

He has him. He has this man. This is the real quarry. Ben Hapgood was a distraction, but who was to know that? Ben Hapgood was simply the unwitting facilitator. He painted Kath's portrait, had indeed been mad keen to paint Kath's portrait, but for entirely painterly reasons, and who wouldn't? But as soon as the portrait is put on exhibition, is offered for sale, it is pounced on. By whom? By someone waiting for it? Someone Kath had been talking to about it? Someone Kath was seeing that summer?

All that remains is to disentangle himself from the Hapgoods. Who remain remarkably good-humored and hospitable, given it is now clear that Glyn's interest in the artist's work is entirely self-serving. In an attempt to improve his record, he pays belated attention to the works by which he is surrounded, asking questions,

offering the occasional deferential comment. Hapgood is a figura-
tive artist, and so presumably right outside the contemporary
swim, judging from what is to be picked up from the Sunday
newspapers. This deduction allows Glyn to line himself up on the
side of the angels, with some disparaging remarks about unmade
beds and pickled animals, which seem to go down satisfactorily.

Hapgood is now distracted from discussion of contemporary
art by a sudden thought. It has occurred to him that he will have a
slide of that painting of Kath, should have, if he can find it. Let's
see now. . . . He plunges once again into drawers and files. Glyn
finds himself mesmerized; somehow he had not reckoned with
the actuality of the thing, in this form or any other. Kath. Here,
now. Ben Hapgood shuffles through folders and albums; Glenda is
saying something about Kath—she is saying that it was a problem
for Kath, looking the way she did. Problem? Glyn notices this
Glenda, briefly—she is dumpy, fresh-faced, wholesome-looking,
she reminds one of a small brown loaf, she is the antithesis of
Kath. Problem? But now her spouse is saying, Ah, here we go; he
has opened an envelope and is holding slides up to the light.
Should be here, he says, this is the lot from that exhibition. And
then—"Yes!" He passes a slide to Glyn.

Here is a tiny, jewellike Kath, glowing in the light from the
window. The slide is too small to make out detail, but there is no
mistaking that stance, the way she is sitting with her legs curled
beneath her, head turned aside, chin on her hand, elbow on the
arm of the chair. Glyn peers into this crystallized moment, this
time when Hapgood saw Kath sitting thus, when Kath spent so
many hours thus arranged, perhaps in that chair there, looking
probably out of that window. He feels oddly excluded. There she
was; there he was not. And now he is here, and she is not, and this
fact is suddenly chilling.

Hapgood talks about the painting. It was not so much her

beauty, he says—one doesn't necessarily want to paint someone because they are handsome—it was the way she composed herself. The way she stood, sat, moved. Arresting. And so absolutely natural. Like some elegant animal. He had agonized over the pose—had thought of having her sit, stand, be this way or the other—and then one day had noticed her settle herself like that in a chair and had thought, Yes, that's it.

Glyn scarcely hears him. He is intent upon the little translucent shape in his hand, this Kath preserved in amber light. He finds that he does not want to give it up. He searches for Kath's features, but the scale is too small. Eventually he hands the slide back to Ben Hapgood. "Thank you," he says.

Glyn drives home in a trance. He pays scant attention to anything; the landscape whips past unobserved. He makes none of the usual mental notes about place names, about a road arrangement to be checked out later, about buildings, about field structures. He can think only about that slide, about the lost and unknown Kath that he held for a few moments in his hand. Kath is interfering with his work again, but he does not notice.

She came this way. Not once, but several times. She went to that house, talked and laughed with those people, played with their children, was welcomed. She sat in the basket chair in Ben Hapgood's studio, for many hours, gazing out of the window. Thinking about what?

He had never been jealous of her friends, had never resented that shifting pack who drifted in and out of the house, who kept her forever on the phone. They did not much interest him, truth to tell. Lovers would have been one thing; friends were neither here nor there. He is in pursuit of lovers right now, but it is these others who are unsettling his life, stirring up these unaccustomed feelings of . . . of what?

Feelings of exclusion, of ignorance, of deprivation. He is glimpsing a Kath whom apparently he did not know, a Kath known to these others who are themselves mysterious, so far as he is concerned. Strangers, who were nevertheless entirely familiar to the person with whom he lived in that ultimate intimacy.

You knew that at the time. You knew she had friends.

Of course.

So why is this now causing difficulties?

How should I know? How the hell would I know? Glyn sweeps onwards round the M25. Counties wheel past to one side; London lurks out there on the other. He sees none of it. Faces are streaming through his mind, the alien faces of the Hapgoods, of Peter Claverdon, faces that are underpinned by words, the continuous repetitive refrain that plays unprompted—from just now, from long ago: "What a shame it all went wrong. . . . It was a problem for her, looking like that. . . . You're not listening, are you?"

He steps from the lift of this block of mansion flats. The place is hushed and carpeted and proposes solid wealth. The voice of Saul Clements on the entry phone has told him to come up, and Glyn is preparing himself for this man. He knows better now than to second-guess; he has no image in his head, but he is on guard, he is in his corner, waiting for the bell. This is where he is going to need all his perceptions, all his powers of deduction, for the man who so urgently bought Kath's portrait.

The door to the flat is already open. And there stands the ugliest man Glyn has ever seen. This man is a toad, a gnome, a troglodyte. He is as squat as a barrel, his nose is bulbous, his mouth is a letter box. He is seventy-five years old at least. This man was never Kath's lover?

The troglodyte leads Glyn into a room whose furnishings are deep and rich and darkly gleaming. The world beyond has been turned into exterior décor—a glimpse of the London skyline framed in thick glowing brocade curtains, the faintest purr of traffic sound. There are velvety sofas and chairs, desk and tables of museum quality, all the wonders of the Orient underfoot. Oh, there is the smell of money here. And the walls are covered with paintings, each softly and precisely lit. This is perhaps a William Nicholson, and that one maybe an Ivon Hitchens, and over there is possibly a Lucian Freud. This man likes art, it seems. He likes it a lot. He has splashed out, over the years.

It is impossible to imagine Kath in this room. Except that there she is, there in that corner, suspended above a delicate little eighteenth-century davenport. Spotlit Kath. Kath framed about two foot by three, wearing a plain green dress, arms bare, legs tucked under her, sitting on the basket chair that Glyn saw in Ben Hapgood's studio, her face in semiprofile, turned to the light of the window, the light of another time, a time of which Glyn knew nothing.

The man who cannot have been Kath's lover steers him over to the painting. He is speaking. His voice is firm, patrician, modulated—as elegant as his appearance is uncouth. Glyn finds himself silenced. He feels suddenly chastened. He feels like the guest who has committed a solecism, he feels like some hapless schoolboy. He wants out, but he is here now, he got himself into this, he has only himself to blame.

Glyn gazes at Kath. He sees her face—pensive, abstracted. Oh, he knows that sideways look, that partial removal of herself, that retreat into reflection. He stares at Kath, at this vanished Kath, who lives on in this man's gilded cage, who has lived here for years, locked into another time, other days, sealed within a frame by Ben Hapgood. He wonders about those hours. What did they talk about, she and Ben, and Glenda, who perhaps wandered in and out with cups of coffee, or a summons to a meal? He strains to hear Kath's voice. In the most bewildering way, he wants, he needs that voice—here in this alien place, amid the man's great sofas and his groomed antique furniture.

The man is talking. He says that when he bought the painting Ben Hapgood's work was not familiar to him, but that as soon as he saw this painting in the exhibition he was at once struck by it. He was entranced: "A quick and easy decision. One rather welcomes those—the knowledge that one must have this picture and that is all there is to it." He smiles at Glyn, a collusive look as though to a fellow collector. He draws Glyn's attention to the modeling of the face. He indicates the use of light, the way that it falls upon the arm, upon the protruding corner of a yellow cushion.

He is all courtesy, this man. His letter was all courtesy, in which he replied to Glyn's inquiry—Glyn's ever-so-carefully phrased inquiry as to the whereabouts of the portrait of his late wife, which he has been given to understand Mr. Clements purchased back in 1989, and which he would so very much like to see and photograph. Glyn's camera is in his pocket.

And now the man asks a startling question. He asks what Kath's name was. He has never known, it seems; the portrait was sold to him as that of a friend of the artist, unspecified. When he is told, he looks long and hard at the painting.

"Kath," he says. "So. Kath. I have always thought of her simply as—she. Respectfully, you understand—but she has always been anonymous. Now, it will be oddly different. Kath. And knowing that she is no longer alive."

Glyn files away Mr. Saul Clements, who was never Kath's lover, who did not know Kath, but now lives with her in a strange daily intimacy. He files away Peter Claverdon and Ben Hapgood, who also were not Kath's lovers, but who was to know? He has been up several blind alleys, but that is always the case with a research project. Glyn is well used to the sense of frustration, the need for patience and tenacity. But he is not accustomed to the feelings generated by this particular project. He is unnerved, unsettled, he is not in control of his own reactions. Instead of a calm commitment to the objective—which is to establish whether or not Kath was in the habit of infidelity—he finds himself waylaid and distracted. He should be able to discard these various unfruitful areas, now that they are investigated and seen to be unpromising, instead of which he broods upon them. He thinks constantly of that studio in which Kath sat, and talked, and laughed. He sees the spotlit portrait. He wonders about the summer of that festival, when Kath was so radiant in the group photograph. He wants to go back there and ask her questions—questions he never asked at the time. Where are you going? Why? What is it like there?

Nick

Nick is in a daze. He doesn't feel very well. He loses track of time, of the day of the week. He wanders about London, because it is worse to sit in Polly's flat, but he cannot think of anything he wants to do. A jaunt to London used to be an indulgence; now he feels as though he has been dispatched to Siberia. When he is hungry, he must find food, because Polly is out all day and most evenings, and her fridge is not like the richly furnished fridge at home. Home? But he no longer has a home, apparently. Goaded by Polly, he goes into estate agents' offices and asks about rentals. But he barely hears what they say, and the lists that they give him lie about unread.

This cannot be. This is all some absurd mistake. He telephones Elaine, but she is never available. Either Sonia answers, and is evasive and diplomatic, or the answerphone is on. He leaves messages—appeals that are initially dignified, but which soon degenerate to petulant cries and abject supplication. Elaine does not respond.

Polly goes to see her mother, and returns cross and flustered. "You'll have to give it time, Dad," she says. "And, look, have you been to see the place in Clerkenwell? I thought that sounded just the sort of thing you want."

But Nick does not want a stunning loft conversion in EC1. He wants to go home, not after time, but now. He wants this nightmare over, stashed away in the past where mistakes should be, out of sight and out of mind. Which is where the whole Kath thing belongs, and where it safely was until this . . . this ludicrous accident, this insane intervention by bloody Glyn.

It was over and done with. All right, it shouldn't have happened, but no harm was done, only *now* is harm being done, and that is so unnecessary. Nick cannot believe that something long since laid to rest can thus come bubbling up and wreck his life. He is affronted, run ragged; no wonder he has these headaches, this heaving gut. He and Elaine should be working this out together, quiet and calm, as he is sure they could if only she would give him the chance.

Instead of which, here he is pacing horrible London, occasionally meeting up for a drink with some old acquaintance. But such arrangements have lost their kick. Furthermore, he no longer wants to go and potter around Northumberland for a few days, and the various projects he was considering are not of the slightest interest to him. Can Elaine seriously think that he is able to work under these circumstances? He can barely focus for long enough to buy himself a newspaper. He sits on park benches with a beer in his hand, like some wino, staring at the ground.

And staring also at what happened back then, which should not have happened, which should not be roaring up to clobber him like this.

He looked at Kath one day and saw that she was *so* pretty. Had he never realized this before? Well, yes—but in a casual, take-it-or-leave-it sort of way. Now suddenly her prettiness was of another order: it was relevant, it related to him, it made him feel he needed to do something about it.

He wanted to go to bed with her. As soon as he recognized this he was shocked. Look here—this is Elaine's sister. Elaine's *sister*, for Christ's sake, whom you've known for years.

And it made no difference. None whatsoever. So? said some still, small voice. So she's Elaine's sister? Things like this happen, don't they? Nothing anyone can do about it. It's not your fault or hers.

He remembers that onslaught of . . . well, lust. He remembers looking and looking at Kath, astonished that he should be looking so differently, that Kath's familiar presence was suddenly something quite other. Astonished but also quietly thrilled. He remembers how the days took color, how he brimmed with energy.

He remembers all that. He remembers less about the sequence of that time. How long did it go on? Six months? A year? How many times did they make love? Not that many. In his head, the whole thing is now compacted into a handful of vibrant moments: Kath's face, her body, her voice.

She rolls away from him. "Why are we doing this?" she asks. She stares at him—he sees that look still, an intent gaze, that has something of resignation about it. It is a look that bothers him, and he should not be bothered at this particular moment. "*You're* doing it for the reasons that men do"—she corrects herself—"that people do. But why am *I* doing it?"

He tries to hush her. At least he supposes that he did. When he listens to her now, it seems to him that there are things he should have said, but apparently he did not.

"You're Elaine's husband. Is that why I'm doing it? Is it *because* you're Elaine's husband?"

He remembers the day of the photograph. That bloody photograph, but for which he would not be here now, sitting on a bench with crisp packets swirling round his feet, alongside an old fellow reading the *Sun*. I can't go on living like this, he thinks, I can't.

Why did they go to that place? Was it Kath's idea? But Kath was never into Roman villas. It seems to Nick that maybe he himself proposed that excursion, tenuously linked perhaps to some project. But in reality it was an excuse to see Kath, because at that point it was essential to be with her, even if it was in the company of others. So there they all were—Elaine and himself, and Kath, and that woman Mary Packard with some man, and Oliver. Fateful Oliver, who went and brought his camera along.

He remembers a picnic. All of them sprawled around on the grass, and him intensely conscious of Kath—being careful not to pay her significant attention, assiduously behaving normally, treating Kath just as he always had, for years. He remembers her wandering off with Mary Packard, the two of them looking at some mosaic, laughing together. He had wondered if Mary Packard knew; Kath's great friend, she was. How much did Kath confide in her? He half wanted to think that Mary Packard knew.

He remembers that they were standing around, and he found himself beside Kath. Found himself? Positioned himself, probably. And he had not been able to resist reaching for her hand—had reached for it and clasped her fingers and pushed their two hands back behind them, out of sight, hidden by her billowing skirt. The secret intimacy had given him a thrill, intensified perhaps by the fact that Elaine was there talking to them: he had felt guilt and euphoria all in one. For seconds only they had been like that, and then Kath's hand slipped away. But Oliver had chosen that snatch of time in which to raise his camera to the eye and commemorate the outing. Unwittingly—that Nick is quite prepared to believe—but fatally.

It is so *unfair*. Elaine is being so unreasonable. He has been given no opportunity to persuade her that, in time, this thing could be seen in perspective. He is being quite disproportionately punished.

You should have considered this outcome back then, says another sultry voice. Did he? Did they? Well, yes, sort of . . . if guilt and the occasional bout of nerves amount to consideration.

One was so swept up in it, there was an inevitability about everything, it was unstoppable. Of course one was worried, of course one agonized, from time to time. But there was always this feeling that it would be all right, it would work out. . . .

And Kath? What about her?

Nick finds that Kath is inscrutable. He can see her and hear her still, but he has no idea what she is thinking or feeling—correction: what she thought or felt. He is annoyed with her; look, there are two of us in this, it was you too, and you kept that wretched photo and that note.

Why? This thought introduces a further level of disquiet. Were they kept because she was careless, or because they meant something to her? This notion makes Nick profoundly uncomfortable: he does not want to think that there was a dimension to their involvement of which he knows nothing. It was a temporary madness, that was all, something quite irresistible, and eventually quenched, as such passions are.

Indeed, the memory of passion makes him uncomfortable. There is recollection not with tranquillity, or yearning, but a sort of incomprehension. Had one really felt like that? Well, evidently. But he tunes in now as though to some alien persona. He hears himself with a certain incredulity. He hears himself saying to her: "I want you—God, how much I want you."

She stares at him—considering. Those marvelous eyes. "Want . . ." she says. "Want . . ." And the look is not right; he needs responding fervor, not that querying gaze. He seems to have fallen short in some way. What is he supposed to be saying?

He can't really remember what they used to talk about. Well, probably he did most of the talking: Nick is the first to admit that he does tend to go on a bit. He was up to his ears in publishing enthusiasms back then, there was always something absorbing on the boil, he would have assumed that she'd like to be involved. And there seems to be an impression of a listening Kath, of a Kath who sits across the table from him in some pub, smiling, apparently intent. Yes . . . and Oliver turns up there, which is a bit of a problem, and Nick has to deal with that later, have a quiet word.

"Is it *because* you're Elaine's husband?" Nick does not care for that. He would prefer not to have that still in his head—Kath going in for amateur psychology, which does no one any good, and anyway it wasn't very flattering, was it? And he hears her again: "When I was younger I wanted to *be* Elaine. More than anything I wanted to be like her—to be organized and sensible and confident." A little laugh, a rueful sort of laugh. "She won't ever have realized that, I imagine."

"Maybe I'm doing this because I still want to be Elaine," she says. "What do you think?" She stares at him; she sits on the other side of a table in that pub, that quirky look on her face. But he does not think anything, not then or now.

He feels a touch resentful towards Kath. She should be with him on this; she should be in it with him. Instead of which, she is this impervious presence in his head, reenacting frozen moments. Saying the same things again and again. And it seems to him that there was something unreachable about her even then, even when she was flesh and blood beside him, beneath his hand. You never really knew where you were with Kath; she listened and she looked and she talked—oh, she talked, but she never told you much. Just inconsequential stuff, about where she'd been and what she'd done. And she was always slipping away; she was that suddenly vacated chair, the phone that rang and rang with no one answering, the car disappearing round the corner.

And, eventually, of course, she went altogether. Nick does not care to think about that, even now.

Kath is no help whatsoever, and Elaine has turned into someone else. She has become this implacable stranger, who has pronounced judgment against which there is apparently no appeal. Nick has had to tread warily for some while now—for the last few years she has been getting ratty for no good reason at all—but this is of another order. He sees her stony face in the conservatory that morning: "I want you to go."

It is *so* unfair. He is too old to be treated like this. Old? And as the word comes swarming in, Nick's distress is notched up higher still. Yes, he is getting old. Oh, *shit*.

Elaine and Kath

Elaine is full of vigor. She feels calm and purposeful. She has done the right thing, of that she is certain. She has done the only thing that rang true, under the circumstances. To have continued to live with Nick as though nothing had happened would have been impossible; the thing would have stared her in the face every day, each time she looked at him, each time he spoke. As it is, she will be able to give herself entirely to work, and that will enable her, in time, to digest this business. She is revising her decision to wind down, to do less; on the contrary, she will do more. She will firm up that American lecture tour, plan a new book, make a determined pitch for a space at the Hampton Court Show next year.

Today she is judging a garden competition in a prosperous London suburb. This is an exacting process—not so much on account of the footwork, the relentless progress from garden to garden, but because of the diplomatic neutrality of manner that is required. She must remain polite but noncommittal; her reactions must be tempered—all right to indulge in the occasional indication of approval, but aversion must be contained. The garden owners are hovering, smiles glued to their faces, laser eyes trained on her. They would dearly like to get a look at the notes she makes on her clipboard. The organizers move around with her, a protective cohort. The atmosphere is fetid; the whole area steams with rivalrous emotion. A charity is involved here—most of these gardens are open in aid of something this weekend—but charity is not much in evidence right now.

Elaine walks amid roses. She notes the black spot on "Madame Alfred Carrière," assesses "Paul's Himalayan Musk," suppresses a shudder at "Peace" and "Piccadilly," communes with "Cardinal de Richelieu." She winces before a blaze of pelargoniums, appreciates some *Dicentra eximia* and *Polemonium carneum*, deplores a ghastly magenta *Lavatera*, takes attentive note of an unfamiliar *Corydalis*. It is impossible to sideline personal taste, but she tries to give proper credit to the demonstration of gardening skill and commitment, even when the products of these are a tortuously constructed rockery or a rash of carpet bedding. The nation gardens according to whim, and there is whim on show today by the spadeful, though the dictatorial hand of television is also much apparent. Water is being moved around on the scale of the Hanging Gardens of Babylon: rills, channels, miniature rapids, fountains, ponds. Contemporary gardening is a question of engineering quite as much as of plantsmanship. The furnishings are diverse and elaborate; some gardens are ankle-deep in gravel, others have absorbed a lorry-load of beach pebbles, one has a fifteen-foot plastic totem pole, in another a Roman bust rears from a shrubbery. Occasionally Elaine finds herself in a time-warp space of rectangular lawn surrounded by a border of annuals; the accompanying organizers glance nervously at her, wearing deprecating smiles. They hurry her along the street, where a wild garden is on show, a tangle of poppies, scabious, oxeye daisies, and meadowsweet tucked into the end of a fifty-foot plot.

She is looking for structure, for imaginative use of plants, for interesting color combinations, for evidence of horticultural prowess along with individuality. She seldom finds all of these together. Too often the gardening skills have been applied to some disastrous concept, or a promising design is betrayed by unfortunate plantings. Take this long, narrow back garden, for instance: its length and narrowness have been quite cleverly disguised, the space broken up by bold groupings of shrubs, a wandering path to one side leading away to a focal point at the end. But the focus is a clump of pampas grass, that old stalwart of the suburban front garden, which sits there harsh and uncompromising amid the bosky setting. What went wrong here? Elaine frowns at the pampas grass, and makes a note on her clipboard. At the same moment, Kath floats into her head, along with another garden.

Kath says, "Can I do it too?"

"No," says Elaine. Kath is four; she is ten. And she is making a garden. The base of the garden is an old tin tray. She has lined it with soil and she is now intent upon the design and the planting. The lawn is made of moss; there are little clumps of hairy bitter cress, some forget-me-not, a tussock of sedum from the garage roof—Elaine knew the names of things, even back then. The tray garden is clear in her head, to this day. She can see it. Maybe that is how it all began for her, on that spring morning when she was ten. But now as she fetches it up, sees the sprig of catkins that was a weeping willow, she becomes aware also of Kath, lurking on the periphery.

"Shall I find more of that stuff?" says Kath, pointing to the moss. She has crept closer—a small, insignificant figure. Pleading.

Elaine ignores her. Kath is a local disruption on the fringes of her vision. Elaine is pondering what might serve as a tree, just there, and how to do a pond. Of course! A mirror! How is she to get hold of a tiny mirror, like the one her mother has in her purse? Is it conceivable that her mother would let her have it?

Kath is there again. "I've got this." She is holding out a pansy—a great, fat, blowsy pansy. It is her offering, for the garden.

Elaine frowns. "You shouldn't have picked that," she says. "You know you're not allowed to pick things." And can't she see it would ruin the whole garden? It is wrong in every way—size, shape, color.

A kind older sister would have taken the pansy, thinks Elaine. Incorporated it, adjusted, accommodated. She stares at the discordant pampas grass in this London garden, and wonders if someone arrived triumphant with it as an unsolicited gift—spouse, mother-in-law, friend.

Her view of this garden is now skewed. She can no longer judge dispassionately. She cannot give it a gold medal, or indeed a silver, but finds herself awarding a bronze, despite the pampas grass, or perhaps because of it. Kath has intervened, again.

The tour of inspection completed, Elaine is taken to the house of one of the organizers for rest and refreshment, and to pronounce judgment. She is treated with great deference and solicitude, which is rather good for the ego, and she has of course given her services free: good public relations, and you never know what may spring from such an appearance. Book sales, naturally, but possibly some interesting commission. So she remains resolutely polite and cooperative, over and beyond the call of duty, even to the extent of a supernumerary visit to the deplorable garden of the chairman, to advise on a problem with a recalcitrant pittosporum. She is allowed a period on her own with a cup of tea and her notes, for the judging process—a welcome interlude, since it is now five o'clock, she left home at seven, and still has to fight her way back through the South London traffic. She allocates the gold, silver, and bronze medals—a decision which will no doubt further fuel the animosities in this Arcadian suburb. And then at last it is time to be extensively thanked, to smile and smile again, and to get gratefully into the car.

A working day. And a relatively lenient one, in the general scheme of things. I could have been stacking supermarket shelves, thinks Elaine, or pushing millions around on a screen in the City. Instead of which, I come and go as I please, and have done so for many a year—subject, of course, to commitments made, and to the overriding need to earn a living.

She cannot now detach herself from what she does. Her work identifies her, both for herself and, presumably, for others. She cannot imagine a life that was not dominated by the requirements of the occupation. If it were removed, if it had never been there, she would not be the person that she is. She sees herself as shored up by alley and arbor and knot garden, by pergola and parterre, by vista and axis and drift and focus. She is activated by emphasis, harmony, contrast. She flourishes on the rich compost of all that she knows—a library of botanical knowledge into which she can dip at will, bolstered by pruning lore and growth habits and species attributes and a thousand plants that she can conjure up in the mind.

Elaine finds herself considering this as she picks her way out of London and onto the familiar route home. Her current state of heightened purpose is owed entirely to the fact that she is fortunate enough to have something to be purposeful about, she supposes. Without clients and engagements and plans and schemes and the trainees and the Saturday garden openings, she would be at the mercy of what has happened. She would spend all her time in resentment and bitterness. Instead of which, she is able to sideline the whole business, put it away out of sight and out of mind.

Except that that is not quite what is happening.

Right now, as she pulls out to overtake a Golf, she is reminded that Nick's car is still sitting outside the house. Does he propose to remove it at some point, or not? If not, she must get rid of it. But in order to find out his intentions she would have to speak to him, and she is not yet ready thus to expose herself.

And then there is Kath. Kath seems to be with her all the time, these days. Sometimes she is in the wings, as it were, but ready to invade at any moment—a constant preoccupation. At other times she steps center stage, as she did today, aged four, or twelve, or in some adult incarnation. And these last versions of Kath give Elaine trouble, these adult versions: Was this before the day of the photograph, or after? Was this when she and Nick were having their affair, if that was what it was, or not? There is now an innocent Kath, and one who behaved inexplicably. Why? Why *Nick*?

There were so many men, over the years. Before Glyn. When Kath turned up, there was frequently some suitor in tow: "Oh . . . this is James." Or Bruce, or Harry, or whoever. And "suitor" is somehow the word that springs to mind. Not "lover." They were always supplicants, these men, on probation. Did she sleep with them? Not always, Elaine feels. Perhaps not that often. They were followers—that old below-stairs term is neat—and when they followed too assiduously Kath disengaged herself. Next time she came, there would be no man, or a different one. And in all that time, she never looked twice at Nick, Elaine is sure of that. She treated him with casual familiarity; he was just someone who was always around—brother-in-law, Polly's father.

She came for Polly, as much as for anyone, thinks Elaine. And suddenly she sees Kath approaching along the maternity ward, the day Polly was born. Kath is carrying a cornucopia of blue sweet peas, she is joyous, at each bed that she passes heads swivel to eye her. Polly is in a crib at Elaine's side. "Oh—" says Kath. She leans over the crib; she is very still, absolutely intent; there is something in her eyes that startles Elaine. "Oh . . . you." She looks at Elaine: "Could I hold her?"

Elaine lifts Polly from the crib; she puts her into Kath's arms. And Polly opens her eyes, her tiny crumpled face comes alive. For a moment she and Kath seem locked in intimacy.

Elaine reaches out. "I'll take her," she says. "She's due for a feed."

Kath and Polly were always as thick as thieves. And, yes, I was sometimes jealous. Kath descending like the fairy godmother. Polly going on about Kath says this, Kath does that. Kath was everything I wasn't, it seemed.

Is that what Nick felt too?

This thought flies in as Elaine is on the home straight, almost at her own door. It contaminates the relief that she always feels at the end of a demanding day, with an inviting, unsullied evening ahead. And this is not what is supposed to happen; Nick is gone, she must not allow such considerations.

But there of course is his car, another thorn. Elaine hurries into the house and sets about the routine inspection of letters, faxes, voice mail, the kitchen blackboard. This nicely disposes of any intrusive thoughts. She is on track once more, busy with client queries, requests, the daily quota requiring her attention. Polly has rung, sounding fraught; Nick has not, which is a bonus. Her publisher looks forward to their session together tomorrow, and has some exciting work to show her by a new young photographer. The blackboard points out that the weather forecast for the weekend is excellent and hence that visitor attendance will be high; Jim proposes enlisting a nephew to help with the car parking. Pam too has noted the likelihood of high visitor numbers and has been potting up hellebore seedlings and some cuttings from the greenhouse—hardy fuchsias and penstemons—in expectation of heavy demand on the plant-sales area.

Elaine sits in the conservatory with the paperwork on her lap and a glass of wine in hand. Another beautiful evening—*Euphorbia griffithii* glowing ruby-red in the late sunshine, the ornamental grasses shimmering. The sight of these induces reflections on the volatility of taste where gardening is concerned. Nowadays, people do not much care for pampas grass (because people like me tell them that they should not, she thinks . . .); once, it was all the rage. Now, we prefer *Stipa* and *Miscanthus*. The dictation of fashion, of course, but such fickleness invites you to wonder about the whole concept of beauty. A large subject. Elaine plans to include discussion of gardening foibles in the book that is currently at the planning stage; clearly, a glossy publication of this kind is no place for an in-depth review of aesthetics—her concern will have to be strictly limited—but right now she finds her thoughts drifting from plants to people. Knowing as they do so that once again Kath is moving in.

Kath was defined by her looks; she was immediately noticed. Would that have been so a hundred years ago? Two hundred? Elaine thinks of Victorian faces, of eighteenth-century beauties. Are there abiding aspects to a woman's charm—certain proportions, a particular quality of eye, of mouth? With Kath, it was the entire package—not just a face, but her stance, her movements. Even I could see that, thinks Elaine, and I'd been seeing her since she was—well, since she stepped out of childhood and became this surprising new person. She remembers that fifteen-year-old Kath had seemed suddenly like a stranger. "Why are you looking at me like that?" she had said one day, to Elaine. "Is something wrong?" And then—puzzled—"People keep doing it." She hadn't known, back then, genuinely had not known.

And later? Later, she knew. Well, she knew in theory, but it was something she pushed aside, turned away from. Even when Elaine was at her most grudging, she would never have accused Kath of vanity.

She hears Kath. Kath is not speaking to her, but to someone else; this is an overheard conversation. "It's no big deal," Kath says. And now the other half of the conversation comes floating up—what the other person had said. "What's it like to be so incredibly attractive?" The other person is not a man; this is a woman, asking out of genuine interest and curiosity. And Kath replies thus; she is not being evasive, or arch—the reply is as genuine as the question.

When was this? Where? Who? Elaine has not heard this exchange before, or, if she has, she has not paid attention to it. Now, she wants to know more. It seems to her that this took place at the old house, at some gathering, one of those many occasions when there was a crowd of people for Sunday lunch, or one of those impromptu book launches that Nick used to organize. Who is this other woman? She does not really matter, but her anonymity is irritating. She seems to be a relative stranger—perhaps someone meeting Kath for the first time, striking up an acquaintance that day. The question could be taken as presumptuous, intrusive; but Kath is apparently not offended. She gives her honest answer.

And what was I doing? wonders Elaine. She imagines the scene—the kitchen full of people, herself moving to and fro with plates, food. Yes, that would be it—she passes Kath and the woman, and picks up this fragment, which hangs on to this day, as such things do. Why that snatch, rather than some other? It had caught her attention, presumably: the directness of the query, the oddity of Kath's reply. "No big deal." What does that mean? That her looks meant nothing to her, or did nothing for her?

The paperwork has been set aside. Elaine sits staring out into the garden, seeing Kath. Is that what I always wondered myself? How it was to be Kath? To be in possession of that guarantee of instant attention and interest? But of course I never asked her. We never talked like that. I was her sister, but probably knew her less well than her friends did. I never cared for that kind of heart-to-heart stuff; I'm not cut out for intimacy.

And as she thinks this, Elaine finds other Kaths crowding in. These Kaths are not clear and precise, they do not say anything that she can hear, they are not doing anything in particular; they are somewhere very deep and far, they swarm like souls in purgatory, disturbing in their silent reproach. Child Kaths are mixed with grown Kaths, so that the effect is of some composite being who is everything at once, no longer artificially confined to a specific moment in time—no longer ten years old, or twenty, or thirty, but all of those. This is a hydra-headed Kath, who is nevertheless entirely convincing; a multiple Kath who is the continuous, changing person who was there through all of Elaine's life, all that she can remember, and then suddenly was not. This Kath is not happy; these Kaths are not the brimming, busy Kaths of life, but mute witnesses to something unspoken. There is this abiding sense of appeal: "Talk to me. . . ." Does she hear this? "Be *nice* to me. . . ."

Unsettled, Elaine drives these Kaths away. She sweeps up her papers and goes through into the kitchen to fix herself a meal. She puts a quiche to heat in the oven, sets about making a salad. There is some Stilton, and wholemeal biscuits. She lays a place at the table, and as she takes down one of the old Provençal plates from the dresser, there is a small seismic heave of memory and she knows when it was that Kath replied thus to the question from that woman, because the same woman had commented on the plates: "I've got some like that. You must have been to Aix." And Elaine hears herself say, "No. Heal's in Tottenham Court Road, I'm afraid." Furthermore, she knows now that the woman was the wife of the author of a book being celebrated that day, some recent find of Nick's, a man who was the last word on pub signs. Elaine does not give a damn about either the man or his wife, but she is suddenly interested in when this took place, because a further seismic jolt has told her that this was just after the time Kath was ill. She had vanished, in the way that she did, and then one day was on the phone: "I've been ill. I'm fine now. Can I come on Sunday?" And this illness was never defined. "Nothing much," says Kath. "All done with now." And Elaine knows that she never probed, never asked further.

Young Kath, that was. Well, quite young Kath. Twenty-something Kath. When, exactly? This arbitrary memory is now disturbing Elaine; it has brought with it uneasy glimpses of other matters. She wants to push it away, shelve it—but there is also a maddening compulsion to nail it more precisely. Nick would know. Nick remembers all his past publications, he cherishes them to this day. She turns to Nick to say, "That pub-sign book . . . when did you do that series?"

But Nick is not there, and for a moment she is startled, confronting the empty kitchen.

The proposal for Elaine's new book lies on her editor's desk, all three pages of it. A skimpy thing, thinks Elaine, eyeing it as Helen picks it up, puts it down, continues to enthuse. Helen Connor knows little about gardening, but she knows all that there is to be known about the production of a lavish publication that will sell nicely up and down the land, rich with illustration and sealed with the stamp of Elaine's marketable name. Right now, she is handing Elaine a sheaf of photographs—wonders of light and shade, depth, detail, composition. This young man is a genius, he'll do the most amazing job, I'm really keen to use him, what do you think?

Elaine thinks that if she is not careful this book is going to become the vehicle for some adventurous photography. What she has in mind is text, substantial text, supported by constructive and appropriate illustration. She wants to extend her range in this book, to move away from design and plantsmanship into discussion of garden fads and fashions, the social significance of gardening practice, gardens as icons, and indicators. She is bored with telling people how to create a bog garden, or cope with shade, or use challenging color combinations. She has shot her bolt on such matters. She is more interested now in what she has seen and learned over the years of looking at other people's gardens, and wondering why they do what they do. She has done with the practicalities of gardening and wants to consider theory.

Helen is making all the required noises of enthusiasm, but it is evident also that theory has her running scared. Her solution is to temper things with sumptuous presentation—the quality, style, and quantity of the photographs will persuade the reader that this is a standard work. Their gardens will profit if this lies about on their coffee tables.

Elaine knows quite well that she has a bargaining counter. There are other publishing houses out there. Maybe it will have to come to that, but there would be certain inconveniences involved; she will go as far as is possible with negotiation. So she and Helen will be engaged now in a delicate skirmish, neither of them prepared to concede all, both unwilling to part company, each privately considering some gestures of compromise.

Two hours later, Elaine emerges from the publisher's offices. She is neither satisfied nor dissatisfied. She will not be looking for a new publisher, but she has had to curtail her proposed text, give up a potentially rewarding chapter ("It's going to get a bit *wordy*, don't you think?" says Helen). Helen has been persuaded to pull some proposed full-page-spread photographs in favor of a more subdued and relevant approach. Elaine can see that she will have to fight her corner throughout the production process, but the book has yet to be written. For the moment, she can relax on that front; she is reasonably content with the outcome of this meeting. Though she will mark up a few reservations where Helen Connor is concerned.

Elaine has in mind a quick foray to the Royal Horticultural Society's fortnightly show in Vincent Square before heading for home, but first she needs a break. She buys some coffee and heads for a nearby Bloomsbury square. Only when she is sitting there on a bench, amid the patrolling pigeons and the great presiding plane trees, does the place become resonant. She and Kath were here once.

She hears herself: "I'm not your mother." And she hears Kath. "I know," says Kath. "I haven't got one anymore."

Kath is eighteen; Elaine is twenty-four, and a working woman. Today she sees and hears the occasion as though at the end of some time tunnel. The leafy presence of the square is stronger than the two of them; she does not know how they looked, what they wore, but she remembers that even as they talked she was noting the plane trees, with their splayed elephantine feet and their peeling bark. The trees are exactly the same today; thirty-six years is a mere trifle to them. She picks up an echo of that distant self, eyeing the trees and talking to Kath—a distant, muffled voice declaring that, yes, exactly, they are on their own now, they are *grown-up*, for heaven's sake, and Kath must face up to this, must buckle to. . . . Words to that effect.

"I suppose it's all right for you," says Kath. "It isn't for me."

Their mother had been dead two years. Elaine sees Kath with her, intimate in a way that she never was. Hugs and kisses, those long cozy consultations, laughter. Elaine could never be like that; she was impatient with their mother. She saw her as dull, she saw home as a place from which you had to move away. And their mother in turn became wary of Elaine, conscious that she was measured and found wanting. She stood back from Elaine, she mollified, she apologized. But with Kath their mother was someone different; she was at ease with herself, confident, comfortable.

There is more to that meeting under the plane trees. Something that came earlier. Kath on the phone: "I can't go on living there. Jenny doesn't like me. Can I come and see you?" Elaine has heard this often, over time, but now she is hearing herself as well. Not words, or phrases, but a jumbled effect that comes across clearly enough today, also conjured up by the square, the pigeons, the trees: Well, if you can't you can't, but I don't see what you're going to do, I mean it's not as though you were at college or something, had a *base*, you're talking about drama school, well, fine, so long as you realize there's no job guarantee attached. . . .

I'm not your mother.

Elaine finishes her coffee, disposes of the container in a rubbish bin. She is rattled, bothered, she is experiencing a further and different level of disquiet. She is angry with Kath: What did you think you were doing? *Nick*, for Christ's sake . . . And Kath has nothing to say; she is safe, beyond reproach. But she is also forever there, and forever provoking some new testimony.

Saturday. Garden-opening day. And it is all that was promised by the weather forecasters: Wedgwood-blue summer sky with trails of rippling cirrus, warm sunshine, the lightest of breezes. And there is a steady flow of cars from the lane into the paddock car park; Jim's nephew is kept busy. So is Pam, dodging between the plant-sales area and the till in the shop. They are short-handed today; the girl who usually helps out with sales phoned in sick, so Pam must deal with that side of things rather than provide a cheery and informative presence in the garden. Elaine herself is doing garden duty. There have been the usual idiot queries, and a woman presuming to offer advice on epimediums, and various unrestrained children, but also the gardening correspondent from one of the broadsheets, which might be promising, and several genuinely well-informed and appreciative punters. So she is in reasonably good humor when she finds herself confronted by a person in straw hat and sunglasses, who places herself foursquare in Elaine's path, saying warmly, "*Hello!*"

In the person's wake is a girl, also hatted and shaded, but with something about her that causes Elaine a faint stir of disquiet. Elaine offers the woman a somewhat frosty smile, and at the same instant she sees that this is Linda. Cousin Linda—whose mum, Auntie Clare, was Elaine's mother's sister. And still is—festering in some nursing home, one has heard.

"Oh—hello." Elaine's greeting is barely more robust than her smile. She has not set eyes on Linda for many a year and has had no particular desire to do so. She remembers Linda—ten years her junior—as a pasty, importunate child, and Auntie Clare as an occasional tedious visitor with whom her mother engaged in mild competition over cookery skills, dressmaking, and the charms of their respective children. In adult life, she and Linda have exchanged Christmas cards from time to time, and that has been about the size of it.

Linda now lives in the west country, it seems, and is on her way home after a trip to London: "And Sophie was looking at the map and said, Hey! Auntie Elaine's famous garden is on the way—why don't we look in? So here we are!"

Sophie steps forward, demure. Elaine knows now whence the disquiet. There is a whisper there of Kath. She is not Kath, she is not even a pale shade of Kath, but there are flickers and glints of Kath: the curve of a nostril, the tilt of an eyebrow, a way of standing. Genes have skipped sideways and downwards, and surfaced in dumpy Linda's offspring.

"How nice," says Elaine. Few would be fooled, but Linda beams appreciatively. She waves a hand vaguely at the surrounding garden—at the terrace with its clouds of roses and clematis, at the grass walk edged with tree peonies, at the rill and the ginkgos and the lawn sweeping away to the ha-ha. "You've made it really nice here. I must get you to come and sort out our little patch—we've not got green fingers at all, I'm afraid."

Elaine sees that she is going to have difficulty keeping civil. She looks round for help. Why does no one come up to ask what that blue flower is called, or why their roses keep getting mildew? But the garden is ticking over nicely, with little groups of satisfied customers cruising to and fro.

Linda's attention has shifted. "We've been looking out for Nick too."

"He had to be somewhere else today, unfortunately," says Elaine. No way is she going to explain to this intrusive relative that she has recently required her husband to leave home because he once had an affair with her sister.

Linda is disappointed. "What a shame. Sophie wanted to meet Nick. She's working in publishing, you see." She shoots a proud glance at Sophie, who glimmers prettily. No, she is not like Kath—it is just that there are these eerie reflections.

Linda asks what Polly is doing. Elaine counters with Web design. At least this is saving her from any more crass garden-observations, though she is uncomfortably reminded of her mother and Auntie Clare trading child achievements.

Sophie pats her mother's arm: "Don't forget . . ."

"Oh—" Linda reaches into her bag. "I've got something for you, Elaine. We were going through old photos and I found one I thought you'd like. I daresay you've got lots of her. But still—" There is a respectful lowering of the voice; she holds out an envelope.

Elaine knows what is coming. She feels like saying: Thank you, but I've seen enough old photos of Kath to be going on with.

This one is inoffensive enough. Kath sits in a white plastic garden chair, under a striped sun umbrella. She looks directly at the camera, with an air of compliance. Some obligatory photo call.

"In our garden," says Linda. "A couple of years after she was married, I think. She dropped in, quite out of the blue—off to see friends in Cornwall. But I gathered she'd just had that nasty little upset, poor dear, so she was rather under par." Linda gives Elaine a furtive look—regret, and complicity. "Such a shame—"

Elaine thrusts the photo into her pocket. "Thank you. How kind." She becomes brisk. "Have you been down to the woodland garden yet? At its best in spring, of course, but the *Astrantia* are just coming out. I wish I could take you indoors for a cup of tea, but I should be around in case anyone needs me." She is ignoring what she has just heard, and also stashing it away for future contemplation.

But Linda is not to be disposed of quite so easily. She is talking about Kath. It becomes clear that this was not an isolated meeting. Elaine is surprised; apparently Kath had kept up a spasmodic relationship with Linda, over the years. Why? Linda is not Kath's style at all, she has probably never set foot in an art gallery or a concert hall in her life, she would never attend an arts festival, she does not pot or paint or take arty photographs. She is the opposite of the kind of people Kath sought out as friends. So why did Kath bother with her?

Linda is saying it was always a red-letter day when Kath breezed in, a real tonic she was. . . . Kath is cocooned in clichés as Linda talks, and Elaine is further exasperated. Can't the woman see that this is a travesty of Kath? She is reducing Kath to her own humdrum vision, she is re-creating her as some cheery health-visitor. She has no right to this tone of knowing intimacy. She has no right to Kath.

And now the winsome Sophie chips in. She simply loved Kath. I mean, Kath was just *so* cool, she always looked so marvelous, and she was such fun, she'd turn up with these lovely silly presents.

"Actually," says Linda, "we think Sophie has something of Kath about her." A fond glance at her daughter, and a shift to the tone of regretful respect. "Sophie was devastated when—when she—so sad. We couldn't believe it."

Enough. Elaine can stand this no longer. These two helping themselves to Kath. It is an invasion, a presumption. "I'm sorry," she says. "I'm going to have to leave you. I need to check out the car park. Do go and see the woodland garden. Nick will be sorry to have missed you."

Later, she cannot think why she said that. Nick did not give a toss about Cousin Linda. And Nick is not here, he is no longer a part of the place. Why did this hollow remark insert itself, as though she needed the armor of marital solidarity, of normal service?

Later, she hears Linda again. "That nasty little upset . . . under par."

But later is on hold until after six, when the garden empties, the customers and the cars depart, Jim and his nephew pile into the red truck, Pam goes off to the pub with an admirer from the village. Alone, Elaine checks the ticket sales and is quietly pleased with visitor levels, locks up the shop, goes into the silent house. Only then does that other aspect of the afternoon come bustling in. Cousin Linda hangs around all evening, saying that again. And again.

■ ■ ■

Something is happening to the empty house, the Nick-free house, the tranquil and compliant house. Initially, it had been just that: there was no longer the hovering irritation factor, the Nick-generated annoyances, the intermittent requirements and provocations. Elaine's grateful relish of solitude is marred by some subliminal disquiet. She is fine, just fine; she is sitting there at the end of a demanding day, a glass of wine in her hand, something simple in the oven, and then a creeping malaise sets in. The place is too still; its small disturbances are all mechanical—the phone rings, the fax clicks and grinds, the microwave beeps. Its blankness makes Elaine restless; she finds herself wandering around, turning on the television—the background chatter that always so exasperated her in Nick's time. She makes phone calls just for the sake of it, needing to be occupied and purposeful.

She keeps the phone on answer, in case Nick rings, but hovers near to listen, picking up at once if it is not him. When she hears Polly's voice she experiences a mixture of pleasure and apprehension, but is clipped and careful in her responses. Polly's voice brims with agitation and concern, which frequently spill over into further exhortations and appeals.

"Please," says Elaine. "Can we not talk about this."

"But, *Mum*—"

He doesn't know what to do with himself, says Polly. (Did he ever? thinks Elaine.) It's pathetic, says Polly, and I mean *really* pathetic. He doesn't shave some days, and incidentally he's buggered up my washing machine—I had no idea he was so untechnical. And he won't go and look at flats, in case you're wondering; he says he'd rather be here.

I can't believe my *father* is living with me, says Polly.

Actually, Elaine can't quite believe it either. Much of the time she is on course, she is calm and cool and ordered. She deals with each day in a systematic manner, as she ever did. Her attention is on

the matter in hand, whether it is a session with Sonia over paperwork or a client visit or a stint at the drawing board on some design.
She is operating at full strength. But then there come those moments when she is suddenly adrift. She is dazed by events, and she
is confused. What exactly is it that has happened? Nick is no longer
here, apparently because she sent him away. Kath is in her head
more than ever before, but her response to Kath swerves wildly.
Sometimes she is angry with Kath: "Why Nick?" she demands. At
other times she is trying to recover a shadowy, elusive Kath who
seems to be saying something that she cannot quite hear, and occasionally she is startled by some uncontrollable reaction of her own.
She had been affronted by Cousin Linda, jolted into resentment by
that tone of casual intimacy; Linda was nothing to Kath, nobody,
she had no business talking that way.

After a long day visiting a health retreat under refurbishment, for
which she is designing the grounds, Elaine returns home and at
once has the sense that something is not quite right, even as she
turns in at the gate. There are a few moments of disorientation
before she realizes that Nick's car has gone. The Golf is no longer
sitting in the drive.

Elaine goes into the house. Sonia has left the usual pile of letters and memos; there is no reference to Nick. A note on the
kitchen blackboard tells her Pam has detected some suspected
honey fungus on one of the old chestnuts; below this, there is
Nick's scrawl: *"Sorry you weren't here."*

He has taken a few more of his clothes. The almost bare
wardrobe is disconcertingly eloquent, as is the empty space on the
driveway where his car is not.

Children talk a lot about love. "I love you," they say. "Do you love
me?" they ask. Elaine remembers this of Polly. As language began

to flow from Polly, there came this word, flung casually around, in a house that had not much heard it hitherto. It is a word with which Elaine has always had some difficulty; it did not much pass between her and Nick. Polly's carefree usage had reminded her of Kath, when Kath was young. Kath too had bestowed love in all directions, and had asked for it in return. "Do you love me?" she would say, appearing suddenly at Elaine's side, interrupting her homework or her hair washing or her preparations for an outing. And she hears herself: "Don't be silly, Kath."

Don't be silly, you're my sister. That is what she had meant. Sisters don't talk about love. And anyway I don't talk about love. I'm not that sort of person.

Polly and Nick

Listen, I'm not seeing Dan anymore. It wasn't going anywhere. As of last week. All perfectly sensible and grown-up—at least I was. So that's that. A free woman. Though actually there's this guy . . . No, there *might* be this guy. Early days yet—I could be quite wrong. So enough said.

Yes, my dad's still in the flat. I mean, I'm really sorry for him, but it's driving me crazy. Here I am, I'm thirty, and I'm apparently living with my *father*. Yes, of course I've tried that, the place is ankle-deep in stuff from rental agencies, he won't even go and *look*. He says he needs to sort himself out first, get his head together. What does my dad do? You mean work-wise? Well, basically, my dad doesn't really do anything. He talks about doing things, and messes about with ideas that might eventually lead to doing something. It wasn't always like that. He had his own publishing company, way back. Rather successful, actually. But Dad wasn't so hot on the money side, got overstretched or something, and it folded. And by then my mum was doing so well. . . . Actually, my dad's lovely, in his way. I mean, he's still about ten and a half—fifty-eight going on ten and a half. It's always rather driven Mum round the bend, I can see that, but that's how he is, like a sort of overgrown boy, enthusing away about this or that, and actually it's eating me up seeing him like this. Mooching around. Not talking much. Looking *old* suddenly.

My mum? Well, frankly, I think my mum has flipped. I mean, I'm just hoping and praying it's temporary, because my mum isn't a person who flips. My mum is someone who has been on course since she was about five. Well, yes, of course it's *about* something, but all this is so over the top, because what it's about is over and done with. Long ago. I won't go into it but . . . well, I do feel a meal is being made of it, and everyone just needs to calm down. God, *families* . . .

Ah—stepparents. No, I don't know about stepparents. We're the old-fashioned nuclear family. *How* many? Wow! A serial marrier, evidently, your mum.

Anyway, so there it is—my dad on the sofa and beer cans in my fridge and dirty shirts all over the bathroom and various arrangements on hold and my mum saying can we not talk about this. Plus, I've got some really complex client stuff going on right now. I mean, I just don't *need* this.

Listen, I'll have to go—oddly enough they pay me to work here. That's another thing—I can't really talk to people from the flat anymore. It's not that he's listening—it's just that, well, I've lost my personal space.

Actually, no—tomorrow evening's no good. I'm seeing this guy Andy.

Don't jump to conclusions. I've said—it's early days. We'll see.

Oh . . . *hi*! No, this is just fine. Yes, I enjoyed it too. Oh . . . No, no, that wasn't it at all. . . . Look, this really is crossed wires.

This is so embarrassing. The thing is—I couldn't ask you up to the flat because my *father's* there. He's—well, sort of staying with me at the moment. It's a long story. That's why. That's absolutely why.

Oh, I *see*. You thought . . . God, no. Definitely not. I mean, yes, I've been in a relationship, but that's over. Actually, this is quite a difficult time for me—nothing to do with that, that's not a problem at all, we just weren't going anywhere—no, this is, oh . . . *family* stuff. Look, I'm not going to load this onto you when we hardly know each other.

Are you? Well, I think that's nice. I mean, a lot of men don't want to, frankly. They'd rather not know. Listening's just not their thing. Actually, that was a big problem with . . . with this person I'm not with anymore. I just felt he wasn't there for me whenever I had something going on. Know what I mean? Oh God, I'm making myself sound like I'm in perpetual crisis, it's not like that at all, it's just that, well, when you're involved with someone, you expect . . . Look, I'll have to go—I've got a client meeting in half an hour.

Thursday? Yes, as it happens I could do Thursday.

Mum? You all right? Well, good, because everything's not all right here. First of all, I've realized I can't bring people to the flat because of Dad—well, not some people, if you see what I mean. And actually that's really inconvenient just at the moment because . . . well, there's this man I may be interested in.

Oh, Mum, I *told* you I'm not seeing Dan anymore.

And then last night I came home and he wasn't here. No, no— not the man—and he's called Andy, by the way. *Dad.* Dad wasn't here. I mean, usually he's just sitting in front of the telly every evening—and incidentally he's drinking too much. I wasn't going to mention that, except frankly I think you should know. But he wasn't here, and at eleven o'clock I'm like some mother with a teenager out at a disco, watching the clock and thinking accidents and stuff.

The car? Yes, of course the car was gone. And he doesn't

understand about parking in London—he leaves it on yellow lines and gets a ticket just about every day. And by the way he was really pissed off you weren't there when he went to get it—that was the point of going, if you ask me. Seeing you, not getting the car.

Oh, he came back, yes. Nearly one o'clock. By which time I'm climbing the wall, about to start reaching for the police. He's been out of London, he says. Someone he had to see. And it was a long drive and he stopped off on the way back and he got a bit lost. And then he went to bed, and of course I'm so wound up I can't go to sleep, and now I'm wiped out today, just when I've got a panic on with a job that's overdue.

No, he wasn't drunk.

Mum, don't mind me saying so, but if you need to know whether he's remembered that the car is due for its MOT, I think you should ask him yourself.

Oliver and Nick

"No!" Oliver abandons his screen, swivels round in his chair. "I'm not here!"

Sandra is unsympathetic—downright uncooperative, in fact. "Mr. Hammond rang earlier," she says, the receiver held out at arm's length. Does she realize who Mr. Hammond *is*, by any chance?

Oliver attempts to face her down, and fails. He crosses the room, takes the phone. "Ah. Nick. Hello there."

He is in a lather. Not more of this blasted business? First Glyn. Now Nick. Heaven preserve him from Elaine. He can hardly follow what Nick is saying. Nick rattles away. Something about wanting to catch up, out of touch for far too long. Must meet.

"I'm pretty tied up just now," says Oliver. He talks of deadlines, urgent schedules. "Maybe in the autumn." Sandra is listening with interest.

Nick forges on. He talks in broken sentences. He seems to be saying that he is not at home right now, that he has had a few problems recently, that he'd like to have a talk about the old days. He sounds slightly manic.

No! wails Oliver—speechless, defenseless. Nick is saying that he's got nothing much on today, as it happens, so he'll drive over.

Be with you about six, OK? Pick you up at your office—I've got the address. Take you out for a meal.

Well, unfortunately . . . protests Oliver. This evening I . . . But Nick is no longer there. And Sandra is gazing at him, speculative: "Remind me just who this Nick Hammond is?"

When Nick walks into the room Oliver is horrified. This is not Nick, surely? This paunchy figure with thinning hair? With melting jawline and bags under his eyes. Yes, we've all of us matured, some rather more than others, but Nick? Nick was eternally young, it seemed, stuck forever at about twenty-eight, as the rest of them hit forty and edged towards the big five-oh. Well, evidently even Nick is not exempt.

Nick is talking as soon as he is in the room, without preliminaries—a feverish account of his drive, and some difficulty with a recalcitrant clutch, and being jinxed by the one-way system. He is on edge—that is immediately apparent.

Oliver gathers himself. Sandra is observing intently; she has found that for some reason she needs to work late and thus is still there when Nick arrives. "Well, *hello*," Oliver says, genial but not overintimate, for Sandra's benefit—the greeting appropriate to an associate. "Good to see you. Sandra Chalcott—my partner." He turns to Sandra: "We'll be off, then. See you later."

"Is a curry all right with you?" he says to Nick. "There's a place just near." He steers Nick along the street. Nick talks. At least in that sense he is the old Nick, but his talk skitters off in all directions, it is doglegged, herringboned, it leaps from one unconsidered trifle to another. He is in London a lot these days, he says; possibly he may do a book on London squares—fascinating subject, London squares; Polly sends greetings, at least Polly would if she knew he was seeing Oliver, but come to think of it she doesn't; Elaine is extraordinarily busy these days—one doesn't seem to set eyes on her from one week to the next; he has been thinking of writing something on Brunel, but is finding it hard to get down to it, things get in the way so. . . .

Eventually, over a plateful of chicken tikka masala, he falls silent. He stares at his plate. His hair no longer flops over one eye, Oliver notes; it has somehow peeled back from the front. Without that pelt, Nick seems exposed, laid bare.

Nick looks up. He puts down his fork, picks up his beer, drinks deeply. "The fact is, I'm a bit bothered about something."

He shoots Oliver a wild look. He seems now like a schoolboy in disgrace; a chastened sixteen-year-old peers out from the softened jowls and the pouchy eyes.

"Ah . . ." Oliver assumes an expression of neutral interest: Continue if you must.

"Elaine's got herself into a terrible state about a photo. Do you remember a photo of me and Kath?"

Oliver contemplates his lamb korma. "Yes," he says, at last.

Nick pushes his plate to one side. "There's the most awful fuss, actually."

"I know," says Oliver.

"You know?"

Oliver sighs. Bugger it all! "Glyn came to see me."

Now panic flies across Nick's face. "Oh Christ! What did he want?"

"He wanted to know if Kath went in for . . . for that sort of thing. For having affairs with people."

"What did you say?"

"I said I didn't know. What would you have said?"

Nick hesitates. He seems to be reflecting—not a process Oliver associates with Nick. "I'd have said the same."

Silence. "All very unfortunate," says Oliver, at last. "But I don't see what I—" He starts to eat again, determinedly. No doubt he is going to be picking up the tab, so why let a good meal go to waste?

Nick now lets fly. He bursts out with a spasmodic, incoherent litany of concerns. Well, of course Kath must have had affairs, he says; I mean—there were always men around, weren't there? After all, she was *so* pretty. But not for the sake of it. Not in a *frivolous* way, right? Any more than I did. Frankly, Olly, I don't know what got into me. Or her, come to that. Crazy. Stupid. But the point is, it's over and done with, so why, now, all this? I mean, it's so unfair. Elaine's being . . . Well, I won't go on about it, but I wouldn't be surprised if I weren't heading for some sort of breakdown. I'm in a terrible state. Someone's got to do something.

Oliver is barely listening. He is thinking of Kath. She has become like some mythical figure, trawled up at will to fit other people's narratives. Everyone has their way with her, everyone decides what she was, how things were. It seems to him unjust that in the midst of this to-do she is denied a voice.

He interrupts. "Did you love her?"

Nick's spiel is chopped off. He looks shocked. "Well, of course I—" he begins. "Naturally, one . . . I mean, when you're caught up in this sort of thing that's not quite—" He retrieves his plate and picks up his fork.

No, thinks Oliver, sadly. You didn't.

Nick has recovered himself, insofar as this is possible. "The thing is, it might help if you had a word with Elaine."

Oliver stares. "What about?"

Nick sighs—a nervous, juddering, confessional sigh. "She's thrown me out, Olly, that's the long and the short of it."

Startled, Oliver considers this. He is surprised at such emphatic action on Elaine's part. Time was, he had always thought that Elaine rather let Nick get away with things. Admittedly, this must have been quite a bombshell.

"I want to go home," says Nick. He sounds like a querulous eight-year-old.

Oliver is now seized with desperation. He would like to snap at Nick that he is not in the marriage-guidance business, but he is held back by some irritable sense of responsibility that he recognizes from their former partnership. But, for Christ's sake, he is no longer responsible for Nick or anything that Nick does or has done.

"After all," says Nick, "you took that photograph."

Oliver bounces in his chair. "No!" he cries. The people at the next table turn and look at them.

"But you did."

"I mean—no, you can't start blaming me for all this."

"I'm not blaming you," says Nick, in tones of sweet reason. He seems now very much in control of himself. He is shoveling down his food, and pauses to finish a mouthful. "I'm just saying that you are involved, after all."

"I am not," says Oliver sullenly.

"Elaine always liked you."

"I haven't seen her for years."

"She was always going on about how sensible and levelheaded you were. As opposed to me. I think she used to feel sometimes she'd be better off married to you than to me." Nick grins. "It's OK—I didn't mind. I could always sort things out with Elaine then."

So sort this out, thinks Oliver sourly.

"But she seems to have gone completely off the rails about this. All it needs is someone to sit down with her and have a friendly talk. You, Olly."

Oliver glowers.

"It's just a question of getting her to see that I don't *deserve* this," says Nick plaintively. "Right? I mean—OK, it was silly and wrong, but that's *all* it was. There's absolutely no point in every-one going berserk, Glyn charging around, Elaine behaving as though I'd robbed a bank."

"*No.*"

"No, what?"

"No, I won't talk to Elaine."

Nick gazes across the table in silence. He becomes reproach-fully dignified. "As you wish. Entirely up to you. I would have thought you might feel . . . well, a certain involvement. Never mind. So be it."

The meal is finished to the accompaniment of a few con-strained exchanges. When the bill arrives Nick has fallen into a de-pressed silence; Oliver pays it.

They part outside the restaurant. "Good seeing you, Olly," says Nick. He manages to appear generous, forgiving, and leaves Oliver experiencing a grating mix of guilt and resentment.

Oliver and Sandra

"So what was up with your friend?" inquires Sandra.

"Oh, nothing really," says Oliver.

"Come on—I know a man in a tizz when I see one."

They are in bed. There is no escape route. "He always was a bit like that."

"First that Glyn someone," says Sandra thoughtfully. "Then this Nick Hammond. Your former partner, right? And Glyn was married to Nick's wife's sister? Her that died?"

No possible escape. Oliver agrees that this is so.

"And suddenly they're all needing to see you. Has something come out of the woodwork?"

Fleetingly, Oliver considers telling Sandra about the whole business. Well, you see, the trouble is that Glyn found a photo taken by me which indicated that at one point Nick had an affair with Glyn's wife, Kath. He knows immediately that he will not. Bald facts are a travesty, a distortion. That is what happened, but it is also misleading, confusing. Left out is what Nick was like, and what Glyn was like, and above all who Kath was, and how she was. Without the ballast of personalities, of how things were back then, such an account is threadbare, it invites a knee-jerk reaction. He knows just the sort of comment that Sandra would make.

She is waiting. This is evidently to be one of those rare occasions on which Sandra decides to pay close attention to Oliver's past. He knows those indications of terrierlike purpose.

"It's just a question of clarification," he says. "People need to get straight about some dates—that sort of thing."

"A publishing matter?" says Sandra. "To do with the business?" Her tone is deceptively bland.

Oliver is no liar. He is fluttering now. "Well, in a sense, I suppose . . . Not absolutely specifically. Sort of indirectly."

There is a telling silence.

"I see," says Sandra. Then: "That Glyn—striking-looking man. Laid on the charm too. An academic, you said?"

"That's right." Oliver contrives a suggestive yawn. "I'm wiped out, love. I think I'll—"

"The wife," says Sandra. "The one who died. Kath—is that right? I don't have much impression of her, except that she was very attractive. You knew her well, I suppose?"

Oliver is now in full flight. He lays a calming, propitiatory hand on Sandra's thigh, turns away from her with an exaggerated sigh of weariness, and hopes for the best. After a moment, Sandra too rolls over, and is silent.

It is a long while before Oliver sleeps. They all come crowding in—Nick, Glyn, Elaine. And Kath above all. He sees and hears Kath fresh and clear: "Hi, Oliver!" she says, breezing into his office back in the old days. "Where is everyone?" She sits on the window seat in Elaine's kitchen, plaiting Polly's hair. She is beside Nick in the group at the Roman Villa that day; he raises his camera. And when eventually he drifts on the interface between consciousness and sleep, she is still there, but now she has become very young— a girl Kath that he never knew—and she is talking about love. He cannot follow what it is that she is saying.

Glyn and Myra

It is Glyn's birthday. He does not remember this until he notices the date on his newspaper. Birthdays never rated highly with Glyn. But he knows how old he is—sixty-two. This reminder of the relentless process is unwelcome. The passage of time is indeed his stock-in-trade, but when applied personally it is as though there were someone out there gleefully chuckling: You too—oh, dear me, yes, you too.

It is Saturday. He plans a weekend dealing with paperwork and ordering his thoughts on a projected article. This will be therapeutic. Glyn is in a curious state these days. He recognizes this, knows that he is not operating normally, that application requires an effort, that his mind wanders, that it is willful, that he cannot seem to control its direction. He has always been able to work; work has been the imperative, ever since he can remember. He has been able to switch into work mode under any circumstances. No, it is not like that. He stares for long minutes at the screen, he does not turn the pages of the book in his hand, or he reads without comprehension.

Kath. Her fault. Except that something odd has happened also with the attribution of blame. He is finding that his former drive to discover her guilt, her duplicity, her involvement with a raft of suspected lovers has evaporated. His various encounters—with Claverdon and his companion, with the Hapgoods, with Kath's portrait and its courteous guardian—have eroded his sense of purpose. They have left him feeling uneasy, even chastened. He is no longer interested in that obsessive pursuit of what she may have done, in whom she may have known. He is not even much interested in Nick, he finds.

He thinks about Kath. She rises up in front of the screen, she is superimposed above the page. He listens to her.

But this morning he will work. Grimly applied, he heads for his study.

The front doorbell rings. It is Myra. With a birthday smile on her face and a present in her hand, which turns out to be a rather nice piece of early Victorian china. He receives both with the best possible grace, but she is out of order. Very definitely out of order. The unstated terms of their relationship are that it is conducted at her place, and there alone. She has only visited this house on two or three previous occasions. If he runs into her in the university, he gives her the polite greeting he might give to anyone else on the staff; no doubt their association is known to some, but it is not to be asserted. On the rare occasions that they go out somewhere together, he ensures that it is well away from common ground.

Glyn takes her into the kitchen and makes coffee. He could hardly do less. And, truth to tell, her arrival has given him a lift. The significance of the date had induced a mawkish feeling of self-pity, a sense of solitude quite alien to his usual stern defense of privacy.

Myra is in her late forties, veteran of a failed marriage that Glyn does not wish to hear about; he has made this plain. She has dark, ripe good looks and a vivacious presence that he finds invigorating at the right moments. And the moments, normally, are chosen by him; during the several years of their association, Myra has acknowledged its boundaries. If she once sought a firmer commitment, she has now abandoned any expectations. And, equally, Glyn accepts that if something more satisfactory to her came along, he would no doubt be required to relinquish Myra. He does not think much about this; and if it happened, well, one would have to look around.

Glyn enjoys sex with Myra; Myra too gives every indication of satisfaction. There is a degree of intimacy between them, tempered by the recognition that this is an arrangement of mutual benefit, and that is all. When he is with Myra, Glyn obliterates any thought of Kath. It is not that Myra is no substitute for Kath; it is rather that she is not on the same plane as Kath, nor ever could be.

"You were working, I suppose," says Myra.

"I was." But some uncharacteristic note of apathy in Glyn's voice gives her the advantage.

"Such a nice day."

He notices that it is indeed. He begins to see where this is leading. And within a minute or two, he has somehow fallen in with Myra's scheme. An outing. A sortie into the landscape. A walk, maybe—lunch at the pub. Or . . . As it happens, she has been doing a spot of research, and there's this country house which is open today that hardly ever is. But I expect you know it already.

He does not. And actually he wouldn't mind having a look at it. Myra is in luck. He agrees, surprised at himself. But first he must have a spell at the desk to deal with a few urgent letters.

Myra is entirely happy about this. She'll find something to do. And within the next hour she has scoured his saucepans, removed various moldy items from the fridge, bagged up the rubbish, and had a runaround with the vacuum cleaner. This is just the sort of thing he has always anticipated, where Myra is concerned, and one reason why he has kept her away. His gratitude is not effusive.

She picks up on this, and is tactfully apologetic. "I'm afraid I got a bit carried away. You know what I'm like." He does indeed, and she is reminding him that the appeal of her own place, for him, apart from the solace of her bed, is the provision of home comforts. "And you haven't got the time or the inclination, have you? Your cleaning lady seems to have a few blind spots. Of course your wife would have—"

Now she is really transgressing; Kath is a forbidden subject. Glyn cuts her off: "Kath didn't do that kind of thing," he says shortly.

Myra is baffled, as well she might be. Does he mean that Kath neglected her domestic duties? Or that she was above such trivialities? But she sees that she has overstepped the mark and makes a judicious retreat by producing a road map with the suggestion that they check out a route to this country house.

Glyn realizes that the excursion has been well planned; he cannot but admire her strategic skills. He has been ambushed. That said, he is not as resistant as he would expect to be. Once again, he recognizes his own abnormal state. He has allowed himself to be manipulated by Myra, something which does not happen. But there is this unusual lethargy, where work is concerned, and he would not be averse to an inspection of the house, which, he recalls, has fourteenth-century origins and will undoubtedly throw up something worth his while.

Glyn drives. Myra navigates, making much of it; she is exuberant with the success of her plot. Perhaps she sees this small triumph as an erosion of Glyn's position, where the conditions of their alliance are concerned. At any rate, she fails to note that he is quieter than usual and she rattles on uncurbed. Her talk skates the surface of things, as always, glancing from one train of thought to another; this has never too much bothered Glyn, for whom her conversation is not her appeal and who is abundantly well qualified to dominate where talking is concerned, when he so wishes. But today he does not so wish, and Myra has full rein, until arrival at their objective and the dictation of a guided tour eventually force her into silence.

A country house, for Glyn, is a fine assemblage of coded references. The roped-off furnishings and the artworks pillaged as successive generations undertook the Grand Tour are of little interest to him; he is busy sniffing out the implications of this accumulation of wealth and patronage. How has this particular pile affected its environment? What has been obliterated by its parkland and its lake? How far has it determined the local economy?

For Myra, it becomes apparent, a country house is merely the decorative extension of a decent cafeteria and an inviting gift shop. The tour is the necessary preliminary, an agreeable enough hors d'oeuvre which she undertakes in a businesslike way, with housewifely attention to detail. She is gratified to spot a cobweb or a grubby surface. But she does pay attention to the pictures, and joins Glyn as he inspects the art displayed in the building's most lavish public room.

The paintings are all about either sex or fame, except for the few that celebrate a woodland scene, a vase of flowers, or some idle arrangement of slaughtered animals. Sex comes in the guise of mythology; but there's no doubt what it's all about, thinks Glyn, wandering from a rosy recumbent nymph being eyed up by Bacchus to an ivory-fleshed Leda tucked beneath a sinuous swan.

"Oops!" says Myra. "What's going on!"

He ignores her, thinking now of fame, which blazes all around. A giant cloaked Napoleon glowers from a rocky crag; Nelson dies on a bloody deck; an armored Caesar glitters amid a thousand spears. Glyn has never paid too much attention to fame, being more concerned with the effects of the toiling masses, but as he prowls from painting to painting he sees that fame displaces its subjects—they float free of any context and become iconic figures. Everyone knows them, but as images, as symbols. This is how these people are perceived, and thus are they portrayed, forever.

Myra is getting a mite restless. She wants her lunch. She draws Glyn on through the next room, and the next. He is unusually compliant, intent upon his own thoughts, which are no longer directed towards the surrounding display—the tapestries, the weaponry, the inlaid cabinets—but in feverish pursuit of quite other matters.

Myra sorts things out in the cafeteria. She installs him at a table and goes off to forage, returning with a tray of food and a couple of glasses of wine. Glyn pulls out his wallet, reminded of decent procedure.

"Birthday treat," says Myra expansively. She raises her glass: "Here's to it!"

Now she looks closely at him. "You seem off color. You're not coming down with something, are you?"

Glyn gives himself a shake. He replies briskly that he is fine, fine. Myra has occupied quite enough new ground today. He is not going to cede any more. Confidences are out of the question, and ever have been. All Myra knows from him about Kath is that she died. No doubt she knows a fair amount more from others.

He forces himself back on course. He remembers where they are. He gives Myra a simplified account of the changing fortunes of the landed gentry since the Middle Ages, to which she listens with apparent interest, though she asks no questions. His intention is to clarify her perception of this place, but by the time he has got to the Victorians his own commitment is waning. Myra takes advantage of a pause to suggest coffee, and goes off to fetch it. She returns talking determinedly of her son, who is reading engineering and about whom she needs Glyn's advice. Glyn has always resisted being thrust into any sort of pseudofatherly role and avoids visiting Myra when the boy is in residence. His only defense now is to speed up the coffee stage and suggest that they get out and see the gardens.

Myra goes off to the ladies'. Glyn wanders out onto the wide terrace overlooking a green vista of southern England, and as he does so he is joined by Kath. She comes with a rush, not just in his head, but all around him, it seems, so that he is with her as he once was at some similar place, to which he hustled her during that ferocious accelerated period of courtship. They stand at a stone parapet, overlooking tree-studded parkland, and she puts a hand on his arm: "There's something you never say." And then, "Never mind—" This rings now in his head: "There's something you never say—"

Myra appears, and they start their tour of the gardens, a couple enjoying an outing amid all the other couples and the families and the straggling coach party. The weather remains idyllic, the roses are out. Myra is high with satisfaction. "Well!" she says. "This *was* a good idea."

For Glyn, it is no longer Myra who is at his side, but Kath: Myra talks, but anything she says becomes irrelevant background interference; he reaches beyond it for Kath.

"You're not *listening*," says Kath. But he is. He is listening with all his might. Listening and seeing. And along with the familiar signals that endlessly repeat themselves, the reliable structure of the years with Kath, the received interpretation, there come odd vagrant challenging flashes—like the hitherto undetected stars that periodically excite astronomers. But Glyn is not excited; he is disturbed, perturbed, awry.

He hears Kath on the phone—a low voice that falters, crumbles. Is she *crying*? He comes into the room, and she is putting the phone down: "I'll have to go, Mary." Her face is odd, distorted. He is in a hurry, he is leaving for a conference in the States, and he has mislaid a crucial paper. He cannot dwell on Kath's face, that shriveled look, but he must have stashed it away because now, here, today, it comes swimming up to him.

Elaine and Polly

Long ago, Elaine considered not having Polly. That is to say, she considered not having children at all. Being childless. There is a choice. She could see that life is a good deal less cluttered without that. One would be able to get on with work a lot more easily. She looked around at her contemporaries and took note. There were those who toiled from day to day, burdened with sleepless nights and howling days, and those who cruised free, accountable only to themselves.

It could have gone either way. For a couple of years, she thought of the matter from time to time, but would push it to one side. And then she noticed that if she forgot to take the pill, she was not particularly bothered about the lapse. She forgot quite often.

When she knew she was pregnant, Nick said, "Oh, good. What fun." She had never discussed with him her own doubts about becoming a parent. Of course there were two of them in this, but it had seemed to her that in the last resort the issue was a personal one. She knew who would be taking the brunt.

Nick was not a bad father. When he was around, and had nothing better to do, he fathered with a boisterous enthusiasm.

From the age of about two, Polly saw him as some kind of engaging but wayward family pet—good for a romp, but not to be taken entirely seriously. As she grew older, this attitude firmed up into one in which affection and amusement rode upon an undercurrent of mild exasperation: "*Typical!*" "Trust Dad—" Polly seemed to shoot past him, becoming the responsible and efficient adult, while he remained in a time warp of feckless adolescence.

Polly's phone calls are now more circumspect. She has given up on direct appeals, defeated by Elaine's polite deflection: "Can we not talk about this." Instead she skirmishes around the edge of the subject. She mentions the trouble involved in fixing the washing machine ill-treated by Nick. Elaine offers at once to pay. "It's not the money," says Polly. "It's the *bother*." She describes how she has hauled Nick into the offices of a rental agency: "On Saturday morning, when actually I had a million things to do . . . And we went to see this really nice flat and he said yes, OK, fine. And then as soon as we're back at my place again, he does a U-turn and it's no, he's not sure, maybe, he'll sleep on it. And there's my Saturday morning down the drain." She makes dark references to drinking sessions. She says Nick has lost weight: "Not that he couldn't do with that, but all the same—"

All this has an effect on Elaine. She is distracted. Her resolve is faltering. Instead of concentrating smoothly upon work, upon the demands of each day, upon future plans, her thoughts come homing back to what Polly last said. She pictures Nick wandering aimlessly around London. She wonders about this weight loss, and the drinking.

Polly visits. She visits at short notice, as usual, dashing down on a Sunday. "Dad knows where I've gone," she says pointedly. "He . . . well, he sent his love."

She and Elaine sit and eat lunch in the conservatory. "I can't believe Dad's not here," says Polly. "I keep expecting him to walk in. All right, all right, I'm not going to start up again. Just . . . well, it's so *unreal*."

Elaine agrees, but she is not going to say so. Polly talks about a man. This Andy. "Not that I'm rushing into anything," she says. "But it's *interesting*, put it that way." She looks speculatively at Elaine. "Did you and Dad fall in love with a great wham, or what?"

Elaine is thrown. She is not open to this kind of exchange, nor is Polly in the habit of such questioning. Have normal family conventions been abandoned?

"Oh—" she says. "It's such a long time ago."

Polly is having none of that. "Oh, come on, Mum. Everyone remembers falling in love."

Elaine is busy over the salad. "All home produce," she announces. "This is a kind of rocket I've never tried before. Grows like a weed." She piles herbage on Polly's plate. "And the first baby beetroot. Here—"

Polly eyes her. "Mum, don't mind me saying so, but you'd feel better if you let go a bit more. You're *so* buttoned up. I mean, I know it's the way you are, but it can't be good for you."

Elaine is used to being scolded by Polly. Polly has been scolding her ever since she was about three. Usually it has been over questions of diet, or dress, or household management. Now, it would seem that she is going for basics.

"I seem to remember a process of gradual drift," she says.

"Drift?" yelps Polly. "*Drift!* For heaven's sake, Mum!"

Actually, Elaine is trying to be honest. That is what she remembers. She searches for passion, and something does come smoking up: an incandescent day when she and Nick walked on the Sussex downs, not long before they got married, and she had brimmed with well-being, with anticipation—yes, with love.

"Well, there was more than that."

"So I should hope," snaps Polly. She becomes reflective. "I mean, I've been in love, but I'm accepting that I haven't been definitively in love. Not the full five-star menu, the earth moving, the real thing. Just a few appetizers. I'm waiting."

"Plenty of time," says Elaine. "How's work going?"

But Polly is not interested in talking about work. "Was Kath in love with Glyn?"

Why is Polly so exercised about love? Is it love in the past or love in the future that concerns her? Elaine's love, or her lack of it? Or a potential love of Polly's own? Whichever, Elaine is uncomfortable.

"I suppose—" she begins. "Well—she seemed very happy."

Kath comes down the register-office steps, again and again, smiling and smiling. She smiles into the camera, at Elaine on the other side of the road. Her skirt is crooked.

"When didn't Kath seem happy?" cries Polly.

Elaine wants to stop this conversation, if conversation it is, but can see that Polly is in a relentless mood. Nor can she say, "Can we not talk about this," because Polly is not doing so; she is keeping the matter of Nick at arm's length.

But now Polly plunges in another direction. "The thing is, I don't *understand*. I don't understand how people can be so . . . *mysterious*. I don't understand *people*. You think you've got them pretty well sewn up, and then they go all flaky on you. They fly apart. They even fly apart in your *head*, for goodness' sake! I don't understand Kath. I mean, I knew Kath. I don't understand Dad. I look at him—and he's a real mess these days, Mum, I can tell you, grubby shirts, needs a haircut, doesn't bother to shave—I look at him and I don't know *what's* in his head. And I don't understand you, Mum. Absolutely I do not."

There is a butterfly tapping against the conservatory window, beating furiously up and down: a tortoiseshell. Beyond, in the garden, the sunlight sifting through the crab apple trees has turned the lawn to a brocade of green and gold. Pam wheels a barrow across the end of the grass walk; some stuff falls off and she stoops to pick it up. Elaine is aware of all this, the stable and consoling backcloth to her daughter's discordant presence. Polly no longer sounds thirty; this wail is coming from a person of eight, or ten, or twelve.

"I don't understand how everything can suddenly go completely off the rails. I mean, the point about life surely is that it moves on. It goes forward. On and on, regardless. It doesn't . . . loop backwards. Which, as far as I can see, is what yours is doing. Yours and Dad's. There's Dad, and he's a zombie. He's completely out of it. I'm beginning to think therapy. There's a woman I've heard of—"

Elaine is jolted into reaction. "No. Definitely none of that." She stares at Polly, who has pushed her half-eaten lunch to one side and is managing to look both martyred and mutinous.

Elaine realizes that what she is now experiencing is guilt, and that she has perhaps been experiencing this for some while. She is feeling guilty about Nick. How can this be? She is the one who is sinned against, but there has been a reversal of roles. It is Nick who is apparently some sort of victim, who is at risk, who invites concern. Whereas she is unreasonable, implacable, unkind.

She says, "You do remember what this is all about?"

"Oh, *Mum* . . . of course I do. But look at you. . . . Frankly, Mum, you're all over the place. I mean, I can tell—you're twitchy, you've got baggy eyes, you're not you."

Is this so? Elaine thinks of the way in which Sonia glances at her from time to time. She remembers Pam's solicitous offers to take on extra tasks. Is this how she appears? Is this, indeed, how she is?

There is a silence. "There—" says Polly. "That's all. I'll shut up." She reaches for her plate and starts to eat again. "The salad's good. Can I take some of this rocket stuff back for Dad and me?"

Kath

Oliver finds himself thinking about Kath's men. Those who came with her when she turned up at Elaine's house. They are a shadowy crew—for the most part he can no longer put a name to a face, and frequently the faces too are lost. There were not that many of them—four, five, six maybe, over the years. A couple who came only once; others more tenacious, who have left a stronger impression. An assorted lot—taller, shorter, younger, older—but the common denominator that Oliver remembers is a certain triumphal quality. They were men in possession of a trophy, successful competitors in some contest with which Oliver was not involved. Oliver knew that he was not the sort of man who aspired to a woman like Kath. These men were better-looking, rich with confidence, purposeful. Kath was their purpose of the moment, apparently. They accompanied her with complacent ease; she was their due, they were owed someone like this.

He remembers an actor whose name he vaguely recognized, a roguish charmer; he remembers an urbane fellow with a BMW convertible. Both of these turned up on more than one occasion. And, homing in on recollections of these men and on the way in which they melted away, over time, he finds himself in Elaine's garden, with Kath, companionably gathering windfall apples. She has come alone this time: no man. Polly darts round them, busy with apples. She rushes up, laden: "Look how many I've got!" "Clever girl!" says Kath. "Put them in the basket."

"Where's Mike?" demands Polly. "He promised he'd give me a ride in his car without a top."

And Kath replies, "Mike's not coming anymore." Offhand, inspecting an apple. Polly pulls a face and goes back to the apple hunt.

Kath turns to Oliver. Was he betraying interest? Or surprise, or sympathy? She smiles: "It's all right, Olly—my heart is not broken. Did you like him?"

And Oliver, flustered, prevaricates—unable to say that so far as he is concerned, they are jammy beggars who don't know their luck, the lot of them.

Kath sighs. She polishes an apple on her sleeve, takes a bite; he sees her white teeth against the shiny red. "The thing is to move away before it's too late." Is she talking to herself, or to him? He does not know that look: something anxious about it, lost.

"Too late?" he says firmly, to bring her back.

And she smiles—familiar cheery Kath. "Before they change their minds. Have you got a girlfriend, Olly?"

How did Oliver reply? Oh, he can guess. He would have floundered about, and Kath would have laughed, and teased him, and they would have gathered up the apples, and Polly, and gone back to the house for lunch, or tea, or supper.

Indeed, the whole scene is now a fluid mix of imagery and supposition. He sees Kath, and small Polly flitting about in the long grass, and experiences the satisfaction of lighting on a perfect apple—no bruising, no scabs or holes. He sees that alien look on Kath's face. Snatches of what is said ring out: "My heart is not broken. . . . The thing is to move away . . . Before they change their minds." The rest is unreliable—perhaps that is how it was, perhaps later wisdoms have imposed themselves, perhaps the need for narrative and sequence has stepped in. Suffice it that he was there, then, with Kath, and it was thus, or very like.

Polly does not remember the day of the apples. It is subsumed into the crowded simultaneous present of her childhood, when she is just a pair of eyes and ears—seeing, hearing, storing. She has stored Kath many times—she can conjure up different incarnations of Kath. Kath gets smaller as Polly gets larger, until eventually they are shoulder to shoulder. Kath is now like some kind of big sister.

Once, Polly wanted her to be something else. She wished that Kath was her mother. This is no reflection on Elaine, it did not mean a repudiation of Elaine, it meant simply that Polly wanted to have Kath with her all of the time, in an attentive, available mother role. She remembers this longing and she remembers also an accompanying guilt; she knew she must not voice this need, least of all to Elaine.

Nowadays, Polly can see this with adult wisdom. She had doted on Kath, and so, naturally enough, wanted more of her. But she had been sufficiently mature—at six? seven?—to realize that there was a whiff of infidelity in this: you can only have one mother, you should love your mother most of all.

And I did, she thinks, as one does. In the last resort. I suppose.

Not that there was anything particularly maternal about Kath. You could not imagine Kath pushing a buggy, dishing up a family meal, waiting outside the school gates. All of which Elaine did as a matter of course, alongside her other concerns. Polly recognizes this, and gives Elaine her due.

Once, Polly and Kath sit drinking coffee in Polly's college room, during her student days. Kath has come to visit. Polly has shown her off, displayed her around the campus, and now they are having the leisurely heart-to-heart that Polly so relishes. She lays out various friends for Kath's inspection. She is heady with the whole student experience. But she is working, she tells Kath sternly, she is working like crazy. Already, there are objectives, there are goals. She will maybe aim for business, for finance, for the City. Or possibly journalism. Web design has not yet raised its head, though Polly is a whiz with technology.

Kath listens. She sits cross-legged on the bed, with a mug in her hand, as to the manner born. She could be twenty, not forty-something. She listens, apparently rapt. "Lucky you," she says, and there is an unfamiliar note in her voice. Polly is brought up short: lucky? her? But it is Kath who is lucky—just for being Kath. To look like that, to be like that—breezing through the days, through life.

They talk about love. Polly thinks she may be slightly in love; not madly, desperately, mind—but there is a definite disturbance. She is interested in her symptoms, and questions Kath. There is no sleep loss, but she does find that she thinks about him a lot and in . . . um . . . a sexual way. She cannot help making a point of en-gineering that their paths cross. Is this a low-grade response, un-likely to escalate? Do you know at once when it is serious? She is assuming that Kath is an expert.

Kath laughs. "Oh, all *that*—" She says that she first fell in love when she was five, with the postman. And then with the Rentokil man and with the vicar and eventually with the boy at the paper shop when she was fifteen, and that lasted all of two months. But Polly is not interested in this juvenile stuff, and she senses flip-pancy. She is after informed guidance. But now Kath seems to withdraw; she is not so much evasive as oddly muted. "All I know is that I'm no good at it," she says. "Mistakes, mistakes—" She stares at Polly: "The thing is, do *they* love *you*?"

Nick thinks that he has slept with six women, apart from Elaine. That seems modest enough. There is a possible seventh when he was eighteen, but he is not at all sure that she counts; it was a particularly inexperienced session. But this is not the track record of a libertine, is it? And three were premarital encounters that can be viewed as perfectly normal steps in sexual development. The other three are indeed infidelities and cannot be explained in any other way, though one is a borderline case, he feels, being a short-lived lapse triggered by getting drunk at a party and fetching up in this woman's flat. The liaison with a publishing associate long ago is more reprehensible, looked at with detachment; but Elaine never knew, no one got hurt, the thing is dead and buried.

His eye has wandered, during married life—he is quite prepared to admit that. He has looked, and occasionally lusted. He has entered into understandings that have somehow stopped short of sex, and he would admit also that these might well have progressed, if the opportunity had arisen.

It is not a particularly admirable record, but neither is it despicable, surely? There are worse husbands, for God's sake.

If it had not been for Kath, Elaine would have reacted otherwise, in all probability. If that photograph had shown some other woman—some neutral, impersonal figure—Elaine would have been angry, he would have groveled, but he would not be here in London, exiled.

Why? he asks himself. Why did it happen? But he knows. He looked at Kath one day and saw her afresh. And now he cannot see her thus anymore. That fatal compulsion is quite gone; the Kath he experiences today is neutral, and the Nick to whom she responds is not himself.

Kath sits on the window seat in the kitchen at the old house, with Polly on her knee—an infant Polly. This is in the time of innocence, long before he looked differently at Kath. Nick has come into the room and he thought at first that this was Elaine. He says as much. "I thought you were Elaine," he says, or must have said.

And Kath looks at him over Polly's head: "No. It's me." She says it thereafter, again and again, and he is arrested still by her tone, by how she is. She is not vibrant Kath, but is suddenly bleak.

Glyn took Kath to the Lake District for their honeymoon. There was a strategy to this choice; he was interested in early hill-farming at the time and needed to do some fieldwork on boundary systems. That week is now a blur, one image melting into another: Kath lying on her stomach to drink from a tarn, the attentive gaze of people in a pub as she comes in through the door, her rain-wet hair glinting in the light. She follows him up a valley; he looks round and sees that she has stopped, her back to him, hands on hips, wearing a scarlet jacket, a small vivid figure, like some romantic affirmation of human existence against the spread of sky, lake, and hills.

They climb: the steep grassy slope, the winding trail. "Does this thing have a name?" she asks. "They all have names. This is Cat Bells." There is soft, caressing wind, and sunlight that flees across the hillside. She comes close and wraps her arms around him. They kiss. Pressed up against him, she runs her hand down and finds his erection: "I think we'd better get off this mountain," she says. They skid back down the track. Somewhere below there is a low stone wall, sheep-cropped grass and bushes beyond. They are over the wall; she is laughing; she says, "I can't take *all* my clothes off—it's freezing!" He spreads his coat on the grass, puts her down on it. She kicks off her trousers. It is the most urgent sex he can ever remember, a glorious immediacy, pinned forever in that place—the wind, the smell of crushed grass, some small piping bird, sheep moving about. Afterwards, he is suddenly euphoric, richly alive; he hugs her to him, pushes his hands under her sweater, feels her warm skin. She is laughing again: "Oh yes," she says. "*Yes*."

And now, today, he is filled with outrage that all this survives only in the head. He wants to retrieve the moment. He wants to retrieve Kath, as never before.

"I'm going to have five children," says Kath. "Mostly girls. A couple of boys—twins maybe. Not just yet. In a few years."

Elaine listens with cynicism. She is pregnant: heavy, hampered, irritable. Kath has blown in; soon she will blow away again, off back to her unfettered life, to whatever it is she is up to these days.

Elaine observes that Kath may find that she requires a husband.

"Oh yes, definitely. I'm looking for one." Kath is twenty-four. And spoiled for choice, Elaine assumes. On occasion, she is accompanied by some attentive man. Not today.

This is a time when Elaine's feelings for her sister rampage from one extreme to another. If Kath disappears for weeks on end, Elaine is on edge about her. Why does she not phone? Where has she got to? When she shows up, need is replaced by a gust of annoyance: there she is—carefree, the fiddling grasshopper amid the striving ants, her beauty a repeated surprise. One had forgotten its effect.

"Well, look carefully," says Elaine. She has little faith in Kath's judgment. She sounds sour, and knows it.

Kath laughs. "Oh, I do. You've no idea how careful I am." The laughter stops, abruptly. She is suddenly concentrated, serious. Her glance sweeps the room—the cluttered domestic place. It homes in on Elaine's fecund belly. "Is it wonderful?" she says. "All this?"

Voices

"Look," he says. "It's Nick. I know I'm absolutely the last person in the world you want to have on the end of a phone, and I don't blame you if you hang up, but I had to give it a try, OK? I just felt if you and I could talk a bit, and frankly you've every right to tell me to piss off, but I thought, No, I bloody well will, I'll ring him up, there's nothing to lose, things are bad enough anyway, at least they are at this end. And, Christ, I know what *you* must have been feeling. Believe me, Glyn. What I'm trying to say is—and I know you must be thinking this is a bit rich coming from me—I'm trying to say it's . . . well, I'm trying to say it's not absolutely what it looks like. I mean, I know it must look pretty wretched from your point of view, but that's where I feel if I could only have a chance to explain a bit, just kind of talk it through, you might be able to see it differently, see *me* differently. It's a question of perspective, really. The thing is . . . Are you still there, Glyn?"

Glyn growls that he is still there—wondering in fact why the hell he is.

"Oh God, thanks. Thanks for giving me a chance. Look, what I'm trying to say is . . . it was all so bloody stupid, it wasn't such a big issue, it was a crazy sort of *mistake*. I don't know what came over us—came over me. Oh, that's what people always say, isn't it—except I'm sure you don't, you've got more sense, I always thought you were such a levelheaded sort of bloke, knew what you were doing, which is why I thought, Let me just try to *talk* to him."

"You seem to be doing just that," says Glyn. "To what end?"

"Ah. Well, it's kind of several things, you see, Glyn. I mean, firstly, me and Kath. What you've got to understand is, it was all over almost as soon as it began. It wasn't some great long-drawn-out business. And it made absolutely no difference to—to other things. Me and Elaine. You and Kath. Those were what mattered, believe me. We both knew that, at the time. She . . . well, I tell you honestly, and I absolutely mean this . . . I always knew her heart was never in it. And for myself, well, I got carried away. She was after all incredibly . . . I just sort of lost my head. But only temporarily, that's what I'm trying to say. It was just this brief kind of lunacy. And that's really the point of my getting in touch, Glyn. I mean, it's long since over and done with, and Kath's not here to . . . Surely the sensible, reasonable thing is just to bury it, let it be, and all of us get on with life—"

Glyn interrupts to say that, personally, he is doing precisely that.

"And that's where you're so sensible, Glyn. I mean, you're seeing it in proportion, you're being rational about it, and frankly I'm so relieved, talking to you, thank God I did phone, and, believe me, I've had to screw myself up to this, but I feel so much better now. But the real trouble is . . . Elaine's taken it rather differently, and that's what I wanted to talk about too. She's really gone over the top about it all, completely overreacted. Actually, Glyn, she's thrown me out."

Glyn has swung from extreme irritation through contempt to boredom. Now, he is interested. Well, well. That's a turn-up for the books.

"I'm staying with Polly. I don't mind telling you, Glyn, I'm in a pretty bad way. It's so . . . well, I just feel it's so extreme. I mean, yes, of course, I can see how she feels, but does it have to be like this? She won't talk to me—nothing Poll says has any effect. What's occurred to me, Glyn, is . . . Elaine always had a lot of time for you, she respects you, I know that—maybe what's needed is someone a bit more detached, like yourself, to sort of have a word, put it to her that she's going too far. I just have this feeling that she'd pay attention to you, Glyn."

"Do you, now?" says Glyn.

"And of course it was through you that she knew about it."

"Oh, I see. It's really all *my* fault," says Glyn.

"Christ, no—that's not what I mean. I can entirely understand why you felt you had to—"

"Good," says Glyn. "Just as well."

". . . of *course* I understand that. And you and Elaine have known each other a long time—though I wish you'd come to me first, if you and I could only have had a talk at that point—"

That does it. "Quite," snaps Glyn. "Elaine and I go way back."

"Sorry?"

"We . . . considered one another for a while. But you may be aware of that."

"Actually, no—I wasn't."

"Again, no big issue, put in perspective. You take my point?"

Afterwards, Glyn has no idea why he said this. Exasperation? Mischief? Somehow, the words just fell out.

"Oh," says Nick. "You and Elaine—" And is silent.

"So, I could, I daresay, have a word, as you propose—but on the whole I think it inappropriate. You have to deal with this for yourself, if I may say so."

"Mum? Look—I'm worried about Dad. Nothing new about that, but I'm differently worried. He's gone all quiet. Not that I see him that much—I'm flat out this week, working all hours, someone's off sick and . . . oh, never mind—but when I do, it's as though I'm not there. He just looks at me—as though he's miles away. I'm thinking therapists again, frankly."

"It's me. I've got to talk."

When Elaine puts the phone down she can hardly believe that this conversation with Nick has taken place. In which she has had to agree that, yes, she and Glyn were once . . . interested in one another . . . that, yes, she met Glyn on a few occasions. But that, no, they were never lovers. She is experiencing a brew of emotions: fury at Glyn, embarrassment, defensive cool with Nick, who has bypassed the answerphone because she forgot to put it on. But now that their exchange is over, and she is angry and undermined, she realizes that Nick's tone was not what she might have expected. There was neither challenge nor reproach; rather, he seemed bemused, incredulous. He was not out to make capital from this, it would appear. The phone call was to seek confirmation: "I thought he might be making it up."

And whatever had Nick been doing talking to Glyn? She can hardly believe this either: "I wanted to ask him to speak to you about . . . everything. Put in a word for me."

Only Nick could have come up with such a ruse, or only Nick in some manic state. Provoking Glyn to this backhander. It is as though we are all possessed, she thinks.

Glyn goes back to basics. Research. A hunt is on once more. He trawls directories, he harries the Crafts Council, he picks up false leads and goes down dead ends, but eventually he is able to make a phone call and arrange a visit.

Elaine finds that she needs urgently to call in on a well-known garden in Gloucestershire which she has not seen for some while;

it would be professionally remiss not to check up on their new water garden, and see what the tree peonies are like this year. This trip will take her very close to Winchcombe, where there is someone she would rather like to talk to right now. She picks up the phone: "Hello. This is a voice from the past. Elaine—Kath's sister. I was wondering if by any chance—"

Oliver goes through old address books. He does this furtively, of an evening, while Sandra is in the kitchen or the bathroom, slamming them quickly back in the drawer when she returns. This is one of the aspects of coupledom that is always a trifle irksome—the fact that any harmless little activity that one does not wish to have to explain must be circumspect. Where basics are concerned, you cannot fart or pick your nose. At another level, anything that may give rise to casual queries that one would prefer to avoid becomes surreptitious. Whyever should he be feeling guilty about a search for the phone number and address of an old acquaintance?

Eventually, he is successful. Here it is, not in any address book but scrawled in the back of a notebook, amid jottings about printers and suppliers and pages of figures and costings. All this dates from the Hammond & Watson days. And next to her address he has written "photos," and circled the word. He must have scribbled this down at the very end of the picnic at the Roman Villa; he must have promised to send her photos. And presumably did so, though that he cannot remember, but in making the selection he would have come across the fatal frame. Which he presumably did not include in the batch that he sent to Mary Packard.

Nick cannot get rid of Glyn's voice. It reverberates in his head, a voice not heard for a number of years, but at once entirely familiar—a dark voice with a lilt to it, conjuring up the man himself. "Elaine and I—" The sound of it flings Nick back into that other time, when Glyn was a frequent visitor, with Kath, always talking, holding forth, quenching Nick himself, whose role that had been. Even then, Nick was prepared to admit himself outtalked.

Elaine's voice rings loud too. What she said. How she said it: frosty, but with an undertow of confusion. Nick himself is in a turmoil now, but it is in some ways an oddly reassuring turmoil; actually, he is feeling better rather than worse, though he cannot quite work out why, and maybe it doesn't matter anyway. Glyn has refused to be drawn in as an intermediary, and Nick wonders now how he can ever have imagined that he would, but instead Glyn has thrown this bombshell. Or is it just a small firework? Nick is trying to get himself sorted out about this. What does he feel about it? Well, he is surprised. Elaine and *Glyn*? Though it would seem that there wasn't all that much to get excited about. But even so . . . Does he feel angry, jealous? Well, not exactly. Though perhaps a little . . . upstaged. And it puts a rather different complexion on things, does it not?

Most of all, Nick finds himself plunged suddenly into endless replays of Glyn's voice. Not only now, but back then. That day. When Kath. He hears him then, sounding the same, but different. The phone rings again, and it is Glyn: "I need to speak to Elaine."

That Day

A Thursday. Glyn left early for the university on account of a nine o'clock seminar. He had woken late, reached for the clock, said, "Bloody hell, look at the time!," and saw Kath lying wide-eyed beside him.

"Why didn't you wake me? I've got to get in early."

Everything about that day stood out in bold relief, later. What was said; what was seen.

He showered, he shaved. He saw his own face in the mirror, foam-flecked, and a reflection of Kath passing behind him—a bare shoulder, her profile. When he went back to the bedroom, she had gone; he dressed. Downstairs, she was in the kitchen, wearing that blue toweling bathrobe, making toast; bare legs below the bathrobe, her hair brushed behind her ears. There was coffee on the table. She said, "Boiled egg?"

"No, I haven't got time." He went into his study, gathered up papers he needed, returned to the kitchen, poured coffee, glanced through a student essay.

"A boiled egg takes four minutes."

"No, no—"

Afterwards, he would home in on this repeated offer; usually, it was take it or leave it—or he fixed something for himself.

In the garden, the sound of an autumn robin. He looked up from the essay: the grass freckled with fallen leaves, the skinny branches of the trees.

She said, "How about we go out for supper tonight? The Italian place?"

"I shan't get back till nine or so—there's something I have to go to. Bit late—"

"OK. I may go to the pictures with Julia." She had friends in the city, people he hardly knew, people she saw on her own.

She was sitting opposite him, reading the front page of the newspaper; the shape of her face, its perfect planes—intensely familiar, but always catching the eye.

She looked up, held out the paper. "Did you want it?"

"No, thanks. I'm off in a minute." He went back to the essay.

She said, "It's nothing but death and disaster." He saw a headline about famine in Africa, the wizened features of a ragged child.

"It was ever thus. This student is telling me—somewhat inadequately—about the demographic effects of the Black Death."

Kath said, "I wish I was one of your students."

He did not know what she meant, nor would he do so subsequently—examining the words. "Why?"

"Oh . . . just, they know someone I don't. Do you get fond of them?"

"Some leave an impression. It's a relentless tide, you know. One lot goes, another comes." He swept the pile of essays into his briefcase, took a final swig of coffee. "Right—"

"Glyn—" She put her hand out as he stood up, as he moved past her towards the door—she touched his arm. He paused: "Yes?" Hurried, distracted.

"Nothing." And there was nothing in her face, nothing that he could see then, or would see later. A smile. "You get going. See you—"

Thus, that morning. The beginning of an autumn day, a working day, unexceptional. Her voice, her presence, as on a thousand other mornings. He went out of the front door, heard the robin again, got into the car. He may have glanced back at the house, in which Kath was sitting in the kitchen, drinking a cup of coffee, reading the paper. Perhaps picking up the phone to say, "Hi! What about a film this evening . . . ?"

At the university he gave a seminar on eighteenth-century agrarian reform to third-year students. In his office he went through the mail, wrote some letters and a student reference, took a completed paper to the departmental secretary for typing. He stopped to chat with her for a minute: Joy, a chirpy young woman who served as the hub of local activity, pestered by staff and students alike. At twelve, he lectured.

What did you do that day? While she was home, alone.

At one o'clock he went over to the cafeteria for something to eat, joined a couple of colleagues, got into an argument about student expansion, discussed a proposed new course, had a beer. At one-fifty he returned to the department in haste, to collect a file on his way to the library. Joy beckoned as he passed her open door. "Your wife rang. She tried your direct line, but you weren't there. She asked if you could call her back."

He picked up his file, and was at once waylaid by an importunate student; the student occupied his attention for ten minutes, driving other thoughts from his mind. At two-twenty he was on the steps of the library, and briefly remembered Joy's message. The phone call to Kath would have to wait—he had only an hour and a half in which to finish off some crucial checking of references.

In the event, he got back to the department five minutes late for his four o'clock appointment with a research student, already waiting patiently outside his door. That session overran, which meant that by the time the man left, Glyn's five o'clock seminar group was also camped in the corridor.

At a quarter past six he was through with them. There could be a further quick foray to the library before the inaugural lecture and ensuing reception, which he planned to attend. He was going to this not out of intellectual curiosity and support of a colleague, but in order to confirm his view that this appointment, which he had opposed, was a disaster. He was halfway down the stairs when he remembered that he should phone Kath.

He went back to his office, made the call. No reply. He listened to the ringing tone for a minute or so—maybe she was in the bathroom—then hung up. Gone out, presumably.

A useful hour in the library. Then the lecture, which was satisfactorily poor. Finally, the reception, at which he stayed for rather longer than he had intended, carried away by a couple of glasses of wine.

At ten past nine he arrived home. The hall light was on—but he knew at once that there was no one here: the inert feeling of an empty house. He went into his study, dumped his briefcase. Then to the kitchen for a glass of water; the breakfast things were still on the draining board. He looked in the fridge: some cold meats, and the wherewithal for a salad. Kath would no doubt eat out.

He went up to the bedroom to shed his jacket and find a sweater. He switched on the light, and saw that the bed was occupied.

She lay on her side, turned away from him so that he could not see her face. He knew, as he stood there. He knew before he went over and touched her, looked at her. There was no one here; the room was empty of life, just as the house had felt barren as he entered.

When at last he walked over to her—looked, touched—it was as though she were a husk. This was Kath, but also it was not Kath at all; the face hers, but also a mask, a void. She had vomited; her mouth was open, there was a mess on the pillow. He wanted to cover her up; no, there were things that had to happen now. He saw the glass on the bedside table, the little capless brown bottle, some empty packets. He seemed to be acting like an automaton; he could move about, respond, but at some other level there was rampaging disbelief. This was not possible. Impossible that he was here, in these moments, with this around him; the proper place to be was hours ago, back this morning, dressing in this room, while downstairs Kath made toast and coffee, picked the newspaper up off the mat. That was real, this was not.

The ambulance came, and went. Later, the police arrived, two of them, a man and a woman. They went up to the bedroom, incongruous invaders, and came back down with the things from the bedside table. They sat with Glyn in the kitchen and asked a few questions—dispassionate, perhaps apologetic.

What did you do that day? While she . . .

The woman asked if there was anyone he would like them to call. He shook his head.

When they had gone, he sat there; the automaton struggled with the rampaging disbeliever. He made a cup of tea, but never drank it.

Then he reached for the address book and looked for Elaine's number.

That morning, Elaine was planting the two *Sorbus cashmiriana* which had arrived the day before. Perfect circumstances: crisp dry late-autumn weather, the ground still nicely workable. She and Jim moved the young trees from position to position until they had it right, dug the holes between them, carted compost. It was an hour or so before the job was done, the stakes in, the two stems of future promise standing bravely alongside the grass walk to the orchard. Returning to the house, she turned to look back at them, visualizing how they would be ten years on—tall, sturdy, with those jeweled, snowy clouds of autumn berries. To garden is to harness time.

Eleven o'clock by now, and the day snapping at her heels. Sonia needed guidance, Nick wanted to talk about buying a computer, which would give him a head start with this exciting new scheme he had to tell her about, there was a tricky phone call to be made to a new and exacting client. Elaine set Sonia straight, deflected Nick, was relieved to find the client unavailable, and turned at last to her largest current project—landscaping the grounds of a refurbished country-house hotel. She spent a couple of hours on design and costings.

A sandwich lunch in the kitchen with Sonia and Nick ("The thing about the technology, sweetie, is that in a couple of years it's paid for itself, in terms of cost efficiency"). By now Elaine was watching the clock; she planned to catch a train to London. In the early evening there was the reception and press launch of the new wing of an art gallery, for which she had designed a courtyard garden, and before that she intended to visit the Royal Horticultural Society's Lindley Library, in pursuit of information about an extinguished Edwardian garden of which she had once seen photos, which might prove inspirational for her current project.

Nick drove her to the station. He had given up on the matter of the computer; both he and Elaine knew that he would return to the subject and that Elaine would probably have to concede, and provide the money, given that he was indisputably in tune with contemporary thinking on this matter. Well, the thing could be set against tax. At the station, he dithered for a moment with the thought of coming with her, tempted by the notion of the champagne extravaganza at the art gallery, and then decided he couldn't be bothered. He would pick her up when she got back.

At the library, Elaine was instantly immersed in her search, absorbed with catalogues and a growing pile of books. An hour later, breaking off to take stock, she realized that she had forgotten to ask Sonia to get together and dispatch some papers needed urgently by the accountants. Not too late to get her before she left at the end of the afternoon.

Elaine found a public phone, got through to Sonia, sorted things out. Sonia reported on a call from a client: "Oh, your sister rang too."

Back with the books, Elaine filed this away; she could ring Kath when she got home. Or tomorrow. The afternoon was nearly gone; the gallery *Festschrift* loomed.

The press photographers were gratifyingly attentive to the courtyard garden. And indeed it did her credit, a vibrant floodlit oasis at the heart of the austere quadrangle of the gallery. She received compliments from an assortment of strangers. There were several indications of possible future commissions. She took a close look at the garden, which she had checked out only a few days before anyway, decided that a cordyline was wrongly sited and made a note to get it moved. After forty minutes she left to catch the train.

Nick was not at the station. She waited, irritated, until the car came sweeping in ten minutes later: "Sorry, sorry, I forgot the time—"

During the course of this day Elaine thought about Kath three times—but "thought" is not the right word for that involuntary process whereby a person surfaces in the mind of another. Rather, she experienced Kath. As she planted the trees, the worm tumbling from a spadeful of earth brought a sudden glimmer of Kath as a small child, crouched intent over a flowerbed, crying,

"Look, look! A *thing*—" Not thought so much as consciousness. Later, in London, a woman glimpsed through the window of a bus had Kath's stance, her shape, and briefly Kath flowed in again—a concept, not deliberate thought—and was chased away almost at once by consideration of how to find an account of this half-remembered garden in the library.

After the phone call to Sonia she did indeed home in upon Kath. Kath occupied her full attention for . . . a minute, perhaps longer. It was several weeks since Kath had last rung. There had been talk of a visit, which did not happen: "Maybe I'll come over next Sunday. Depends what Glyn's up to. I'll let you know." But there had been no subsequent call, and Elaine had been mildly irritated: typical Kath. She intended to phone, but the days had piled up, and the call was never made. But she would make it now—this evening, once she got home.

It was a quarter to nine when they reached the house. Elaine put the oven on to heat the remains of a casserole. Then she went to the telephone.

There was no reply from Kath's number. No answerphone, either, but Kath seldom remembered to put it on. Glyn also out, presumably.

The casserole was eaten. Elaine read the paper, joined Nick to watch the news. She had a bath. She was drying herself when she heard the ringing phone; it stopped—Nick must have picked it up downstairs. She came into the bedroom and heard him call: "It's Glyn—for you." She went over to the bedside phone.

Glyn said, without announcing himself, without preliminary: "I've got to tell you something terrible." And at once she knew. Not how, or why—but what. Kath.

For much of that day Nick was thinking about computers. If he had one of those things—a really good one with masses of giga-whatsits and the latest whatever it was, software—then undoubtedly he would be able to do just so much more. Indeed, the equipment would be inspirational in itself—it would be a stimulus, it would give him ideas. You couldn't work without this technology, nowadays. Especially not in his field. With it, he would be able to . . . well, he'd soon see what could be done once he was up and running.

Elaine was going to take a bit of persuading, that was clear. But Nick felt reasonably confident. If he went about it the right way—calm, businesslike, knowledgeable—she would eventually capitulate. Yes, these things were quite pricey, but it wasn't going to break the bank—not the way Elaine was pulling it in these days, and all credit to her.

Fired by these considerations, he drove into town after he had dropped Elaine at the station, to do some reconnaissance on the different makes. He spent an hour in a big office-supplies place, where the twitching screens were a bit intimidating, and he could not understand a word of the sales talk. Never mind, he'd get his head round it all soon enough.

Back at the house, he made himself a cup of tea and took one to Sonia. It was nearly four now, so there was no point in getting down to anything today. He settled himself in the conservatory with the tea and a book. At one point he went back to the kitchen to forage for a snack, feeling peckish. Sonia was on the phone as he passed her door; she held the receiver aside to say, "Kath, for Elaine. Do you want to—?"

He shook his head. Not that there was any *problem* with Kath since . . . since that time. Absolutely not. Everything was always quite normal and natural. Just they both sort of avoided any one-to-one situation.

He got hooked on a TV program, and was a tad late meeting Elaine's train.

Judiciously, he made no further mention of the computer.

Elaine was in a good mood, quietly chuffed from the praise apparently lavished on her art-gallery garden. They ate a companionable meal, watched the box for a bit; she went up to have a bath.

Glyn's voice on the phone was terse: "I need to speak to Elaine." Nick called up to her from the bottom of the stairs. He returned to the sitting room, decided he'd had enough of this program, switched off the television. He wandered around for a few minutes putting out lights, and then went up. When he came into the bedroom Elaine was standing with the receiver still in her hand, and an expression on her face that he had never seen before, a look that gave him a jolt of wild unease.

By the time Polly heard about Kath, that day was yesterday. She was visited by a sense of guilt, of culpability—all these hours in which she had gone about her business unknowing, carefree, while elsewhere Kath . . . Polly could not bear to think of that.

Polly was a working woman. She was twenty-two years old, she had a degree, an overdraft, three credit cards, and a studio flat in Stoke Newington. Her feet were planted firmly on the bottom rung of the Prudential Insurance Company, which might not turn out to be the best place to have put them, but it would do for now, while she sniffed the air, took stock.

And so, that day, she had breezed through her work, which was not exacting—not exacting enough, indeed; she had socialized usefully with colleagues, she had conducted an interesting flirtation over the photocopier with a guy from the sales department. In her lunch hour she had bought a pair of expensive shoes without which she could not live for a moment longer. After work she had met up with an old friend from college and had luxuriated in an extended gossip over a pizza.

She had been occupied, intermittently interested, she had been stimulated, entertained, uplifted by the flirtation and the shoes; at one point she had walked amid the city lights, the bustle, the energy, and had experienced a surge of well-being. If asked, she would probably have said that she had been happy that day. She had once or twice been irritated, she had remembered the overdraft with compunction when buying the shoes, she had had a flicker of envy for the friend, who was in the throes of an ecstatic love affair. None of these add up to unhappiness.

When Polly looked into that day—Kath's day—she knew that she was staring at something far beyond her experience, beyond even her conception of experience. Kath, that day, had visited some terrible place that Polly found unimaginable. Kath—so intimately known, so familiar, so . . . well, in a way so ordinary, except of course ordinary she was not.

Polly realized that she had never known someone die. Someone close, someone in your life. And she was incredulous—not so much grief-stricken as in a state of incredulity. No, no . . . this could not be. Impossible. Not Kath. There must be some absurd mistake.

When eventually she knew that there was not, all she could think was: But where has she gone? Where *is* she? Where, where? She imagined some great dark void, and Kath out there in it, helplessly drifting, unreachable.

When Oliver read Elaine's letter his first reaction was one of shocked recognition: yes, it never occurred to me, but, yes, this was always on the cards. He found himself searching for times with Kath, and each sequence that arrived was subtly changed by what had happened; that day last week had kicked away old assumptions—what had seemed unexceptional was now quite other. "Are you happy, Oliver?" asks Kath.

He mourned Kath. He read the letter, which told him little, the bare facts—when, where, how. But not, of course, why. He read, and then he put the letter down and was filled with sadness. He had not seen or spoken to Kath for years, but he realized that there had always been a sort of quiet satisfaction in knowing that she was out there, somewhere. And now she was not.

He did not wonder why; he did not want to know why. He saw—dimly, inexplicably—that in some disturbing way what had happened was heralded, that there had always been something troubled about Kath, something that set her apart. Behind and beyond her looks, her manner, there had been some dark malaise. But nobody ever saw it, back then, he thought. All you saw was her face.

Mary Packard

Mary Packard watches each of her visitors as they arrive: The car pulling up in the lane outside her gate, the driver getting out, looking around, checking that this seems to be the right place. Coming up the front garden path between the lavender bushes towards the cottage door, while Mary observes from the window of her studio to one side. She will emerge when the visitor puts a hand on the knocker: "Hi," she will say. "I'm in here."

To Glyn Peters, to Elaine, to Oliver—whose other name she always used to forget, and still does. Not all at once, of course: separately, spread out over the course of several weeks, this curious little epidemic of arrivals, each preceded by a phone call—brief and purposeful (Glyn), diffident but determined (Elaine), equivocal (Oliver). After the first, she had no longer been surprised by the others.

Mary's studio is a converted dairy, detached from the cottage: cool in summer, cold in winter, whitewashed walls, tiled floor, large strategic window that floods the room with light. There is a sink, and a great cluttered table, and the clay and the wheel and shelves of finished pots. Mary's work is displayed in galleries and craft centers; it is expensive. It seems astonishing that those poised shapes can have arisen from the dumpy, glistening mound of clay.

Kath used to say: "Can I just sit and watch?" She would be over there, on the old cane chair—a silent, companionable presence.

Mary is short, compact, sturdy. She seems to have more in common with the clay than with the elegant reincarnations that she conjures from it. Today, years on from the time when Kath was often here, her cropped dark wiry hair is badger-gray. She is alone; various men have come and gone, which is fine by her. The man of the day at the Roman Villa is so effectively gone that she has to hunt around for an image of him, when Elaine makes some reference: "Oh, he's someone I'm not in touch with anymore," she says.

This is a woman who is self-sufficient. Which does not imply egotism, or complacency, or indifference to others; just, she is one of those rare and perhaps blessed souls who are able to make their way through life without the need to be shored up by companionship, or dependents, or love.

Mary has both received and given love; but when love is not around she is able to do without. She is childless, and takes pleasure in children; she acknowledges that perhaps she has missed out on something significant there, but sees no point in dwelling on the matter. She is astute, she is generous, she is warm; she is also gifted with the power of detachment.

People have always eddied around Mary, recognizing some strength that they cannot identify. Or that most cannot identify. Some have had a shot: "You've got ice in your heart," said one man. He was wrong; not ice within, but armory without. Mary has a sound shell into which to retreat; those less well equipped are inclined to hover near her, like scuttling crustacean claws in search of a safe haven. Mary accumulates lame ducks, hangers-on, some of whom have been men who had to be gently dislodged when the level of dependency became ominous. Sometimes there have been studio apprentices, girls whose need was not so much to learn how to throw a pot as how to live. Which is something that cannot be taught, as Mary has come to realize. Nowadays there is no one enjoying official waif or stray status, just various people who turn up on a regular basis—friends for whom Mary has been the reassuring backstop, and an assortment of needy neighbors and local connections.

Mary dispenses brisk sympathy, wry advice which is not always heard as such, coffee, cheap wine, and her spare bed. She listens well—the kind of uncommitted listening that induces a sense of catharsis. Those who have leaned on Mary for a while are left feeling cleansed, relieved; their problems look a bit more manageable, as though set in perspective. In fact, Mary has indicated little and said less. Sometimes, her own thoughts would surprise and dismay those who bend her ear. She cannot help feeling a certain impatience with the way in which people allow themselves to be dragged through the fires of hell by others. At the same time, she recognizes that her own immunity is unusual. Since this state is not one that she can transmit to anyone else, all she can do is hear their tales of woe, and reserve judgment. This restraint is quite hard for her at times, when she hears another saga of betrayal from some apprentice who brought the whole thing upon herself, in Mary's view—couldn't she see that the guy was stringing her along? Or when a neighbor's tale of financial woe reveals a subtext of feckless outlay. Mary herself lives frugally, and always has. Those who conspicuously consume must accept that they may be consumed, she thinks—but says nowt. People who pour out their woes to others require commiseration, not admonition.

Mary met Kath at a craft fair long ago. Kath was manning a friend's stall; Mary looked across and saw this exquisite woman behind a display of fired-enamel dishes and a rank of mesmerized customers. The run on enamel was phenomenal. Mary came over to chat; they took a lunch break together. Mary said, "Would you care to sell pots next time?" They beamed at each other, each recognizing an unexpected confederate. "I am your exact opposite," Mary would remark, idly, at some other time, much later. "Yes," says Kath. "That's the whole point. But really I want to be you. Swap?" Spoken as a joke, but in fact not a joke at all.

They were a conspiracy, a tacit alliance. Weeks and months might go by without contact, and then they would resume the association as though they had parted yesterday. Phone calls were elliptical, each knowing how the other would react. "Why aren't you a man?" said Kath. "Or why can't we be gay? Then that would be me all sorted out." If any of her men met Mary they shied away, sensing some sort of competition that they could not match. Kath never asked what Mary thought of this man, or of that; she would just say, eventually, "He was no go, of course." And they would talk of something else. She was blithely agreeable to Mary's occasional lovers; when they were gone she would say, "Poor him. But he wouldn't do. And you don't even need him, do you?"

Over the years, they were close, yet also far apart—separate lives linked only by the crucial semaphore of friendship. Kath observed the lame ducks, the hangers-on, alert to their status; but when such people were around Mary she was at her warmest, her most friendly. Once, when they were alone after a succession of such importunates, she said, "Am I like that? Come on, you can be honest." And Mary had said, "You never could be. Whatever happens to you, that's impossible."

She knew what happened, from time to time. Not always. On occasion, she knew from Kath's shuttered look; she saw that beneath the surface gaiety something darkly thrashed. She knew also not to ask. She saw Kath as in perpetual flight from inquiry, from scrutiny; whatever it was that went on there could only be glimpsed. But once in a while she would learn in full: "Sorry about this," Kath would say. "But I need to dump on someone, and it seems to be you. Actually, there is only you."

Glyn Peters and Mary Packard circled one another like suspicious dogs. On the first occasion that they met, Mary felt her own rictus of welcome to be more like bared fangs. Why him? she was thinking. Why this one? Why now? She had noted Kath's state of tension. She saw Glyn as some kind of opportunist marauder, a sexual freebooter. When Kath told her—when she announced, "Actually, I'm going to marry him"—Mary had said, "You're not pregnant, are you?"

Kath went suddenly still. She looked away. "Oh no," she said. "Oh, *dear* me, no." There was a silence. Then Kath spoke again—a small, quiet voice: "I think he loves me." Mary could find nothing to say.

And so, on this day so much later, when Mary watches Glyn get out of his car, look around, open the gate, and walk up her garden path, she sees a man who carries baggage—the baggage of all those years. He is freighted with her own initial mistrust—mistrust which gave way eventually to tolerance. She sees a man she once disliked, and then got used to, because there was no alternative and he was by then an unavoidable feature of her friend's life. She sees a man she sparred with on occasion, a man she thought too ready with an opinion, a man inclined to talk everyone else into the ground. She is startled to see that this man is now an older man, and then remembers her own grizzled head. All the same, he is palpably the same man, and all around him there float other times, and other people. He brings Kath; he brings Kath's voice saying, Glyn this, Glyn that, Glyn's away for a few days so I'm going to play hooky and come to see you, right? He brings that house of theirs in Melchester, which Mary seldom visited and always found in some way a house without a heart, a house in which two people came and went but in which they somehow did not live. He brings Elaine and Nick and their place—gatherings in that crowded kitchen, Kath with Polly dancing attendance, Elaine dishing up food to a dozen people, Nick on a roll about some project, Oliver whatsit hanging about at the edge. He brings . . .

Glyn arrives at the cottage door. He lifts a hand and knocks. Mary opens the studio window. "I'm in here," she says.

When Glyn opens the garden gate, he is pitched into uncertainty. He no longer knows quite why he has come to see Mary Packard. What on earth got into him? Why did he make that impulsive phone call, so essential at the time?

He rallies. He takes in his surroundings; he sees a limestone cottage with mullioned windows, seventeenth-century, with brick chimney and slate roof of a later date. He heads up the garden path and knocks at the door. And a voice comes at him sideways. He looks round, and sees her. Oh, it is her all right, though he is surprised to see that she too has . . . well, moved on.

"Ah," he says. "Mary."

Afterwards he will try to piece together what was said and will find that what he has is an accumulation of language and of feeling: her words, his mute responses. His own words are not much in evidence; he is conscious of having spoken at the outset and then fallen silent. At one point she too stops speaking and the silence hangs in the room—Mary's deeply inhabited room, which is kitchen, sitting room, office, in which an old railway-station clock softly ticks and the dresser is crammed with seashells, lumps of rock, grasses, and a sheep's skull. "I seem to have rather shut you up," she says. "Sorry about that." And he remembers spreading his hands in a gesture of . . . what? Defeat? Concession? Repudiation?

That would have been way on into the afternoon. After the initial niceties, the move into the cottage, the making of coffee.

After his opening moves, Mary sitting there, saying nothing, that look in her eye. After he had made his pitch; after he had been careful, candid, persuasive.

Some while after that. After Mary had begun to talk, had been talking for what seemed a long time. Talking about Kath. You want to know about Kath? she had said. Right, then, I'll tell you about Kath.

Actually, I'm not fooled, Glyn, she said. Stuff this memoir. There isn't any memoir, is there? I don't know what it is that's bugging you—but, whatever it is, you've become obsessed with Kath, haven't you? Obsessed in a way that you never were when she was alive, I suspect—at least not after you'd married her.

This is when the words begin to pile up, when he simply listens, despite himself, when he is conscious of kaleidoscopic emotions. A tide of resentment ebbs, and is replaced by something else that will surface fully much later on—tomorrow and tomorrow. Mary talks about a Kath whom Glyn seems not to have known. This is when she talks about the miscarriage. You never knew about that, did you? she says. Kath told me you didn't. She wouldn't have you know. You were away somewhere when it happened—in the States, I think she said. She was going to tell you about the pregnancy when you got back. It was a while ago—two or three years after you were married. She was working for some arts festival at the time.

You hadn't realized she wanted a child. How much she did. Neither did I, until then. Afterwards, she said, Maybe just as well, Glyn wouldn't have taken all that kindly to the idea. But it wasn't just as well, it was just about as bad as anything could have been.

It was the second. The second miscarriage. The second non-baby. The first one wasn't yours. Way back, that was. When she was in her twenties. She told me about it once in an offhand way—that way that always set alarm bells ringing. I asked her if

she'd have stayed with the father, if things had turned out otherwise, if she hadn't lost the baby—and she said, Oh yes, for that I
would have. You bet. Anything, for that.

You want to know about Kath's friends? Mary says. Well,
that's me, mainly. But you always knew about me. You want to
know about Kath's men friends, don't you? Is that what's bugging
you? If so, you're on a hiding to nothing, Glyn. There was no
string of lovers. There's nothing under the carpet.

So he tells her what is bugging him. At least he has a card to
play.

Yes, I knew, she says. Afterwards, I knew. When she was busy
hating herself. Hating herself even more than usual.

She told me. She said, I've been doing something so stupid. So
bloody pointless. Nick. She said. *Nick*, of all people. I remember
her sitting there, looking utterly bleak.

And, no, I don't know why. The sort of thing that brings the
analysts out of the woodwork, isn't it? What I can tell you is that
it didn't go on for long, and when it was over it was over. Nick, of
course, is . . . well, you know Nick as well as I do. Better, indeed.
Nick blows with the wind, doesn't he? A seize-the-day man, Nick.
And there was a streak of that in Kath—more than a streak. But
with her it was because it was the only way she could keep the
demons at bay—whatever they were, whatever it was that boiled
away there, every so often. She had to keep on the move—get out,
go somewhere, do something.

So that's what's bugging you. I remember the picnic at the
Roman Villa. She was staying here for a day or two and either
Elaine or Nick rang up and suggested we all meet up. You were off
somewhere, presumably. The photo call I do not remember.

Mary's voice conjures up the photograph, which Glyn does
not want to see, ever again. He sidesteps, he backtracks.

Hating herself . . . ?

You didn't know about that? Well, she was good at smoke-screens. Maybe there was a touch of acting talent after all—perhaps she shouldn't have quit drama school so precipitously. Most people would never have known. But you . . .

You were married to her; you lived with her for ten years. This is unspoken, but rings out between them.

Again, don't ask me why, says Mary. I don't go in for amateur-shrink stuff. But that was how she was. Not always. Sometimes she could coast along fine. Then . . . wham! Oddly, she was often at her most beautiful when she was like that. Kind of glowing. Oh, you'd never have known. I only did because she told me. Once, just once. And after that I watched her.

I'll tell you why she married you, Glyn. Out of all the men who went after her. She thought you loved her. Mary looks intently now at Glyn, and he finds he cannot meet her eye.

And at some point then, Glyn has had enough. He can't manage any more of this, he wants out, he wants to get in the car and head away from Mary Packard, from what she has said. Except that nothing can now be unsaid, her voice will be there always. He must walk down her garden path with her words in his head, and take them home with him.

Elaine knows what she wants of Mary Packard, but she does not know how she will go about getting it. What she wants is precise in her mind, but is also impossible to specify. She wants to hear someone talk about Kath—someone who is not Polly, or Glyn, or Oliver Watson, or Nick—least of all Nick. Who is not maddening Cousin Linda. Someone who, like herself, speaks with authority. But something has happened to her confidence in that authority, over the last weeks; there have been subversive voices, there have been suggestions of lacunae, glimpses of things she does not understand.

She wants that confidence restored. She wants to hear that the voices are misleading, that she has not heard what she thinks she may have heard, that everything is as it always was.

She just wants to talk for a while about Kath to someone who knew her well. That is all she wants. Isn't it?

And so she steps briskly from the car, opens the gate, walks up the path between the two little hedges of *Lavandula augustifolia* "Munstead" and raises her hand to knock on the door of Mary Packard's cottage, which is thickly clad with *Clematis tangutica* and *Rosa* "New Dawn."

"I'm afraid I'm a bit of a bolt from the blue," says Elaine. "It's been quite a while—"

"Not at all," says Mary Packard. "I thought you'd come."

Which is not what she should be saying, and Elaine is disconcerted.

That was at the beginning.

At the end, when Elaine walks away between the lavender hedges, she has this odd feeling that much time has passed, instead of an hour or two, during which she has become someone else. In one sense she is herself, but in another she has been entirely altered. The past has been reconstructed, and, with that, her own old certainties. She sees differently; she feels differently.

The nonbabies are now loud and clear, who did not exist a couple of hours ago. Kath's nonchildren. Because of them—because of these beings who never were—there is a new flavor to much that was said, much that was done. When Kath speaks now, Elaine hears a new note in her voice. Kath says the same things, but she says them in a new way.

Why didn't you *tell* me? says Elaine.

She sees Kath with Polly, dancing with her—small Polly, grown-up Kath—she sees her plaiting Polly's hair, she sees her coming into the kitchen with Polly and a brimming basket of windfall apples.

I always thought you didn't particularly *want* children, says Elaine. She speaks to the wheel of her car, to the driving mirror, to the tailgate of the lorry ahead of her, to Kath.

The nonchildren eclipse much else. She hears the nonchildren louder than anything that has been said. It is the nonchildren above all who have skewed things. They keep coming back—faceless, formless, significant.

Mary Packard knew, and Elaine did not. Friend; sister. Mary is perhaps embarrassed by this: I hadn't entirely realized . . . she says. I knew that Glyn . . . but I thought that probably you . . . I see. Well, Kath would have had her reasons, I suppose, says Mary.

Quite, thinks Elaine. And the principal reason was probably me. How I am. How I was with her.

There is more, though. There is a subversive flow that occupies her as she drives mindlessly in the direction of home. The thing is, says Mary Packard, Kath always wanted to be someone else. She wanted to be you. She wanted to be me. She was stuck with the dictation of what she looked like, which pretty well determined her life, one realizes. If she hadn't looked like that, quite different things might have happened. Different men. Different directions. She might have set to and learned a trade, like you and me. She once said—sitting out there, in my studio—she once said, There isn't a single thing that I can do well, I've fiddled away at this and that ever since I can remember.

She wanted to be loved. Most people do, I suppose. But her more than most.

Your mother dying when she did. That accounts for much, says Mary. Didn't you know? There is an edge to her voice; Elaine is uncomfortable.

The business with Nick . . . says Mary.

And Elaine, who would not have spoken of that, goes rigid. Oh, so Glyn has been here. I see, no wonder I was expected.

That sodding photograph, says Mary. Yes, I remember that day. Who? Oh, him. Someone I'm not in touch with anymore.

Forget it, says Mary. That business. Nick. A crazy aberration. God knows why. Do we need to ask?

Halfway home, stationary at a crossroads behind a line of traffic, Elaine discovers that she does not need to ask. This news comes as a relief, a release from something oppressive, and adds to her sense of a change in perception. When the line of cars advances, and she gathers speed once more, it is as though she were moving into some new age, a time when things would be apparently the same but also rather different.

What the hell am I doing?

Oliver sits in his car, outside Mary Packard's gate, and for two pins he would start the engine up again and be off. What is he doing here? This is daft. Embarrassing. Entirely unnecessary. Except that for a few hours, several days ago, it seemed an imperative.

He gets out, locks up, opens the garden gate.

He had forgotten quite what Mary Packard looked like, but she is immediately familiar. Of course—that shock of hair, that cool, calm manner. And as soon as he is sitting in her kitchen, with a mug of tea in his hand, it seems quite reasonable and straightforward to be there.

The thing is, he says, I can't get all this out of my head. Ever since . . . Well, you see, there's this bloody photograph that turned up.

I know about the photograph, says Mary Packard. And she tells him why she knows, but Oliver has an eerie feeling that this woman might know everything anyway, by some osmotic process, like the wise woman of folktales.

It's all my fault, says Oliver. I mean, it isn't, of course—but actually it is, because I took the photo and then like an idiot I gave it to Nick instead of just throwing it away and saying nothing. If it weren't for me there wouldn't be all this fuss. I've had Glyn on my back, then Nick. Elaine threw a complete wobbly, it seems, and gave Nick the push.

Yes, says Mary. People do seem to have been on the move.

Is it my fault? says Oliver.

Of course not, she tells him. And you know perfectly well it isn't. You didn't come here to ask me that, did you?

Oliver agrees that he did not. They have become oddly companionable, he and Mary Packard, as though they were old friends, though Oliver cannot recall that back then they ever exchanged more than stock civilities. There is now some shared, unstated vision.

It was a crying shame, says Oliver. He is no longer talking about the photograph, or Glyn, or Nick. Her, of all people, he says. The blessed of the gods, you'd have thought. But she wasn't, was she? One of the damned, more like.

I keep thinking about her. I mean, one always did, but not quite so—compulsively. Was there anything to be done?

Probably not, says Mary.

The afternoon has turned to evening. The mugs of tea have been replaced by glasses of red wine. Oliver and Mary Packard talk about other times. About Kath, especially. They remember this and that; they bring Kath back to life, passing her to and fro between them—looking at her, listening to her. They are clear-eyed; they do not remember with sentimentality. Oliver hears of things he did not know, and the Kath of whom he talks is subtly changed even as he does so; what he saw and heard is infused with a different understanding. But he is somehow soothed. It is as though in this consideration of Kath they are also performing a kind of ritual, they are paying tribute. He has no idea if this is what he came here for, but he is glad that he did. The visit has served a purpose, if not perhaps the one that he sought—if indeed he knew what that was.

She had an effect, he says.

She still is having an effect, says Mary.

Conclusions

"Can you remember what date Mum and I got married?"

"Actually, I wasn't there," says Polly.

"It was July, I'm pretty sure. And it's July now. But what *date*?"

"You don't *know*?" cries Polly. "All this time, and you don't know?"

Nick replies that he does know. Well, he sort of knows. He knows sort of whenabouts it is—just, the exact day he sometimes forgets.

"Well, then, let me tell you. It's the nineteenth. This Friday. And, frankly, Dad, I'm astonished you don't know. I think you should ask yourself how on earth it can be that you don't know. And listen, Dad, I'm going to be away this weekend. I'm going to the country with . . . with a friend. *Please* remember to take your keys with you when you go out."

Nick goes shopping. He stares bemused into windows, glowing caverns in which watches have been tossed carelessly amid folds of satin, in which headless velvet necks display swags of gilt or shining stones, and miniature crystal trees are festooned with gold chains. Since he cannot imagine going into one of these places and entering into some negotiation, he passes on, and eventually ends up in a department store, where he cruises helplessly up and down escalators. He hasn't been to such an emporium since his mother used to take him on forays to acquire school uniforms. He could do with his mother right now; she would have known how to deal with this.

Nick wanders from Electrical Appliances to China and Glass, through Haberdashery and Lingerie, into Furnishing Fabrics, up to Sports and Garden Furniture, down by way of Baby Wear and Gifts. He is a boat against the current, bumping up against hordes of purposeful people; everybody here knows what they are doing except for him. He is immeasurably dispirited; it seems possible that he will go mad here, pitched finally into the purgatory that has loomed since Elaine told him to go. The store has become a mocking metaphor for a world in which others head confidently for their chosen slots. They know that their destiny is with Lighting or with Hosiery, while he can only drift feckless among them, unable to identify either need or direction. It is all uncomfortably near the knuckle, a parody of some true experience, except that in its way this is indeed real—he is here, by choice, and does not know where to go or what to do.

There are signals from ordinary life. In Kitchenware he passes a kettle like the one at home. He finds himself staring at a chair identical to one in Polly's flat. He brushes past a girl wearing big hoop earrings like Kath used to wear, but immediately slams Kath out of his mind—there is not time nor space for her, she must be put aside, for now and perhaps forever. Occasionally he comes up against himself, a mirrored glimpse of this distracted man—too bald, too old—and is further disoriented. This cannot be him, but apparently it is.

He comes to a halt at last by a desk. A woman sits at the desk:

a calm, benign woman who smiles at him—the first human contact he has experienced in this place. The woman has a sign above her head: she is Customer Services.

There is a chair in front of the desk. Nick sits down. The woman continues to smile invitingly. Later, it seems to him that he bared his soul to her.

"It's the nineteenth," says Sonia. "And we still don't have an estimate for the hard landscaping on the Surrey place. Two weeks overdue."

Elaine registers this—the date rather than the errant estimate. So? she tells herself. So it's the wedding anniversary? Well, it would be, wouldn't it? They come round, like bulb-planting or pruning time. So?

Later, when she has snatched an hour to work in the garden, the date lurks, prompting various reflections: that Nick seldom remembered it, and, if he did, invariably got the day wrong and proposed a celebratory dinner a week too early; that this always riled her; that the wedding occasion itself is now something of a blur. How can such a seminal event have dissolved into a few hazy impressions? Auntie Clare's hat, the rock-hard cake icing that resisted the knife, Kath in a floaty green dress.

Elaine plants out some pulmonarias and tries to concentrate on current projects. She has plenty of work in hand, but since her visit to Mary Packard she has felt disoriented, unable to fix her attention where it is required. It is not so much that she has been dwelling on what she learned from Mary Packard; rather, it is a question of coming to terms with a revised vision, with a new set of responses.

The day proceeds. Elaine spends time on a garden design, and even more time on the phone. Sonia comes in and out with queries, as do Pam and Jim. Elaine achieves a further spell in the garden and, eventually, after five, everyone has gone and she is alone.

Nick's arrival is nicely judged. Elaine has had a bath and is through in the conservatory when she hears a car in the drive. She goes to the front door, and there he is, with a package in his hand.

Elaine is so taken aback by the sight of him that she just stands there. Possibly she says, "Oh—" Polly is right—he is thinner. Otherwise he is simply Nick, and moreover, Nick wearing the furtive expression that normally heralds a long process of exculpation.

He proffers the package.

"It's a scarf," he explains. "It's got flowers on it. Actually, a nice woman in the shop helped me, I must admit. You know I'm not good at shops. I told her all about you, and she thought this one with the flowers. It's Italian, apparently. Silk."

Elaine continues to stand there, now holding the package. An entirely fresh image from that day thirty-two years ago has swum into her head: she sees Nick's hand above hers as he puts on the ring. She remembers her startled recognition that she was now part of a unit of two, whatever that was going to mean.

Nick is on the doorstep, expectant.

"Well," she says. "You'd better come in." She knows as she speaks that he will not be leaving again, and that this will be all right, or as all right as it ever was.

"You know how everything was completely fouled up for me?" says Polly. "Well, now it isn't. Honestly, *life* . . . First of all, I think it may be serious—with Andy. We went away for the weekend and—let's just say it was pretty good. What? Yes, of course there was amazing sex, but that's not the whole picture, is it? The thing is, he's just such an understanding person. You can relate to him. He's not—well, he's not like the men I usually end up with. Oh

God, just talking about him's making me feel all peculiar. Do you know—this may be it.

"And there's more. My dad's gone back to my mum. Or rather my mum's let my dad come home. I got in late on Friday night and there's this message saying actually he's at home now and he'll come and pick his things up next week. Just like that. Sorted, apparently."

In youth, Oliver was good at Latin. Occasionally, a shred of Virgil or of Caesar can still float into his head. These days, he is haunted by *lacrimae rerum*—those plangent words. He remembers that the Latin master considered the phrase untranslatable. He would chalk it up on the board, with some suggested renderings: the pity of things, the tears of the world. "Not right, are they?" he would say. "A beautiful expression, the ultimate in poetry—and it has to be left as it is."

Lacrimae rerum. Oh yes, indeed, thinks Oliver. Admittedly, run-of-the-mill distress such as he has in mind is hardly on a par with the fall of Troy, but nevertheless the language seems apt, and a curious kind of solace. He allows the words to float, and one afternoon he lets them fill his monitor also, in many different colors and fonts—red, purple, yellow, green, bold, italic, Symbol, Tahoma, Times New Roman, you name it. He shuffles them up and moves them around.

Sandra, crossing the room at one point and glancing over his shoulder, says, "What on earth are you up to?"

"Doodling," says Oliver. He clears the screen. "Right. Now, am I doing the Rotary Club job or are you?"

Glyn works. Of course—that is what Glyn does, what he has always done. Term is over, so there is no longer the dictation of students and colleagues; he spends long hours in the library and in his study, preparation for a far-reaching new project on transport systems. He thinks prehistoric trackways and salt and cattle and coal; he thinks road, water, and rail; his mind's eye is concentrated upon the map of Britain, a network of communication, layer upon layer, piled up, intersecting, making nonsense of chronology. He does not think about himself, he does not think about Kath; or he believes that he does not.

That photograph is back in the landing cupboard. Glyn does not wish or intend to look at it again. He might as well destroy it, but the destruction of archival material offends his deepest instinct. Let it lie there.

Glyn works, amid this tide of paper—books, periodicals, offprints, maps. He reads and writes, he marshals information, he interprets and reinterprets. Even when he takes a break he is pondering the route of a canal, the advance of a railway; as he makes a cup of coffee, river systems are imposed upon the kitchen counter; as he walks to the shop to buy a newspaper he is considering connections and survivals.

But every now and then this detachment fails him. He is flung inexorably into contemplation of other things. That day, above all. The day he returned in the evening to this empty house. He moves through the day again and again, and at the end he sees what he saw then. The sight is the same as ever it was, except that it is informed by new wisdoms, and he looks differently.

Glyn knows now that he has to find a new way of living with Kath, or rather a way of living with a new Kath. And of living without her, in a fresh, sharp deprivation.